HEARD IT IN A
LOVE SONG

HEARD IT IN A LOVE SONG

TRACEY GARVIS GRAVES

THORNDIKE PRESS
A part of Gale, a Cengage Company

**LIBRARY OF CONGRESS CIP DATA ON FILE.
CATALOGUING IN PUBLICATION FOR THIS BOOK
IS AVAILABLE FROM THE LIBRARY OF CONGRESS.**

ISBN-13: 978-1-4328-9226-5 (hardcover alk. paper)

Published in 2021 by arrangement with St. Martin's Publishing Group.

Printed in Mexico
Print Number: 01   Print Year: 2022

To Matthew David Graves —
for loving music as much as I do
(especially anything out of the seventies).
I raised you right.

PROLOGUE

LAYLA

Now

Layla Hilding smiled at the man standing next to her. He gave her a thumbs-up and she flashed the peace sign back at him. The room smelled of beer and fried food and sweat and cologne and she would always associate these smells with happiness. Underneath her shirt, she could feel the steamy dampness of her skin, and she knew her face would be glowing from the exertion of doing what she loved.

She had arrived at a crossroads, personally and professionally.

For years, she'd put the hopes and dreams she'd been chasing on the back burner.

Not by choice.

Not without resentment.

Now, she stood on the precipice of a whole new life.

Layla strummed the opening notes, and

as she sang the words written by the man who stood beside her, it was as if she were hearing them for the first time. She'd been singing them for months, but she was finally paying attention to what they said.

She drew in a breath and her voice rose as she belted out the words. The lyrics were an anthem, one she would proudly sing whenever she could.

Her instincts were screaming by then. Layla pictured the words as if they were arrows pointing back at her. Toward the answer.

What do you love? What do you really want?

She'd finally figured out the answers, but what she hadn't expected was that failing would feel so sweet.

She glanced his way again, and they exchanged a triumphant smile, his voice joining hers on the last verse in beautiful harmony.

She had to tell him it wasn't working.

She had to tell him she couldn't chase it anymore, and more importantly, she didn't want to.

But that didn't mean she couldn't have it all, because she could.

Layla didn't need the universe to send her a sign that the decision she'd made was the right one.

Layla didn't need any help at all.

CHAPTER 1

LAYLA

Six Months Earlier

Layla Hilding-Cook stood on the curb next to the drop-off line on a mild day in early September, bracing herself for what she was about to endure. Drop-off and pickup frustrated the staff on the best of days, but that was nothing compared to the confusion on the first day of school. Every year, the district sent out detailed emails with instructions on how to navigate the process. Layla often wondered if the parents ever read them.

"It's nice to see your face again," Tonya said. "I've missed you." Tonya Perkins taught art and Layla taught music and they had gradually evolved from coworkers who started teaching on the same day almost ten years ago to close friends who knew the innermost details of each other's lives. During the summer months, when Layla's split from Liam was still in that raw place that kept her inside with the curtains drawn, Tonya would send a text once or twice a week asking her to go to her front door and open it. Layla would comply and discover whatever Tonya had dropped off. Often, it was Layla's favorite candy, which at the moment was Cinnamon Fire Jolly Ranchers. On especially hot days, there might be an iced hazelnut coffee. Sometimes, it was flowers from the farmers market or a bag of perfectly ripe peaches. Layla would smile, bring the items inside, and respond with a text of her own saying thank you.

Tonya was really into bullet journaling, and one day there had been a gift bag with a brand-new journal inside it sitting on the welcome mat. Layla had brought it inside, and it had sat on the kitchen counter, ignored, until mid-July, because it was going to take more than a bullet journal to put her life back together. She picked it up one day, more out of curiosity than anything. She'd thumbed through it and then put it back down. When she picked it back up again a few days later, she opened it to the first page and in the spot for the ten-year goal, she wrote, *I want my life not to suck so much.* The second time she opened it, she wrote, *I don't think this is going to help but whatever.* The third time she picked it up, in the spot for daily goals she wrote, *I'm going to write in this stupid journal every day, I guess,* and then she poured out her thoughts for an hour straight. It was now part of her daily routine, and she had thanked Tonya profusely.

"The break was good for me," Layla said as they watched the cars creep slowly through the drop-off line. "I did a lot of healing." The divorce would be finalized soon and that would feel like another momentous milestone. When she left Liam last March, Layla still had three months of school to get through, and she limped her way through them with Tonya's support, a spectacular poker face, and a truly astounding amount of compartmentalization. At school, she held it together. At home, she fell apart. And then finally June arrived, and Layla had never been so grateful for a job that allowed her three months off every year. Tonya knew all about the depth of Layla's unhappiness and would have been more than willing to provide a literal shoulder to cry on as Layla navigated the separation process and eventual divorce. But Layla just needed to be alone with her thoughts.

"I'll be fine," Layla said. It was a sentence she'd repeated in her head almost every day during the summer. Most of the time, she actually believed it.

I will be fine.

Tonya smiled. "I know you will. And I, for one, am glad I don't have to look at Liam's stupid face at the Christmas party this year."

"Comments like that are why I love you. Instead of telling me what an idiot I was, you simply pledge your support for Team Layla."

"You weren't an idiot."

Maybe not now, but for many years she'd been living someone else's life.

Annie Hakanson sidled up to them, travel coffee mug in hand. Layla had taught all three of Annie's boys. Rambunctious hellions, especially the twins, but so charismatic and affectionate that most teachers, including her, let it slide. Layla had gotten to know Annie well enough over the years that she considered her a friend. She was also one of the few parents who knew about Layla's marital strife.

"These parents will never, ever understand how this process works. Never," Annie said.

"Is that why you park in the lot and walk the boys in?" Tonya asked.

"Partly. But also, I want an excuse to gossip with the two of you. I know it brightens your morning routine immensely." Annie

14

stepped forward and pointed at one of the cars, motioning for its driver to lower the window. "Move all the way forward. Then you can let your children out. Go on."

Layla and Tonya stared at her. "What?" Annie said. "I'm helping you out."

Layla laughed. "You sure are."

"Oh, hey, hot-dad alert," Annie muttered under her breath. Drop-off and pickup seemed to be primarily a mother's task, so when a dad wandered into the mix, it was hard not to take notice. A handsome one was like chum in the water. *It's probably not him,* Layla thought before looking nonchalantly in the direction Annie had indicated.

But *of course* it was him. And Layla already knew how handsome he was.

"I don't see a ring," Annie added in a low, singsongy voice.

"How can you possibly see that far?" Tonya asked, squinting.

"That's because he's separated," Layla said.

"Wait," Annie said. "How do you know he's separated? Do you know him? Layla, is there something you want to share about what you did on your summer break? Or *who* you did?"

"You're quite the comedienne," Layla said, shaking her head. She was in a *healing*

15

phase and was not remotely interested in pursuing a romantic relationship at this time. The mere thought of it exhausted her. "I met him and his soon-to-be-ex-wife at back-to-school night."

He had walked into the music room holding his daughter's hand. He had short dark hair and was dressed casually in jeans and a navy-blue polo. Mid-to-late thirties, give or take. A gorgeous woman had been holding the little girl's other hand. Her long dirty-blond hair had a few lighter, face-framing highlights. She wore a sundress and had a deep, golden tan, the type of which Layla would never achieve because her fair skin only pinkened in the sun and would burn to a crisp if she spent more than thirty minutes outside without slathering herself in something with an SPF of at least fifty. This woman looked like she belonged in a beach town, Malibu or Monterey.

Not Rochester, Minnesota.

Healing phase notwithstanding, *occasionally* Layla allowed herself to fantasize about the type of man she might fall in love with someday, and this was definitely one of those times. The fantasy was slightly marred by the presence of the woman. It was like that Alanis Morissette song about meeting the man of your dreams and then meeting his beautiful wife. In another lifetime, Layla used to sing a lot of Alanis Morissette songs.

"Hi, I'm Josh Summers," he said when they reached Layla. He shook her hand. "And this is Sasha."

Layla crouched down so she was at eye level with Sasha. "Hi, Sasha. I'm Miss Layla. I'm going to be your music teacher. Are you excited for the first day of school?"

"I have an Elsa lunch box and backpack."

"You do? That's cool. Maybe I'll get the chance to see it. Do you like music?"

"She likes the *Frozen* soundtrack," Josh said. So did Layla. She often sang along to it when she was alone in the car. How could she not? It was awesome. *Frozen II* would be released sometime next year, and when that happened, the elementary school would be hit with a fresh tidal wave of *Frozen* merchandise.

"She certainly does," the woman said. "Hi, I'm Kimberly. Sasha's mom." She stepped forward and clasped Layla's hand.

"I'm sorry," Josh said. "I should have introduced you."

"No, it's okay," Kimberly said.

"It's nice to meet you both," Layla said. "And I'll see you at school in a few days, Sasha."

Josh and Sasha drifted toward the door,

but Kimberly hung back. "Well, that was awkward. We're getting divorced. I mean, we're just separated for now, but we don't live together anymore. We're trying our best to remain united where Sasha is concerned while we figure everything out." She said it as if Layla wasn't the only one she was trying to convince. "We've given the school contact information for both of us."

"Of course," Layla said. "Thank you for letting me know."

Kimberly smiled and hurried off to catch up with Josh and Sasha.

Now they watched as Josh and Sasha reached the sidewalk on foot, the Elsa lunch box swinging from Sasha's fingers. The parents of kindergartners often elected to skip the drop-off line and walk their children into the building on the first day. It was usually a good call.

"What do you think those pants are called?" Annie asked, her voice low. She motioned toward Josh with the slightest tilt of her head. He and Sasha were getting closer.

Layla was wondering the same thing. The pants were khaki-colored and had a lot of pockets. Cargo? Painter? He was also wearing a gray T-shirt and work boots, and until then Layla hadn't realized how much she liked that look. Liam wouldn't have been caught dead dressed like that.

"I have no idea," Tonya said. "But I'm going straight to the mall to buy my husband a pair as soon as I'm done here today."

"Uh-oh," Layla said. "We might have a runner."

Sasha had stopped dead in her tracks. Layla had had enough experience with the first day of school to know that the kids usually fell into one of two camps: super excited or a total flight risk. Josh reached down and picked up Sasha. She threw her arms around his neck and clung to him.

Layla walked over to them. "Hi, Sasha. I'm Miss Layla, your music teacher. Do you remember meeting me?" Sasha lifted her head and peeked at Layla. Then she shook her head.

"Well, I remember you. I was thinking about you this morning because we're going to sing a song from the *Frozen* soundtrack in music class this week. Do you know the words to 'Let It Go'?" She had planned no such thing, but if she could assist in eliminating the first-day jitters of a reluctant kindergarten student, she would.

Sasha lifted her head from the crook of Josh's neck and nodded.

"Could I take a look at your lunch box?"

She nodded and Layla took the lunch box out of her hand and examined it. "Who's your favorite, Elsa or Anna?"

"I like Olaf," she said.

Layla smiled. "Me too." A bell rang in the distance. "We'll be starting soon. Now, are you all ready for your first day of kindergarten? We can't sing if we don't go inside."

"Okay," she said.

Josh placed his daughter's feet back down on the ground. "Come on, Sasha. Let's go find the line for your homeroom." Sasha placed her hand in Josh's. "Have a nice day," he said to them.

Layla smiled. "Thanks. You too."

"Hmmm," Annie said when they were a safe distance away. "I really hope that wasn't a one-off. We need something to shake up the morning routine."

"I think you mean *someone*," Tonya added in the same singsongy voice Annie had used.

"Settle down, you two," Layla said.

CHAPTER 2

JOSH

Josh climbed back into his truck and stifled a yawn. The house he'd bought after he moved out was too close to the school to qualify for bus service, but he didn't mind. One of the reasons he enjoyed self-employment so much was that it gave him the flexibility to take his daughter to school and pick her up at the end of the day. He was already used to filling in the gaps when it came to Sasha's care, and he was happy to do it.

Sasha had awakened at 5:00 A.M., too excited for the first day of school to stay in bed a minute longer. He'd tried to gain another hour of sleep by coaxing her back into her room, but Sasha wanted nothing to do with that plan.

Wide awake with no hope of falling back to sleep, he'd admitted defeat and rolled out of bed. Sasha bounded into the kitchen alongside him as he started the coffee. He poured her a bowl of cereal and sat with her while she ate. When she was done eating and the caffeine had started to clear out the cobwebs, he told Sasha to get dressed while he grabbed a quick shower.

He and Kimmy had a fifty-fifty physical-custody split. It wasn't ideal and neither of them liked the thought of Sasha having to go back and forth between two homes, but neither of them wanted less time with her, so that's what they decided on. A few years ago, Kimmy landed her dream job as a legislative policy analyst for the City of Rochester and often worked long hours as a liaison with the state and federal governments. An important meeting prohibited her from accompanying Josh and Sasha to school on the first day, and she'd been feeling guilty about it all week. Josh tried his best to assuage it. "It's okay," he'd told her last night when she called to speak to Sasha and apologized yet again for not being able to join them.

"I'll be at the house in the morning to see her off," Kimmy said.

Kimmy had arrived half an hour before they needed to leave for school. She took lots of pictures of Sasha: standing by the door, out on the front steps, with and without her backpack and lunch box.

"Can you take a few of us together?" she'd asked, handing Josh her phone.

"Sure." He snapped what felt like hundreds of pictures of the two of them. Sasha finally tired of it, and Kimmy crouched down in front of her and smoothed her hair. "I'll be thinking of you all day today. Tonight, we'll have a special dinner and you can tell me about your first day."

"What if no one plays with me?"

"They will. You'll see. And don't forget that Daddy and I love you very much."

"Okay."

"I'm getting off early and I'll pick her up after school today," Kimmy said, even though she'd already mentioned it twice in the last twenty-four hours. She grabbed her purse and travel mug. Gave Sasha one last hug and kiss. "Gotta run," she said to Josh.

He was leaning up against the counter. "Yep," he said. The screen door banged shut and then it was just the two of them again.

Sasha's early-morning enthusiasm had been momentarily eclipsed by her fear, but once they'd made it inside the building there hadn't been any further delays, and he had Sasha's music teacher to thank for that. Before pulling out of the school parking lot, he'd sent Kimmy a quick text letting her know that Sasha had made it into her classroom without a hitch. Telling Kimmy it hadn't all been smooth would only add to her angst, and the last thing he wanted was to tell Kimmy that something else hadn't gone quite the way they'd hoped.

Josh turned his thoughts away from Sasha and mentally reviewed his day. Lots of people dreaded Mondays, but Josh loved them. Mondays meant putting on his electrician's hat and doing the work he loved. It meant losing himself in an intricate jumble of wires and using his experience and problem-solving skills to figure out a solution. Most importantly, it meant not sitting in an office all day staring out the window or at the clock.

He drove to his client's home, and Carl came to the door and opened it before Josh finished knocking, his shaggy white dog, Norton, at his side. "Morning, Carl," Josh said. He'd learned to speak loudly, because Carl had lost most of his hearing. "We've got a lot of work to do today."

"Long as we're done by noon," Carl said. He was dressed in jeans and a button-down shirt, and the work boots on his feet had probably been purchased sometime in the eighties. Carl was ninety-six years old and still lived alone. His daughter June checked on him daily, and Meals on Wheels kept him fed. His refusal to consider assisted living had less to do with an absence of any serious health problems and more to do with the fact that Norton might not be able to accompany him, and Carl would have none of that.

June had called Josh's business line one day, frantic about the jumble of exposed wiring she'd discovered in the basement of her father's house and in dire need of an experienced electrician. It seemed that Carl liked to tinker in his spare time — of which he had a lot — and though he'd probably been quite handy back in the day, he was not remotely qualified to work with electrical systems. Josh had told June he would make sure that it was safe and that everything was up to code.

Unfortunately, it had taken longer than he'd envisioned. A lot of the wiring was outdated, and each problem he'd uncovered led to three more, most of them critical in nature. How the house had not yet gone up in flames, he didn't know.

Josh had yelled up the basement stairs the first day and asked Carl to bring him up to speed on what exactly he'd been doing down there. Carl had walked slowly down

25

the stairs in his jeans and slippers and appointed himself Josh's unofficial apprentice, offering helpful advice that, had Josh followed it, had the potential to electrocute them both. Instead of following it, Josh offered alternatives that Carl begrudgingly admitted "might work." At one point, Carl had gone upstairs to use the bathroom, and when he returned, the boots had been on his feet. The dog had perched on the stairs and fallen asleep while Josh and Carl worked side by side until the Meals on Wheels delivery person arrived. "I've got to eat lunch and watch the news now," Carl said.

"And then what?" Josh had asked.

"Then I take a nap," Carl said. "Come back tomorrow."

On their third day working together, Carl said, "It's probably going to take us a while to get this all sorted out."

Josh had requests for bids stacking up, as well as a few larger jobs that would require him to be on-site all day instead of arriving in the afternoon after spending the morning at Carl's. He'd hoped to wrap this up in the next couple of days, but a lump had formed in his throat and all he'd been able to say was "Yeah."

CHAPTER 3

LAYLA

That evening, when the first day of school was finally, blissfully behind her, Layla went out to the deck. When the Realtor had shown her the house, there were so many things she'd loved about it, among them its smaller size and rustic charm and, most importantly, the fact that it was ten thousand dollars below her budget. When they'd made their way around to the back and Layla had seen the covered deck, she'd turned to the Realtor and said, "Sold."

Layla had created a sanctuary for herself with comfortable all-weather furniture and a large gray-and-cream-striped outdoor rug that felt soft under her bare feet and would be protected from the elements by the deck's roof. She'd placed lanterns in each corner, and the flameless candles inside them were on a timer that turned them on at dusk. She'd spent most summer evenings here with her guitar and a glass of wine and her journal. She strummed and she sipped, and she poured her thoughts and fears and dreams into the creamy white pages. She made lists and set long-term goals, and those nights on her deck were cathartic in the exact way she needed them to be. She felt energized, alive, and the guitar and the journal lifted her spirits in a way that nothing else had in an awfully long time.

The night she left Liam, between bouts of crying, she'd scribbled a few things down on the hotel notepad at the Holiday Inn Express where she'd fled, too ashamed at first to let anyone know she was there. Too afraid she'd see it on their faces: *I told you so.* Over the summer, she transferred those thoughts into the journal and added to them, jotting down the things she'd always been too ashamed to vocalize. Things Liam had done and said that she'd allowed. Things that she'd even made excuses for. Writing them down was her way of working through them, and her journal had become her therapy. She'd never shared these things with anyone — not her mom, not her sister or brother, not Tonya — because she feared their judgment: Why didn't you leave him a long time ago? they might wonder.

Yeah, why hadn't she?

But now, reading the things she'd written over and over desensitized her and gave her the courage, the strength, to realize that every mistake she'd made was a blessing and a lesson. Layla wasn't perfect. She was human and she'd made a few wrong turns. It was time to forgive herself and get her life back on track. But sometimes, when she'd had one glass of wine too many, she retraced her relationship with Liam in an attempt to figure out how it had happened. Where it had started to go so wrong. Wondering what he'd done that had led to her falling so hard for him, because for many years, she had loved Liam Cook fiercely.

The band was headlining at a bar called Connie's, where they played so often the customers had started referring to them as the house band. Layla had majored in music, with an emphasis on performing, and she'd met the other three band members when they were still in college. Kevin played drums, Rick played bass guitar, and Sam played the keyboard. Layla played a variety of instruments, but she was the band's lead guitarist, and handled most of the vocals. What had started as a drunken jam session at Kevin's off-campus house her junior year had slowly and steadily turned into a viable source of income. There hadn't been much Layla could do with her music degree unless she wanted to teach somewhere, and she absolutely did not want to do that. Layla wanted to be the lead singer in a band, and that was exactly what she'd become. She dyed her shoulder-length hair a vibrant shade of neon pink and stood before the microphone front and center, basking in the glow of the lights. She had been born with a natural flair for performing, completely devoid of anything resembling stage fright. The others, who enjoyed the band perks like free beer and an endless supply of adoring women almost as much as they enjoyed playing, were happy to let her take the lead, and she capitalized on it, because under the spotlight was where she shined.

One year after graduation, the four of them — now known collectively as Storm Warning, their nod to Minnesota's frequent inclement winter weather — had started rising through the ranks of the local music scene. Layla also gave guitar lessons on the side, and her earnings, combined with her cut of the band's profits, were enough to live on. It wasn't a great living, but it was enough for a twenty-three-year-old to get by on if she was frugal, which she was.

The crowds had gotten bigger, more enthusiastic, which only fueled her desire to keep on doing it. Her parents had not been thrilled, and they told her it was time to get serious about finding a real career before it was too late. Her friends were the only ones who were supportive, but that was mostly because they didn't quite have their lives figured out, either.

Layla refused to be swayed by anyone's opinion of what she should have been doing with her life, and there wasn't a lot anyone could say, since the money she earned paid the rent on her studio apartment with just enough left over to cover her basic needs.

She had her guitars and she had her freedom and that suited Layla just fine.

That night at Connie's, the crowd cheered when she launched into the opening riff from Eric Clapton's "Layla." The band seldom performed the actual song, but Layla loved how the crowd understood why she played the iconic intro. When their first set ended, a sea of enthusiastic fans — most of them male — surrounded her. One thrust a beer into her hand; another asked her to pose for a picture, and he slung his arm around her shoulders as she looked into the camera and smiled.

Liam had bumped into her as she was making her way back from the bathroom. "Oh, hey. Sorry," he said, placing his hands on her shoulders to steady her. "Great set."

"Thanks," she said.

"You're really talented," he said, resting his arm against the back of a nearby barstool, creating a protective little bubble around her. "I'm Liam."

"Layla."

"Ah, now I get it," he said. "I've never heard you play before. Clearly I've been missing out."

"Well, we're about as local as you can get. I think we've played every bar in this zip code."

"I just moved back home. Graduated from Colorado State a month ago and started a new job. I'm in sales." In time, Layla would learn that it had taken him five years to graduate. He'd flunked out his sophomore year and had had to return home with his tail between his legs and work for a year while he saved up the money to return to school after his parents refused to pay his tuition. "Show us you can pay for it yourself and we'll reconsider," they told him. Liam could be very successful when he wanted to be, and he'd shown them all right. He'd worked at a used car dealership for nine months and had made so much money he seriously considered not going back to school at all. But the hours were long, and Liam had his sights on selling something a lot more glamorous than used cars. The big money, he told anyone who would listen, was in medical devices, software or telecommunications, and pharmaceuticals.

"So, were you named after the Clapton song?" Liam asked.

Layla smiled and shook her head. "No. I was named after my dad's sister. She died when my dad was —"

Something had caught his eye and he turned away abruptly. "Oh, hey, I've gotta run," he said.

"No problem," she replied as she watched him take off like a shot toward the exit. His sudden departure didn't bother her in the least, because good-looking guys in a bar were a dime a dozen, and besides, Layla wasn't interested in starting a relationship with anyone. At twenty-three, she could have her pick but was having too much fun to care about finding another boy who she would later find out was only masquerading as a man. She was tired of the beer-can pyramids in their apartments, their filthy disgusting bathrooms that seldom had any toilet paper, and their obsession with video games.

"Who will you take to weddings as your plus-one?" her friend Christine had asked one Sunday morning when they'd met for brunch. It was the height of wedding season in their friend group, and every weekend seemed to be filled with a wedding shower, a bachelorette party, or the wedding itself. Christine's own wedding had occurred three months before, and she had not stopped espousing the benefits since. Layla liked Christine's husband well enough, but being married mostly sounded like Christine never had to worry about whose name she'd write down for the emergency contact on her medical forms, or who would take her to the airport when she was flying solo. Christine was a couple of years older than Layla, and it had seemed like she'd been in an awfully big hurry to settle down, which Layla found perplexing. What was the rush? Weren't people supposed to be marrying later now?

"When is the last time you actually saw me at a wedding?" Layla said. She had, unfortunately, missed a lot of the weddings — although not Christine's — because the band was almost always booked on Saturday nights. "I'd rather be playing weddings than attending them on the arm of some guy who'll probably worry that a wedding will put ideas into my head and have me pining for a ring for my own finger. Please."

"Famous last words," her friend Noelle said. "Everyone knows that the minute you swear off men, you'll meet the love of your life. That's how it works."

Layla laughed. "That sounds like total bullshit to me. Besides, I only have eyes for my music. It never lets me down."

Christine and Noelle laughed then, too — whether with her or at her, she didn't know and didn't really care.

The truth was that, although her music had never let her down, Layla wanted to break into the Minneapolis bar scene so bad she could taste it, and a boyfriend would more than likely complicate things. They were "paying their dues" and would conquer Minneapolis "in due time," according to their manager, a guy named Scotty who was short on personality but some kind of shark when it came to keeping them booked on a regular basis. A boyfriend would be distracting, and besides, she was having the time of her life and it certainly wasn't due to the presence of a guy. Layla was an artist, a musician. For her, performing was as necessary as oxygen. If she had no one to play for, was she even really playing?

As much as Layla wanted to expand their reach, there was something to be said about being at the top of their game, even if the only reason they were big fish at all was because the pond known as Rochester was really quite small.

CHAPTER 4

JOSH

Kimmy brought Sasha back to Josh's house on Saturday at noon. "She slept in this morning," Kimmy said. "I think kindergarten tired her out."

"Maybe she'll start sleeping in regularly," Josh said.

"Well, we can hope."

At thirty-seven, Kimmy barely resembled the girl he'd met in detention his senior year. It wasn't unheard-of to fall madly in love in high school, but it was less likely that two eighteen-year-old kids would take it all the way to the altar. That was probably why his parents hadn't worried about their relationship too much. They often joked that Josh was their fourth boy and they were tired.

Trying to explain to people why he and Kimmy decided to separate had been the most difficult part of the process. They'd beaten the odds, everyone said. Why throw in the towel now? His parents had grown to love Kimmy and she'd become the daughter they never had. Sitting his mom and dad down to break the news of their split had been one of the hardest things he'd ever had to do.

But staying together wasn't that easy, and no one could understand that unless they'd been there from the very beginning, the way he and Kimmy had all those years ago. He just wished Sasha hadn't been the collateral damage, especially when he shared equal responsibility for causing it.

The only good thing Josh could say about February of 1999 was that it was a short month. The news was filled with doomsday predictions about the havoc Y2K would cause the following year, but Josh and his buddies were too busy setting their sights on May, when they would collect their diplomas and finally be free from the shackles of high school. No more books, no more homework, no more sitting in a classroom. Josh might not have had a good sense of what he wanted for the future, but he was crystal clear on the things he wanted to leave behind. When he thought back to those late-winter days right before he met Kimmy, "I Want It That Way" by the Backstreet Boys always popped into his head. Back then, he couldn't turn on the radio without hearing them, which annoyed him, because the Goo Goo Dolls and Matchbox Twenty were more his style. He spent more time than he should have playing video games on his PlayStation and searching for anything that would excite him during those gray days when it seemed like the sun would never shine again.

Back then, his dark, messy hair almost always needed a trim, but his skin was clear, and several female heads had turned when he entered the room where detention was held. He was wearing a flannel shirt — unbuttoned and untucked — a T-shirt, and faded jeans. None of those preppy button-down shirts some of the senior nerds wore. Or worse, any pants other than jeans.

The minutes dragged and he fidgeted constantly — tapping his pen, bouncing his leg up and down, shifting his position every thirty seconds. He spoke to no one but made two trips to the wastepaper basket in the corner of the room, balling up a sheet of notebook paper each time as if engineering a valid reason to get up. Taking the long way back to his seat, he folded his lanky body into his chair and resumed fidgeting.

There was a girl, a blonde in a pink sweater,

and she looked every bit as bored as the rest of them. When she turned around to talk to the girl sitting behind her, she glanced in Josh's direction and a mischievous smile appeared on her face. *That girl looks like fun,* he thought.

When the bell finally rang to signify their release, he shot out of his chair and was halfway down the hall before the other kids had even picked up their backpacks.

He was driving home when he spotted someone up ahead walking along the side of the road. The blond hair caught his eye and rang a bell somewhere in his brain. The air had a bite to it that had stung his cheeks as he walked through the parking lot on the way to his car. Late winter in Minnesota still felt a lot like the dead of winter, and the cold was not something to mess with. He pulled up next to her and slowed the car. She was wearing a thin coat, no hat. Tennis shoes on her feet. She whipped her head toward the car, looking cautious, defensive. Ready to fight. The look turned fearful when he rolled down the window. "Hey, do you need a ride?"

She must have recognized him, because a look of relief spread across her face and she said, "That would be great." She flung open the door and settled herself into the seat next to him.

"Didn't mean to freak you out," he said.

"No, it's just . . . you're not the first person who's ever offered me a ride." She didn't elaborate at the time, but eventually he would learn of her mother's unreliability and how there had been times others slowed down the way Josh had. At best, she said, the person behind the wheel wouldn't look as if they cared too much about her welfare but didn't have the heart not to at least check on her. At worst, it was a man whose inquiry had more of a self-serving angle to it. She told Josh she never accepted rides from adult men. Kimmy might not have been especially book smart, but there was nothing wrong with her common sense and she had no desire to make the front page of the newspaper when it announced the discovery of her body buried in a shallow grave somewhere.

"It's really cold out. I don't think it's good to be outside for so long."

"No, probably not. My mom must have gotten held up at work."

"Which way?" he asked.

"Keep going straight. My house isn't that far from here."

"I'm Josh."

"Kimmy," she said, holding her hands in front

40

of the heat vents.

"I saw you in detention."

"I saw you too." The mischievous smile was back.

"What'd you do?"

"Didn't turn in my homework. What did you do?"

"I cut out of class."

"I cut all the time. That's why I don't turn in my homework and I'm always in detention."

"I went to class, but I jumped out the window."

"No way," she said, looking at him with something like admiration, as if his impulsivity was a plus to her.

"The teacher turned his back and by the time he turned back around, I had the window open. It was a bit of a drop and I hit the ground harder than I meant to, but it was worth it. It's just so boring in class. I couldn't sit there for another minute."

"So boring," she echoed. "Turn here. That's me on the right. Second house."

He pulled to a stop in her driveway. The home was much smaller than the one he lived in. The paint, which had probably once been white, was grayish and peeling.

"Thanks for the ride," she said.

"Yeah, no problem." She opened the door and hurried up the sidewalk, slipping and sliding on the snow and ice that looked like it had been there awhile.

Too late, he realized he should have asked for her phone number and her last name. His detention was more than likely a one-time thing. His parents might have been tired, but if he'd gotten into any kind of regular trouble, his dad would have set him straight. His mom, too. With such a large student body, the odds of bumping into her again weren't great, which was a damn shame, because he wouldn't have minded that at all.

CHAPTER 5

LAYLA

On Saturday, Layla slept in and then changed into an old pair of jeans and the torn and faded Rolling Stones concert T-shirt she'd been wearing since she'd bought it after their show in 2002 and refused to ever part with. Hers was authentic, unlike the current iteration she'd seen on the rack at Target.

She made several trips down to the basement carrying armfuls of supplies: carpet knife, work gloves, bucket of soapy water, paint can, rollers. Her house had been built sometime in the early nineties, and there was an additional living space down there, not that she had much need for it. But what did interest her was the twelve-by-fourteen half-finished room meant for storage. Its poured-concrete walls would provide adequate soundproofing. One egress window at ground level let in a bit of natural light, but it was only a single pane and might allow too much noise to escape. She wouldn't know until she tested its limits. The ceiling wasn't as high as she'd like, but it would do.

Layla took the ponytail holder from her wrist, pulled her hair into a knot on top of her head, and got to work.

By evening, the basement space looked a lot different than it did when she started the project. The old, stained carpet had been cut into strips, ripped up, and put in the garage for the time being. She'd cleared the cobwebs from the corners of the walls and washed the window and window well. The glass sparkled. She'd swept the concrete floor after pulling up the old carpet tack strips, and she daydreamed about what kind of flooring she'd choose. She preferred wood, but low-pile carpeting would make things more comfortable. Now, with the area cleaned and prepped, Layla could truly begin the transformation. Whether that meant the room or herself was anyone's guess.

It turned out that Liam Cook hadn't been interested in a relationship either, but that was mostly because he was already in one. The second time Layla ran into him, a girl named Suzanne, whom she'd known since they were seven, was sitting on his lap.

The ugly lights had come on and the bouncers had begun the thankless task of herding a large number of intoxicated customers toward the door. Layla had finished chatting and posing for pictures and was on her way to the bar for a cold beer when Suzanne yelled her name. Layla looked at Suzanne and thought the guy whose lap she was sitting on looked vaguely familiar, although it took her a few seconds to place him. When Liam put two and two together and realized that Suzanne knew Layla, he'd stood up so fast that Suzanne tumbled from his lap and barely avoided falling on her ass. Once Suzanne righted herself, she enveloped Layla in a hug. "Oh, wow. You're kind of sweaty."

"Yeah, that happens when I play for forty minutes straight."

"Layla and I go way back," Suzanne said. She slung her arm around Liam's neck. "This is Liam. We're dating."

"Yep," Layla said. "We've met."

"Hey," Liam said.

Suzanne was the prettiest girl Layla had ever known. They'd become friends in elementary school and had once been quite close, although they'd drifted apart as they'd

45

gotten older. Suzanne had gone the cheerleader, homecoming-queen route and Layla had immersed herself in music and band. They had gone to different colleges but had run into each other occasionally when they were home on break. Somehow, neither of them had managed to move on to greener pastures yet.

Suzanne was tall and willowy, with a tight, toned body, the result of hours spent at the gym. That night, she was wearing a low-cut blouse with a plunging neckline, and a tight short skirt worn with the highest of heels. Her blond hair still held its artfully tousled curls, and her perfectly applied red lipstick hadn't budged. It was an eye-catching look and, reflecting back on it, Layla sometimes wondered if Liam had been drawn to Suzanne the way birds are drawn to scraps of foil and other shiny objects to take home to line their nests.

Layla didn't remember where she'd picked up the advice, probably a magazine or one of her friends, but before leaving your house you were supposed to look in the mirror, turn around, and then look back into the mirror. Whatever caught your eye, whether it was an accessory or an article of clothing or something weird going on with your hair, needed to be removed, fixed, or adjusted, because that meant it was too much. Suzanne seemed like

46

someone who took that same look in the mirror and then fluffed her hair and put on another necklace and more eyeshadow.

They could not have been more different in terms of style. Layla was wearing snug, faded jeans and a pale yellow T-shirt. And not one of those pastel, girly fitted ones, either. Hers was cut like a man's, although in a much smaller size. It bore the logo of a Key West bar, and it worked on her, giving her an effortless, sexy, rocker-chick kind of look with her long messy hair — which was now blue after she'd grown tired of the pink — and her delicate features. Layla was made of angles, and her slim-hipped, straight-up-and-down figure with its B cups would never fill out an outfit like the one Suzanne was wearing.

"We're going to get something to eat. Wanna join us?" Suzanne motioned toward the guy sitting on the other side of Liam. "This is Phillip. We could make it a foursome." She giggled when she said "foursome."

"Thanks, but I'm starving and can't wait that long. I'm going to see if the kitchen has anything left and then I'm going home to crash. It was nice to see you," Layla said, and then she walked off before they could say anything else.

Now, as she stood in the basement, she wished she had a time machine. If she did, she'd have gone back and cut out all those years that came after that night in the bar, saving herself a load of heartache in the process. Layla had spent way too much time ruminating on the time-machine thing, which was stupid, because time machines didn't exist and the past was in the past.

She reminded herself to focus on the present. There was certainly something to be said for being one hundred percent in charge of your time and your resources, and this freedom felt like drawing a fresh breath of air into her lungs. This time, nobody would derail her from having the life she wanted.

She felt buoyant.

Unencumbered.

Alive.

By Sunday night, the walls gleamed with two fresh coats of snowy white and Layla tumbled into bed, tired, aching, and as close to happy as she'd felt in a while.

CHAPTER 6

JOSH

Josh picked Sasha up from school on Monday afternoon. On the way home he said, "I have a surprise for you and I'm pretty sure you're gonna love it."

He'd stashed the dog in the spare bedroom, and as soon as they were inside, he took Sasha by the hand and led her toward it. She'd been begging for a dog since the age of three, but Kimmy had been lukewarm on the idea and would have preferred a cat. Josh was allergic to cats, so they'd compromised with a hamster that neither of them had been all that thrilled about. It had died a few months ago, and Josh and Kimmy had no desire to replace it due to Sasha's insistence that it come with her every time she changed houses. Plus, the cage smelled awful and required parental help to clean.

Josh opened the bedroom door and a giant, white fluffy dog bounded out. "Dad,"

Sasha screamed. She threw her arms around the dog's neck, and Josh's heart swelled. The dog licked her face tentatively and she buried her face in its fur. "Do we get to keep him?"

"Yes," he said.

Carl hadn't answered the door when Josh knocked that morning. He'd knocked again, because maybe Carl hadn't been watching out the front window and hadn't heard the knock. He'd grumbled to Josh once that he usually just left it unlocked but when his daughter found out about that she'd gotten upset. Josh knocked a third time and then a fourth. He walked around to the front of the house and looked into the living room window. He thought about calling Carl's daughter to see if she had an extra key but decided it might be easier if he did a little breaking and entering in the name of a welfare check. He had the door unlocked in about two minutes and smiled because he figured installing a new lock would give Carl and him another project to work on. This one was flimsy as hell.

Norton came tearing around the corner the minute Josh entered the kitchen. Josh took in the overturned garbage can and the garbage on the floor as Norton jumped up on him, pawing at Josh's chest. "Hey, buddy." Normally the dog was as docile as they came, and Josh proceeded with caution as he rounded the corner into the living room. There was more trash by the couch, and Josh followed the trail. It was a small ranch house, with two bedrooms, a bathroom, the living room, and the kitchen on the main level, above the unfinished basement where he and Carl had done most of their work. The bedroom door was open a crack, and Josh could see Carl lying on the bed. He was fairly sure he knew what had happened but made himself check for a pulse anyway. Norton jumped up on the bed and curled his body around his owner. Except for rummaging in the trash because he hadn't been fed, he'd probably been right here since Carl died, which was probably sometime after his daughter had checked in on him yesterday. Josh took comfort in the fact that the dog had likely been with Carl when he'd drawn his last breath, and it made him happy to know the man had spent his last days doing something he enjoyed. Josh left the room, steeling himself for the call he was about to make to Carl's daughter.

"Where did he come from, Dad?" Sasha asked, her words muffled by the dog's fur.

"The owner couldn't take care of him anymore," Josh said, and that was all she needed to know.

Sasha had not left the dog's side. Josh was happy she didn't ask if she could rename it. The dog was old, and a name change would likely confuse it and it had been through enough already.

"Can he sleep in my bed tonight?" Sasha asked.

"How about on the floor next to your bed?" Josh said. After leaving Carl's, he'd taken the dog to be groomed, and while Norton was being attended to he'd purchased all the necessary supplies, including a large dog bed with plenty of cushioning and support. He had reservations about bringing an older dog into the mix but only because he knew it would be hard on Sasha when they lost him. But Carl's daughter had been distraught over the news of her father's death and she'd been so relieved when he'd offered to find a home for the dog.

Might as well be mine, he thought.

CHAPTER 7

LAYLA

"So, Annie and I were talking the other day and we were thinking it might be time for you to dip your toes in the dating pool," Tonya said as they stood outside on an overcast morning. "Maybe try an app."

Thankfully, Annie had not yet arrived. Layla didn't have the energy to deal with an ambush, and the morning drop-off was still a complete clusterfuck. How could so many grown adults not understand the simple process of dropping off their children?

"I'm not interested in a dating app," Layla said. "Plus, I've heard everyone lies."

"Nobody really says what they mean at first."

Nobody really says what they mean during ten years of marriage, either, Layla thought.

"You're free to browse," Tonya said. "See what's out there."

"I'm not sure I want to know."

53

Layla noted the arrival of Josh and Sasha. Either he had little patience for the drop-off line or Sasha continued to need extra encouragement, because Josh was still walking Sasha in. Layla was quickly becoming a touchstone of sorts for Sasha, and the little girl almost always stopped to say hi. That morning, Sasha barreled toward her shouting, "Miss Layla! Miss Layla! Guess what?"

Layla had no idea what Sasha might say. Teachers were often on the receiving end of some very personal information that parents would be mortified to learn came out of their offspring's mouth in a school setting. A little boy had recently told Tonya all about the farting contest he'd had with his dad that resulted in one of them shitting themselves. "And it wasn't the little boy," Tonya said.

"What is it, Sasha? It must be pretty big news because I've never seen you so excited before."

"We got a dog! It sleeps on my bed."

"That's *hugely* exciting news," Layla said.

Sasha beamed. "His name is Norton and he's big and fluffy. He eats a lot and his poops are really big," Sasha said, wrinkling her nose.

Layla stifled a smile. "Well, that is to be expected, I guess."

54

Josh looked at them and shrugged. "She's not wrong."

"I'll draw you a picture of him," Sasha promised as Josh began nudging her closer to the building's entrance.

"I would love that," Layla said. "Have a good day."

"Okay, I will," she said. Layla watched them walk away. Josh always smiled at Layla, and it made her happy. She would never admit to Tonya and Annie how much she enjoyed the daily interaction with Sasha *and* her dad. They'd lose their goddamn minds.

Annie joined them at the curb. "What are we talking about?"

Tonya answered her. "Online dating."

"Oh, good. You told her. So, there are different apps depending on what you're looking for."

"I never said I was looking," Layla said, but Annie wasn't going to let something like Layla's disinterest deter her.

"There's one for hookups and another one that only allows women to send the first message so you wouldn't have to worry about a bunch of dick pics in your inbox."

"You're making it sound so appealing," Layla said.

"I just said *no* dick pics. What's the problem?"

"The problem is that such a concern exists in the first place."

"This is what dating looks like now," Annie said.

"How do you even know this?" Layla asked. "You're married."

"I like to keep my husband on his toes."

"This is the most depressing conversation I've had all week," Layla said.

"It's only Tuesday," Tonya said.

"Exactly."

The truth was that Layla didn't know if she had the energy to do it all again, especially now that the rules had apparently changed. It exhausted her to think about the various stages of dating. There was the meeting stage followed by the getting-to-know-you stage. Then there was the I-like-you stage, and the falling-in-love stage. Then there was the I-can't-live-without-you and let's-spend-the-rest-of-our-lives-together stage.

At that point, no one was thinking about the other stages. The ones that got progressively hurtful and shouty and ended in the office of an attorney.

Layla considered herself a mood performer,

and that night at Connie's she was feeling a combination of kick-ass and sultry. The band had opened the set with a screaming rendition of Lita Ford's "Kiss Me Deadly," with Layla on lead vocals. Onstage, she was a lot less sugar and a hell of a lot more spice, and she moved across the small space like a lioness stalking its prey. She sang about being kissed once and then twice, and more than one guy in the audience wondered what that might be like. They followed the opening song with "You Oughta Know" by Alanis Morissette, and by then Layla was completely in her element.

They kicked it down a notch with Fiona Apple's "Criminal" and Sarah McLachlan's "Building a Mystery." Layla had loved so much of the music that had come out of the last three decades, especially the releases by female artists that felt like they'd been tailor-made for someone like her.

On "Picture" by Kid Rock and Sheryl Crow, their bass player, Rick, a tall guy with longish hair, stared into Layla's eyes as they sang. The two of them shared a microphone, and a casual observer might have wondered if there was something between them, but she and Rick simply sounded good together and they sang the hell out of that song.

Layla strummed a few opening notes and announced that this would be their last song of the night. "This is a new original tune. We hope you like it."

She sat down on a stool, center stage. Kevin, their drummer, had been writing a lot of original material, and they'd slowly been adding it to their sets. Cover bands brought people into bars and they'd never be able to stop playing crowd favorites. But they hoped their fans would begin to recognize the new stuff and start asking for those songs as well.

A spotlight shined on her and the crowd remained silent as Layla's pure, clear voice filled the bar. Her lean arms flexed as her hands moved up and down the neck of the guitar. Her face looked rosy in the spotlight, flushed, the way a person's skin glowed right before they started sweating. Her chest rose and fell under her tight T-shirt as she took deep breaths, filling her lungs with the air necessary to sustain the long notes. Her eyes were closed, and she was lost in the music as if she were playing only for herself and not a room packed full of people.

When the song ended, Layla thanked the crowd for coming, and removed her guitar strap. People crowded the stage, ready to mob them. The guy whose lap Suzanne had been sitting on a few weeks ago walked by. Layla had completely forgotten his name by then, but there was something about his face that made it easier to recall. It wasn't that he was the handsomest guy she'd ever met, but there was a commanding presence about him that made you sit up and take notice. He cocked his head to the side and held her gaze for a second before smiling.

Now that they were done playing, sweat gathered at her hairline and ran in a narrow rivulet down the side of her face. Her T-shirt stuck to her chest and the area under her guitar strap was soaked. Moments before she would have stepped down from the stage and been enveloped by the crowd, Liam — that was his name — heaved himself up on it like he belonged there. He reached around to her hair and lifted the long thickness of it off her neck, pressing the bottle of unopened beer in his hand against her skin.

"Ah," she said, because it was exactly what she wanted, needed. She looked at him oddly, as if she wasn't sure why he was standing in front of her or how he'd gotten there.

But, in time, she would learn that Liam was a closer. It was what made him such a good salesman.

He didn't wait for permission.

He didn't ask questions that might result in a no answer.

When he was selling cars and reached the point where the customers expected him to crank up his sales pitch, he'd put a purchase order and a pen on the table in front of them instead and say, "Sign here and we'll have you on your way in that beautiful car in no time." When you were well-dressed and confident, you could get away with shit like that. And nine times out of ten, the customer would give him exactly what he wanted.

Liam moved the beer bottle around to her cheek and pressed it against her damp skin. Her fans were crowding the stage, waiting for her to step down. Waiting to mob her. He opened the beer and offered it to her; she grabbed it and drank.

"How does it feel to be a rock goddess?" he asked. He probably expected her to stammer, to protest, because "rock goddess" was laying it on thick and they both knew it.

But what she said was "It feels fantastic."

Because it did, and she never wanted this feeling to end.

She took another long drink and put the beer back into his hand. He paused as if waiting for her to thank him for the beer or the compliment, but instead she turned, and, without warning, jumped off the stage, swan-diving right into the waiting arms of the crowd with a confident arrogance that surprised even her sometimes.

Liam looked on as her fans passed her lithe

body overhead, never letting her come close to hitting the ground. She shrieked in delight as she bounced among them, her weight supported by their arms. When they finally put her down, gently and on her feet, the line of people who wanted to talk to her, to buy her a drink, was at least ten deep, and she forgot all about Liam.

Months later, Liam would tell her that the night she jumped off that stage was the night she'd intrigued him so much he decided that he simply had to know more about her.

When Layla was onstage, microphone in hand, the crowd gazing up at her, she was awfully shiny, too.

Maybe shinier than Suzanne, even.

Every man in that bar would have agreed that Suzanne was beautiful, but Layla was the one everyone — man or woman — came to see.

CHAPTER 8

JOSH

Justin, one of Josh's older brothers and a former self-proclaimed bachelor for life, met a woman he couldn't live without, and suddenly marriage was the greatest, most awesome thing in the world. Josh had listened patiently over beers one night as Justin blathered on like a lovesick fool. Josh didn't have the heart to tell him it was early days, partly because he and his brother were close, and partly because Josh still remembered being so stupidly in love that putting a ring on it seemed like the only gesture grand enough to honor the way he felt about Kimmy. He didn't regret it, but if he'd had a crystal ball and even the slightest bit of impulse control, he might have had a completely different life. He'd been thinking about that a lot lately.

Justin and his fiancée were getting married next Saturday night in a large ornate church in her hometown. It was a four-hour drive, so they'd be making a weekend of it and coming back home Sunday morning after brunch. Sasha overheard Josh making the arrangement to board Norton. "Dad!" she cried the minute he hung up the phone. "Norton has to come with us. We can't leave him behind." In the weeks that had followed Norton becoming a part of their household, Sasha had fallen hopelessly in love with the dog. When Sasha was at Josh's house, Norton could always be found by her side.

"I don't think your uncle Justin, or his bride-to-be, would go for that. It'll be okay. The place is really nice. We can sign him up for extra walks. They even have dog cookies."

"He would be so scared and sad without us."

The dog did seem to have a problem with being left alone for too long. Josh had started bringing Norton to work with him if the homeowner had a fenced-in yard and didn't mind. For commercial jobs, Norton had to stay home, and Josh noticed that he followed them from room to room when he and Sasha returned at the end of the day. He didn't want to board the dog either, but everyone in his family would also be at the wedding. Maybe he could ask one of his

63

friends. When Norton had people around to calm him, he was affectionate and as low-maintenance as they came.

"I'll figure something out," he told Sasha.

CHAPTER 9

LAYLA

After school, Layla drove to the new guitar shop that had recently opened in the strip mall she passed every day on her way home. It was time.

The bell tinkled when she opened the door. Shiny guitars lined the walls, and her pulse quickened. She walked the outer perimeter of the room, pausing now and then to peruse the offerings. The shiny Fender. The gleaming Stratocaster. She had once owned six electric guitars. One by one, she sold them. She couldn't play them in the luxury loft she and Liam had moved to shortly after they got married, because the first time she had, someone complained about the noise. She couldn't bear to part with her beloved acoustic, but for years it sat zipped into its case when she wasn't using it to teach other people how to play. When they moved into the new house they'd bought, she could have played it whenever she wanted. She strummed it occasionally, but eventually it only served to highlight what was missing in her life, so she rarely brought it out. She played it often now, on the deck when she was writing in her journal and sipping wine. But the urge to play electric had been building, especially now that the basement studio was almost ready.

"Is there something I can help you find?" a voice to her left asked. The man was tall and had short, spiky blond hair and an earring. He looked to be in his early forties, although Layla wasn't sure. The earring made him seem younger. "I'm Brian."

"Layla," she said. "I'm looking for a new electric guitar." She ran her hand along the neck of the beer-can-blue Fender on the wall in front of them. So shiny. So magnetic.

He tilted his head and studied her briefly. Glanced at her fingers, which were callus-free.

For now.

"Awesome. Just learning or have you been playing awhile?"

"I know how to play. I've just taken a rather long break. Too long."

"Okay. Tell me what you're looking for."

66

■ ■ ■ ■

At home, Layla brought her new purchases — the gleaming Fender and the forty-five-watt amp — down to her studio. There were now a stool and two floor lamps to illuminate the space. A microphone in a stand, ready and waiting for her to sing into until her voice was raw. But that would come a little later. Right now, it was the guitar strings that beckoned the most.

She removed the guitar from its case, tuned it a bit. When she was satisfied that it was ready, she plugged it into the amp. The acoustics weren't great, but the room was fairly soundproof with its concrete walls and the one small egress window. Layla wanted to play with abandon, without regard for noise ordinances or neighbors who might not share her penchant for fast, loud, wall-shaking riffs.

She wanted to *shred.*

And for the next hour, that's exactly what she did.

CHAPTER 10

JOSH

Josh stopped to talk to Layla on the way back to the parking lot after he walked Sasha into the building.

"Did Sasha ask you to watch our dog?" Sasha had mortifyingly informed him that morning that she was no longer worried about Norton going to the kennel because Miss Layla was going to watch him instead. Apparently, Sasha had asked her music teacher if she liked dogs, and Layla had said yes. He wasn't sure exactly what had transpired after that.

"She did. She mentioned in class the other day that she was very worried about Norton going to the dog babysitter."

"I'm sorry. I certainly don't expect you to do that."

"It's no trouble," Layla said. "The family I bought the house from had two big dogs, so I have a fenced-in yard and there's even a dog door."

"If you're sure about this, that would be great. He really likes it when people are around. The wedding is next weekend. I'm taking Sasha out of school early on Friday afternoon so we can get there in time for the rehearsal. I can bring him over on Thursday night after you get home from school if that's okay. What's your phone number? I'll text you the details and get your address."

She gave him her number, and he saved it and slid his phone back into his pocket. She really had seemed like she didn't mind, and that was one less thing he had to worry about.

Josh's thoughts kept returning to Layla on his way to work. Sasha had decided she loved being walked into school by Josh every day, even on the days she was with Kimmy, so he'd pick her up at Kimmy's condo shortly before eight and drive her. Kimmy appreciated it, because it allowed her to get to work on time, and Josh truly didn't mind.

Layla was never there in the afternoon, but she was always standing at the curb in the morning and he'd started to scan for her as soon as he was close enough to make out the faces of the teachers. It reminded him a little of meeting Kimmy for the first time and how he'd thought he wouldn't see her again and then suddenly she seemed to be everywhere that Josh was.

It was like noticing something for the first time, like a particular make of car or an advertisement for a product that kept appearing. But in this case, it was someone. Josh caught glimpses of Kimmy in the commons before school. He was parking his car three rows over when she got out of the passenger seat of another girl's car. He was in the office one morning when he ducked in to pick up a pass because he'd overslept, and she was there doing what seemed to be the same thing.

He'd done a little checking one night, in his bedroom with the door locked as he looked her up in his old yearbooks. He'd scanned the rows of alphabetical listings until he spotted her face: Kimberly Keller. There was only one picture each year. No candid shot of her in a basketball or cheerleading uniform. No singing in show choir or arguing a case on behalf of the debate team.

Nothing.

Same as him.

It didn't appear that she participated in any extracurricular activities at all.

Same as him.

She didn't seem the type to run with the stoners or the nerds either, which made her hard to figure out. There were people who'd said Josh was hard to figure out, too, because he didn't fit neatly into any one category.

Later, in marriage counseling, when asked to say what she liked most about him, Kimmy had said, "Josh is a caring, salt-of-the-earth individual. Reliable, trustworthy. Loyal. He's a hard worker as long as he's allowed to do what he loves." When asked for his opinion of that assessment, he'd agreed that that was pretty much him in a nutshell.

The next time he spoke to Kimmy, Josh literally bumped into her in the hallway, because he wasn't watching where he was going and they collided. Later, they would have whispered conversations about fate and destiny while lying intertwined and naked in each other's arms. When he thought back on those early days with Kimmy, Josh wanted to punch himself for being so whipped and blinded, and for making ninety-nine percent of his decisions with his dick instead of his brain.

"Oh, hey. Are you okay?" Josh asked, placing his hands on her shoulders to steady her. "It's Kimmy, right?"

She had blushed. "Yeah." Then she had smiled up at him and it was less mischievous, a little more curious.

"You sure you're okay?"

"I'm fine."

"Do you want a ride home?"

"I don't actually have detention today, so yeah. That'd be great."

"I just need to swing by my locker," he said.

She followed him to his locker, which wasn't that far from hers although it was around the corner in a hallway she said she rarely used. "You're really tucked away back here," she said.

"I like it. It's close to most of my classes, so I can mess around and still make it to my seat on time."

Josh threw his books into his locker and slammed it shut. As they walked down the hallway toward the exit that led to the parking lot, they passed signs reading WOOD SHOP, METALWORKING, CONSTRUCTION.

Josh's thing wasn't sports, or show choir, or debate, either.

It was the industrial arts.

Despite his good looks and easy charm, he hadn't had much luck finding a steady girl-friend. The jocks would always have first pick, followed by those who excelled in the fine arts. Then came the brainiacs, normal kids with no obvious issues, and finally the goths, emos, and stoners. Guys like Josh were often mistak-enly lumped in with the stoners, which wasn't at all true, at least in his case. Sadly, there weren't very many girls who were interested in the industrial arts, so his high school years lacked the romantic opportunities afforded to other members of the student body.

In the parking lot, when they reached his car, he opened the door for her, because one of his brothers had told him it was a real power move. Josh didn't know about that, but Kimmy blushed again and looked up at him with a surprised look on her face like maybe that had never happened before.

"No homework?" she asked when they were pulling out of the parking lot and he was still trying to come up with something to start the conversation.

"When you're a solid C student, books aren't necessary. I've got enough credits to graduate and as long as I don't do something stupid like fail one of my classes, it'll be a smooth ride all the way to graduation."

"And then what?" Kimmy asked.

He told her he currently worked for a landscaping business loading bags of mulch and strips of sod into people's cars during the warmer months, but that a friend's dad hired him to pour concrete starting this summer. He'd been warned that it was backbreaking work, but it still sounded a hell of a lot better to Josh than voluntarily sitting in a lecture hall for four more years.

"I've never met anyone else who planned on working instead of going to college," she said. "I'm going to work too."

He glanced at her, surprised. "Really?" He'd figured she'd already decorated her dorm room in her head.

"Yeah."

"Cool. Where are you going to work?"

"I don't know yet. Mostly I babysit but I'd like to find a real job. I want to buy a car. And I need benefits and stuff." That was another thing he'd find out later, that she and her mother had never had health insurance and they'd been lucky that neither of them had ever gotten really sick.

"How do your parents feel about you not going to college?"

"It's just my mom and me. She's cool with it."

"You're lucky," he said. "Mine are not cool with it. 'Josh, you could be a good student if you applied yourself. Josh, you aren't going to get anywhere in life if you don't go to college.'"

"College isn't for everyone," Kimmy said, and it would have been hard for anyone to miss the conviction in her voice.

"Well, I know it's not for me," Josh said. "But no one listens. They think they can convince me like I'll suddenly say, 'You know what?

You're right! I do want to go to college.' It's infuriating. My parents' friends make comments all the time. So do total strangers. They find out you're a senior and they automatically say, 'Where are you going to college?' When I tell them I'm not going, they all say I'll change my mind. Like, I'm going to just flip-flop? It's stupid. I think I'm old enough to know what I want."

It was the most he'd ever spoken about it to anyone, and once he got started, he couldn't stop.

"I've got three brothers. Two are currently in college and one has already graduated from Minnesota State. I pointed out to my parents that they'd finally get a break from paying tuition." That hadn't gone over well, but he'd only been trying to lighten the mood because everyone was so damn serious about the subject and he was tired of arguing about it.

"They'll pay for it?" She sounded a little like she might have considered going to college if there was money lying around for it.

"They set up college funds when we were born. That's another reason they're so pissed. I'm squandering my opportunity. They think I'm ungrateful."

"So, you take a lot of industrial arts classes and stuff?"

"I've taken all of them. I'm not bored in those

75

classes. The As I get balance out the Ds I get in my other classes."

"Which one is your favorite?" she asked.

"Construction. I like building things, but what I really like is doing the wiring."

"You mean like for the electricity?"

He nodded.

"Have you ever been shocked?"

"Well, yeah. A whole bunch of times. It's no big deal."

"Wow," she said, and he grinned.

By the time he pulled into her driveway, he could feel an even more thrilling form of electricity, the kind you felt when two people seemed to be clicking on all cylinders. "Let's go out," he said when the car came to a stop and she unbuckled her seat belt.

"Yeah, okay," she said.

He grabbed a pen from the floor of his car, where it had been rolling around for months. "What's your number?"

She told him and he wrote it on his arm. "I'm surprised we never met before this year," he said.

"I know. I was thinking about that too."

"I'll call you tonight," he said.

"Yeah, okay," she said again, and he liked the way she looked at him like he was someone she might want to know better.

CHAPTER 11

LAYLA

The teachers' lounge was packed on Friday when Layla finally got a minute to heat up her lunch. Tonya waved her over and moved the stack of books she'd used to save Layla a seat. She crunched into her apple when Layla reached the table and said, "Hurry and sit down before someone else does."

"Thanks," Layla said, plunking down her enchiladas. She still hadn't gotten used to cooking for one, but she'd learned to freeze the leftovers, so she always had something to heat up if she didn't feel like cooking. It also made for easy lunches, even if she found herself eating the same thing for multiple meals.

"Tim and I are going to check out that trendy new tapas place by the mall tomorrow night. Come join us, just for a couple of hours. You need to put down that guitar for one night and get out of the house. At

77

least give your hands a break."

"You keep forgetting that I don't want to leave the house." Layla planned to spend the weekend in her basement studio. Maybe she'd also take a long nap or binge-watch something on Netflix.

"You said you were going to try to get out more. I miss the time we used to spend together outside of school."

Their girls' nights, movie dates, and shopping trips had come to a screeching halt when Layla left Liam and she'd gradually become a hermit. But it was time for her to start living her life again. "You're right. I did say that. I'll come for a little while."

"Maybe you can get a manicure tomorrow, too." Tonya shuddered, because the fingertips on Layla's left hand looked a little ragged, and her short nails were devoid of polish.

The calluses were starting to form and a few of them were already peeling. The aching in her hand felt *good* to Layla, because it was a welcome and familiar pain. "You want me to leave the house *and* you want my hands to look nice? Don't push it."

"Just be ready to go tomorrow night, and don't text me with some bullshit excuse."

On Saturday night, Layla put on her nicest

jeans, a cute top, and a pair of heels. At the restaurant, there was a third person sitting at the table with Tonya and Tim — a co-worker of Tim's named Drew who just happened to be free tonight, they hoped Layla didn't mind. Drew was handsome in a Disney-prince kind of way, with his wavy blond hair and gleaming teeth. His smile was genuine, and when he shook her hand she wished she had gotten that manicure after all, because a little nail polish never hurt anything.

"Are you mad?" Tonya asked after dinner when they went to the bathroom to check their lipstick.

"No. I knew it was a setup when you suggested the manicure."

"Well, if you're not even going to consider online dating, I had to get creative. Wait, you knew, and you came anyway? Interesting."

"Don't read too much into it. I'm tired of freezer meals and drinking alone."

"Tim said he's really nice. Everyone likes him at work," Tonya said.

"He seems great," Layla said. "But the thought of starting a new relationship exhausts me. I thought if I came out tonight, that maybe if I met someone in person, I'd feel differently. But if a man like that can't tempt me out of hibernation, the problem isn't with him. It's with me."

"I just want you to find someone who's as wonderful as you are."

"So do I. But it's not going to be tonight."

"Well, Tim and I will be receiving a call from our babysitter in about ten minutes telling us that Ian threw up. Not true, but that's our way of leaving the two of you to your own devices while I make out in the car with my husband across the street in the mall parking lot. The kids keep busting in on us at the most inopportune times and Tim's about to explode."

"The amount of planning that went into this is truly impressive," Layla said. "Go. It won't kill me to converse with a man. I almost remember how it's done."

"Call me tomorrow and tell me everything. Embellish the story to make it worth my while."

Layla laughed and hugged Tonya. "I'll do my best."

Fifteen minutes later, when Tim and Tonya had beaten a hasty retreat, Drew flagged down the waiter and asked him to bring back their menus. "How about dessert? It's not a ploy to get you to stay longer. I'll just never understand the concept of tiny plates of food. I'm still hungry. Like, really super hungry."

She laughed and he smiled warmly at her. When the waiter returned with the menus, she opened hers and said, "I like chocolate cake."

He ordered two, and when they were digging into them with their forks, she felt a pang of regret. So much of what happened in life came down to timing. He was a great catch and he'd undoubtedly make some woman incredibly happy, but she felt nothing, so she had no choice but to remove the hook and throw him back.

"My ex-husband and I divorced a little over six months ago and now my friends are trying to set me up and, well, you know. Everyone seems to think that the answer to a failed relationship is another relationship," Layla said.

"Ah, matchmaking friends who mean well. I remember those days. Don't worry. It'll die down eventually."

"I guess I'm in that weird transitional place," she said. "How about you?"

"I've been divorced for a few years now," he said, and she could sense a sort of desperation behind the words because he'd been at this longer than she had and maybe he'd grown weary of it not working out yet.

Maybe all he wanted was to find the right person so he could stop doing it.

"How did you know you were ready?" she asked when there was nothing left of the cake but a few errant swirls of chocolate sauce on the plate.

"It was just a feeling I had. You'll know it when it happens."

"Please don't think it's you. It's not you at all. It's me. I'm not ready. I just need to be alone for a while."

"That sounds lonely," he said, and he looked at her in a way that cut her to the quick. She wondered if three years from now she'd be the one sitting across from the newly single guy and it would be her desperation that was palpable. She hoped not, but she also knew that jumping into something too soon wasn't the answer, either.

And she wasn't lonely, not really. Layla had been lonely for years while she was married, and she'd take being alone over lonely any day.

CHAPTER 12

JOSH

"Hey, Sash. Go put your stuff in your room. Norton's sleeping on your bed," Josh said when Kimmy brought her back on Friday. He waited until Sasha was out of earshot and then he turned to Kimmy and said, "Am I supposed to be receiving something? I haven't gotten any paperwork or anything."

About the only thing they agreed on when they ended the marriage was that neither of them wanted to pay hefty attorney fees or go through a dragged-out divorce process, so they worked out the terms on their own. It was amicable as far as separations went. Neither of them had any big ax to grind. There hadn't been any cheating. No lying. No one had a drug problem or gambled away their savings. It was more or less an even split, so they'd agreed upon an uncontested divorce and Kimmy suggested an at-

83

torney one of her coworkers had recommended. Josh had given Kimmy the information she'd requested, mostly financial and the rest having to do with Sasha and how they'd agreed to split custody of her, and she'd given everything to the attorney. Once Josh received the documents, he'd let his attorney — someone his dad had used in the past and been happy with — look over everything to make sure it was fair and what they'd agreed upon. It should have been a slam dunk, but he'd been waiting for paperwork since May. Now it was almost the end of October and a couple of people had put the thought into his head that maybe Kimmy had decided to hire a different lawyer. Go for full custody or more assets, although he didn't see how any of that would ever fly in court. But everyone kept warning him how divorce changed people until suddenly they decided that what they'd agreed upon was no longer good enough.

"I've been busy," Kimmy said, and for the first time in a long time her tone was a mix of defensive and wounded instead of the polite, sterile way they now spoke to each other. As if they were merely acquaintances and not two people who had been together since they were eighteen years old and whose child was made of their combined DNA. "Why? Have you met someone?" she asked.

"What? No, I'm just following up," he said.

"I'll call the attorney on Monday."

"Okay," he said. "Let me know if there's anything I can do to help."

She'd left without saying another word, and then Sasha and Norton had come bounding back into the room, and he tried to put it out of his mind. But the niggling worry was still there.

If Josh's parents had strong feelings about the split, they'd kept it to themselves. But one night, when Josh and Sasha had gone over for dinner and he was in the kitchen alone with his mother shortly after he'd broken the news, she was rinsing dishes in the sink and she said, "I just never thought she'd be the one who'd want to leave."

Josh and Kimmy's love had burned brighter and for far longer than anyone could have ever guessed it would. He had once loved her more than he'd ever loved anything in his life, but all he said was "People change," and he left it at that.

Josh had been standing next to Kimmy's locker after the final bell rang on Friday. He'd been there the day before, and the day before that, too, and then he'd driven her home. Since she'd given him her number last week, they'd tied up the phone for hours every night, hanging up only when someone else in the house needed to use the phone, usually one of Josh's brothers. And now the weekend was finally here, and when Kimmy spotted him standing there waiting for her, she lit up. "Hey," she said when she reached him. She reached out her hand to spin the dial and open her locker.

"Hey, yourself. Want a ride?"

"Yeah," she said. One day in the future she would tell him that riding home from school with him had become so important to her that she'd started turning in all her assignments so that detention would be a thing of the past. She joked that even back then, Josh was helping her to reach her full potential, even if all she wanted at the time was to be near him.

Kimmy shared his self-awareness about her place in the social echelon of their high school. She was not popular and had never aspired to be. She was as invisible at school as she was at home, because no one really cared very much about what she did in either place.

But she wasn't unattractive. Not at all. There

was something very wholesome about her, with her peaches-and-cream complexion and long blond hair. There wasn't enough money in the budget for her to wear the latest fashions, but there was nothing wrong with her figure, and by the time she reached puberty, she knew how to accentuate her long legs and tiny waist with a simple pair of Levi's purchased secondhand from Goodwill, and one of the white Hanes T-shirts she bought in packs of three. The other girls could have their Benetton and Guess. Kimmy learned from an early age to embrace "less is more." With her limited clothing budget, she really didn't have a choice other than to make it work for her. Josh liked her look and he liked her social standing. Kimmy was the female equivalent of Josh, and for once he didn't have to see the look of disappointment on a girl's face when he admitted that sports weren't really his thing. Kimmy let Josh be himself, and that was something he'd never experienced before.

That Friday, when Josh pulled into her driveway, he shut off the car. "Do you want to go to Mikey's garage with me tonight?"

Kimmy's face fell. "I have to babysit."

"How about after? I can pick you up if you give me the address?"

"You wouldn't mind picking me up?" she said.

"No, not at all."

"What's Mikey's garage?" she asked.

"It's just my friend Mikey's house. His parents are cool. They let us hang out in their garage."

"Okay."

"So, you'll call me?" he asked. "When you're ready?"

"Yeah. They said they'd be home by nine thirty or ten."

"I'll be waiting."

Josh pulled into the driveway of the address she'd given him. Kimmy had called him right before the parents were due home and he'd headed over. He'd only been there a minute or so before the front door opened, and Kimmy hurried down the steps and into his car.

He'd showered and changed clothes and was wearing jeans and a sweatshirt. She'd changed her clothes, too, and it looked like maybe she'd curled her hair or something. She smelled good.

The faint haze of cigarette smoke hung in the air when they entered the garage. A boom box in the corner pumped out pop hits at an earsplitting volume. Candy wrappers and chip bags littered the concrete floor, which was stained with some sort of automotive fluid, although there were no cars parked inside at the moment.

Everyone was already there, and some of them had undoubtedly been hanging out from the minute they had escaped the confines of the school. They were a harmless, if somewhat unmotivated, group of kids, who enjoyed each other's company while they marked time until graduation, the way Josh was. But that didn't mean they didn't have futures. The people Josh introduced Kimmy to that night would go on to be the diesel mechanics and carpenters. The plumbers and HVAC experts. A few would go on to the community college and study computer programming or fashion merchandising. A couple more would join the armed forces. In time Kimmy would come to know Josh's friends well and become an important member of their close-knit group. Back then, it was unfathomable to imagine that your peer group would ever change.

A couple of the guys were smoking cigarettes, which he wasn't crazy about. "Do you smoke?" he asked Kimmy. He'd smelled it on her clothes a few times, but she never mentioned it.

"No. My mom smokes all the time and I hate it."

All the kids in that garage were holding a drink of some kind, beer mostly although one of the girls sipped punch from a red Solo cup. His friend Jacob handed Josh a beer. "Do you drink?" Josh asked Kimmy.

"Yeah," she said. She told him that her best friend Angie's parents entertained a lot and when they did, they didn't keep a close eye on what the girls were up to. Kimmy had slept over many times when Angie's parents had guests, and they loved cruising through the kitchen and helping themselves to whatever was chilling in a big glass pitcher in the fridge. Plus, they'd also raided the liquor cabinet of all the stuff Angie's parents ignored like the cordials and brandies and some weird peach-flavored liquor.

Kimmy's mom rarely drank alcohol. Kimmy and Angie had once found a dusty bottle of gin in Kimmy's kitchen, shoved way back in one of the cupboards. But when they snuck a glass of it up to her bedroom, they discovered it tasted awful and poured it down the bathroom sink. Kimmy's mom preferred coffee and she drank it all day long, a cigarette in one hand and a cracked travel mug of instant Sanka that she carried everywhere with her in the other.

Jacob came back with one of the red Solo cups and handed it to Kimmy. She took a sip.

"You like it?" Josh asked.

"It's sweet," she said, and she took another

drink. He led her to the old couch in the corner, which wasn't very clean and already had three people sitting on it. They wedged in close together and Josh didn't mind that one bit. "I'm not squishing you, am I?" he asked, and she said no so quickly that maybe she didn't mind it, either. He gave her a smile like the one she'd given him earlier that day when she'd spotted him leaning up against her locker. *I am going to kiss her tonight,* he thought.

He brought her another cup of punch, and when she finished it she asked where the bathroom was. He told her it was just inside and down the short hallway. He stretched out his leg a little so that his knee was holding her spot. He moved it when she got back and patted the tiny pocket of space and she sat down and cuddled right up next to him. He was also a couple of drinks in by then and a warmth had started to spread through him.

Then another group of kids walked into the garage and Kimmy said "Shit" under her breath. One of them, a senior named Colin that Josh had never really gotten along with, shot Josh a look. He looked at Kimmy and then back at Josh again. "So, you two are a thing?"

"What's it to you?" Josh said.

Colin looked at Kimmy and wrinkled his

nose. "I'd wish you luck for later tonight, but you won't need it. I doubt you'll have to try too hard," he said, and the people he'd walked in with laughed.

Josh felt Kimmy tense up beside him and was just about to jump to her defense when she said, loud and clear, "I'm looking forward to it. I'm sure his dick will be a lot bigger than that tiny little thing you have." Josh choked on a mouthful of beer.

"You don't know what you're talking about," Colin said. The sneer on his face and the intensity of his words propelled Josh into action. Mikey was more Josh's friend than Colin's, and it was time to pull rank. He stood up, and Kimmy surprised him again by getting to her feet along with him.

"Well, if we'd been together, I would know, right? I mean, it's abnormally small. And weird-shaped. And there was that thing on the end."

Colin's face went nearly purple in his anger. "There's nothing wrong with my dick. I never touched you."

"What did you say?" Josh asked. "Because if you slept with her, she would definitely know what your dick looks like. And she said it was small and weird-shaped and had that thing —"

Colin cut Josh off before he could finish.

Smart move, because Josh had raised his voice so that everyone in Mikey's garage could hear him clearly.

"I never touched her. She wanted it, though. I'm the one who didn't want to give it to her." He threw his half-full beer can toward the pile of empties in the corner, and when it hit the floor some of the liquid sloshed out.

"Hey!" Mikey yelled. "Not cool."

Colin stomped off and walked toward his car in the driveway, his buddies falling in behind him. Kimmy stood silent, motionless. Maybe she was wondering how he'd feel about the girl he'd brought with him causing so much drama, though it wasn't like she'd done it on purpose. Maybe she was worrying that he wouldn't believe her side of the story. That he thought she was a slut.

If she was concerned about any of those things, she didn't need to be, because when Josh turned toward her, he was smiling. He grabbed her around the waist like something out of a movie, bent her backward a little, and kissed her right there in front of everyone. She kissed him back, and by the time they finally separated, gasping for air and smiling like fools, the others were hooting and hollering and yelling at them to get a room.

She told him about the trouble with Colin on

their way home later that night when he took her to an empty parking lot, where they kissed and talked for hours. How Colin had showed interest in her at the beginning of the school year, coming on strong and showering her with attention in the math class they were both taking. Eventually, he finagled an invitation to come over to her house after school while her mother was still at work. He said they'd go to a movie when the weekend rolled around, but in the meantime, he really wanted to spend some time with her outside of school. Get to know her better. "I believed him," Kimmy said.

Instead, he pressured her to have sex and it took every bit of strength she had to shove him off her when he didn't heed her very loud "No." For a minute, she told Josh she thought she'd been in real trouble, but he came to his senses in the nick of time, leaving her shaking and near tears.

The next day at school, when he was distant with her and there was no mention of weekend plans, Kimmy realized there was never going to be a movie.

Josh leaned in, kissed her again, and then pressed his lips to her ear. "In case you were wondering, I've never really liked that asshole. But I know I like you."

"I like you too," she whispered.

He liked her and then one day he loved her

94

and after that, he couldn't imagine them ever being apart, and for the next nineteen years, they weren't.

they weren't.

CHAPTER 13

LAYLA

Layla didn't register the arrival of Josh and Norton until they were standing at the top of the stairs leading up to the deck. The weather was still holding, and Layla wanted to take advantage of every last minute she could spend outdoors, because winter could come knocking at any minute.

Layla had told Josh the gate would be unlocked and to come around to the back, but she'd lost track of time, which happened often when she was writing in her journal and strumming her guitar. The sun had already started its descent and the air had grown cooler.

"Sorry," Josh said. "I didn't mean to startle you." He set down a couple of dog bowls and a bag of food.

A bird landed on one of her fence posts, and Norton shot down the stairs and took off after it. Just before he reached it, it flew away and landed on another post. Norton followed and came up short again.

"Chase-the-birds is by far his favorite activity," Josh said. "For an older dog, he's remarkably spry."

Layla hadn't heard Josh pull into the driveway or the slam of a car door. "Did you walk here?"

"Yes. When you sent your address, I realized we only live about four blocks apart. I dropped Sasha off at her mom's and then figured I'd walk him here. He moves a little slower than he probably used to, but he loves it."

Her guitar was laid across the other chair and she picked it up and moved it out of the way. "Would you like to sit down?"

"Sure," he said. "Were you playing?" he asked, motioning toward the guitar.

"A little."

"I bet you can play everything. You're the best music teacher in the world, according to Sasha."

Layla smiled. "My students are extremely sweet. They're also not hard to impress."

Her throat was dry, so she reached for her wineglass and took a sip. The pinot was lukewarm, and she grimaced when she spotted the gnat floating in it. She fished it out and it seemed rude to be giving her wineglass so much attention right in front of him. "Would you like a glass of wine?"

He surprised her by saying, "I would, actually. My ex-wife doesn't drink so I didn't much, either. It sounds good, though. Thanks."

She went inside and poured him a glass of wine. When she came back out, she handed it to him and sat down. "So, Norton," she said. "Like the antivirus?"

Josh laughed. "Definitely *not* like the antivirus. And I know this because when I asked his former owner the same question, he said, 'What the hell is an antivirus?'"

"You knew the person Norton belonged to?"

"Norton's former owner was a ninety-six-year-old man named Carl who lived alone and whose house was likely to go up in flames at any moment due to his very faulty and not-even-remotely-up-to-code wiring. I'm an electrician, and his daughter hired me to take care of it. He was fine on Friday, but when I went back on Monday morning to finish the job, I discovered he had died at some point over the weekend."

"Oh my God," Layla said.

"Yeah. Norton had drunk all the water out of the toilet and had been eating garbage out of the kitchen garbage can. When I found Carl, Norton went and curled up on the bed next to him where he'd probably been since Carl died. It tore me up. He has a few abandonment issues because of it. It seems to stress him out when there aren't people around. Sasha has wanted a dog for a long time, so he's ours now."

The story sliced at her heart. *I'm not going to cry,* Layla told herself. She blinked back tears and shook her head. "That is truly heartbreaking."

He pointed at her guitar. "So, now I have to ask. Were you named after the Clapton song?"

"No. My dad's sister died when he was thirteen. She came down with meningitis and was gone in less than forty-eight hours." She winced. More death. *Way to bring it back around, Layla.* "Dad told me his parents were so touched when he and my mom announced my name after I was born."

"Do you know how to play the song?"

She heard the cheering from the audience. Remembered her twenty-three-year-old self having the time of her life. "Yes."

"Do you sing too?"

"A little."

"How long have you lived here?" Josh asked.

"I moved in at the end of June."

"It's just you?"

"It's just me."

He didn't ask for details; she didn't offer them.

She hadn't sat with a man in a long time. Liam had never been home during their last year of marriage, although it had taken a while for Layla to figure out that he was not actually working late the way he told her he was.

They drank their wine and watched Norton chase the birds. "Did you know you've got a light out in front?" he asked.

She had turned on the outside lights to make it easier for him to see the house number in case he arrived closer to dusk or even after dark. There were four lights, and one of them wouldn't turn on even after she replaced the bulb with a new floodlight right out of the box. The homes in her neighborhood were the kind that were still nice but were starting to need a little bit of work, as her Realtor so eloquently put it. The good bones were there, but certain rooms were in dire need of updating. These were mostly cosmetic improvements, and Layla had no trouble hiring the flooring company down the road to install new carpet in the living areas and a good laminate in the kitchen. The painting she was

100

perfectly capable of doing herself, and she had spent a considerable amount of time over the summer, in complete silence, soothed by the gentle sound of a paint roller turning the walls a creamy alabaster. The kitchen appliances worked fine, but Layla looked forward to the day when she'd saved enough to swap them out for something newer. Replacing the cabinets, countertops, and light fixtures would go a long way toward bringing the kitchen out of the nineties and into the new millennium. Of course, once she moved in she discovered a few things the inspector she'd hired had missed, things like the faulty outside light and the slightly unlevel floor in one area of the basement. Then there was the heating and cooling system that technically worked but probably only had a few years left. Same with the roof.

So maybe not good bones and certainly not great bones but definitely okay bones, which was all she really needed.

"I've changed the light bulb, but it still doesn't work," Layla said. Fixing the light wasn't high on her priority list, especially with all the time she was putting into her studio. Plus, she'd have to find someone to do it. Someone who knew what they were doing and wouldn't try and rip her off. It was one of those items she kept carrying forward on her to-do list, and even though she found it mildly annoying that she kept blowing it off, she didn't really care enough to address it.

"I can take a look at it when we get back, if you don't mind."

"Sure," she said.

They finished their wine, and before Josh left he told Layla he'd text her before he came to pick up Norton on Sunday afternoon. "And if you have any questions about him while we're gone, don't hesitate to ask." He bent down to scratch Norton behind the ears. "And if you want to send a picture or something, that would be good too. For Sasha."

He grinned and she said, "For Sasha. Got it. Have a great weekend."

"Thanks. We will."

Layla gathered up the wineglasses and her journal and her guitar. "C'mon, Norton," she said as she led the dog inside. She might not have a husband or a child, but she had decided to be one of those glass-half-full kind of people. She had a guitar and wine and, for a few days anyway, a dog who looked sad that Josh had left but happy that Layla was here, which meant he wouldn't have to be alone.

CHAPTER 14

JOSH

In the church, they rose as the wedding party made their way down the aisle and reached the altar. All they needed was the bride, and they turned toward the back of the church, where Amber was waiting on her father's arm as the opening notes of the wedding march filled the air. Josh lifted Sasha up so she could see. His brother was looking at his bride as if she were the only woman on earth, and Josh knew he believed it, too. He'd been in those same shoes once, but instead of a wedding gown, Kimmy had been wearing a prom dress.

"You look beautiful," Josh said.

"Really?" Kimmy said, grinning as she smoothed her palms over the yellow sequins that dotted the bodice. "Even in this vintage dress?"

"Absolutely," he said.

103

"Vintage" was their own little inside joke, because Kimmy had bought the dress at Goodwill. "It's all I can afford," she told him. "I can't imagine my mom taking me to the mall and dropping hundreds of dollars on a dress." They kept no secrets from each other, and he liked the way Kimmy had confided in him about all the ways her home life sucked. Her mother had never once attended a parent-teacher conference and had always considered the hours Kimmy spent in school to be a break from parenting her. For as long as Kimmy could remember, her mother had worked as a home health aide for an old man whose family didn't want to spend the money to get him a real nurse. The man was disabled in some way and agoraphobic. He liked to play Chinese checkers and smoke cigarettes, which was convenient because Kimmy's mom loved those things, too. The arrangement sounded all kinds of dysfunctional to Josh, but Kimmy said that as she got older, she realized how lucky they were because she feared her mother was basically unemployable in any other capacity. "My mom always said she couldn't do the things other moms did because she had to support us," Kimmy said. "I guess my dad was never in the picture." Maybe things would have been different for Kimmy if there had been someone who'd believed in her before Josh came along.

Josh had offered to pay for any dress Kimmy wanted, but she wouldn't hear of it. And the truth was that the dress was beautiful and looked like it had only been worn once. It skimmed her hips, and the yellow color looked stunning with her blond hair, which she'd left long and straight. All the other girls would be wearing elaborate updos, but even at Goodwill prices, Kimmy had blown her budget on the dress, shoes, and Josh's boutonniere. Angie had done her makeup, and Josh wasn't lying when he said she looked beautiful.

She did.

He'd met her mother for the first time on prom night, and that had gone better than he'd expected. Mrs. Keller was short on personality and warmth, but she wasn't rude, and she shook Josh's hand and told him it was nice to finally meet him. It seemed to make Kimmy happy that her mother had put down her cigarette and even snapped a picture of the two of them with an old camera Kimmy said she didn't know they owned.

It was a different story at Josh's house. His mother took loads of pictures of him and Kimmy, and several times she wiped away tears, because Josh was her youngest son and this would be the last prom. But when they finally escaped and were on their way to the restaurant to meet up with their friends, Kimmy was still talking about her mother and that camera. Josh was only eighteen years old and not very attuned to these kinds of things, but it was clear to him that night just how alone Kimmy must have felt growing up and how such a small amount of attention from her mother had affected her.

Kimmy had met Josh's parents several times by then, and they were always so nice to her. They'd seemed a little dismayed when she told them she wasn't going to college, but if they had an opinion about it, they'd kept it to themselves. They were still pushing hard for Josh to at least go to a trade school in the fall, but he remained convinced that working for a while was the best option for him.

Kimmy had decided she was ready to go all the way with Josh. They had come close several times, but Kimmy said she wanted to be sure. And when Josh told her he loved her one night when he'd taken her out for ice cream, he really wanted her to know that he meant it. They hadn't been making out or anything. They'd just been standing in line holding hands when he bent down and whispered it in her ear.

They had discussed the matter of having sex for the first time, and Josh had booked a hotel room for after prom. The others were going to cram as many people as they could into another room, but Josh and Kimmy wanted their own space. They were both legally adults, and Josh's parents had given their blessing, saying they'd rather the kids were at a hotel instead of driving around in cars. When they left Kimmy's house, her mom hadn't said anything about a curfew or even asked when she'd be home, but Kimmy had given her the name of the hotel anyway, just in case.

They didn't stay at the dance long. It was lame and the only thing either of them cared about was going back to the hotel. The punch Kimmy loved was waiting for them in the room next to theirs, a big batch that a few of their friends who had skipped the dance had been tasked with making.

They had their own room, but they joined the others in the room with the punch. Kimmy downed half of her glass in three big gulps. "I love this punch. I love the way it makes me feel," she said. She and Angie kicked off their high heels and jumped onto the bed, dancing along to the music, punch sloshing over the sides of their cups. There was nothing quite like being young and in love, and everything was going to work out exactly the way they planned.

It made Josh happy that Kimmy loved his friends. She'd also brought Angie into the fold, and Kimmy told Josh she never wanted to be without the garage gang, as she now thought of them. At their age, all that mattered was belonging to something.

"I just love your dress," Cheyenne, Mikey's girlfriend, said to Kimmy as she joined them in jumping on the bed. "It's so gorgeous."

"It's vintage," Kimmy shouted, and she and Angie dissolved into giggles as they hugged Cheyenne and the three of them collapsed onto the mattress, punch flying. Whoever had to sleep on that bed was going to be pissed off and soaking wet.

Later, when she was drunk, Kimmy told Josh she loved him and was ready to give herself to him. He was pretty drunk, too, but when he peeled her out of her dress and ran his hands along her naked body, she smiled at him. He looked at her like she was the most precious thing in the world, and he would never want to be without her. "I love you too, Kimmy. I always will."

She said it didn't hurt, but he wondered later how much she remembered of it. But then they did it two more times before checking out of the hotel the next day, and those were the memories of their first time that always came to mind when Josh thought about it.

When he pulled into her driveway, Kimmy said all she wanted to do was crawl back into bed and stay there until she'd managed to shake off her brutal hangover and feel human again. But before she got out of the car he said, "I love you," and she looked at him and said, "I love you too," and one of the few things he would ever be sure of in life was that they both meant it.

Josh pulled himself away from the past, chastising himself for missing the moment when Justin and Amber were pronounced man and wife. Later, his mother would put on the mantel in the living room a framed picture of the two of them taken moments after their first kiss. In it, Justin was giving Amber a pointed smile meant just for her, one that seemed to say that they were the only two people on earth and that he couldn't possibly fathom living without her.

When Josh held the heavy silver frame in his hand and looked at the picture, it would not conjure memories of his own wedding day. The only image of Kimmy he could think of would be when he'd looked at her one day and realized that maybe he wanted more than just a world of him and Kimmy and that maybe he'd made a mistake.

109

At the reception, his brother James delivered a rousing toast to Justin and his bride after dinner. Josh's arm rested on the empty chair next to him; Sasha was sprawled across his lap, asleep. He wished he felt as hopeful as Justin looked. Mostly he felt tired. Not in the way Sasha was tired. His fatigue ran much deeper than that. His brother Jordan plopped down in the empty chair beside him and put a drink in his hand. "Looks like you're unable to get a refill on your own. Thought I'd help out."

"That's why you're my favorite brother," Josh said.

"How are things going? I'm guessing weddings kind of suck for you right now."

"They're going okay."

"Maybe it's time to get back out there?"

"It's only been six months. Kimmy insisted she be the one to file since it was her choice and everything. But I haven't gotten paperwork yet and I have no idea when it'll be a done deal."

His brother winced. Seemed like he wanted to say something about that but thought better of it. That was another reason Jordan really was his favorite brother.

110

"At least you've got some free time these days."

Everyone said that. Because of their fifty-fifty custody split, Josh had more free time than he'd had since becoming a father. Too bad he didn't know how to fill it. His married friends were busy with their jobs and wives and kids. The chief complaint out of everyone's mouth was how little time they had for everything. They rushed everywhere and were bombarded with so many stimuli during their days that all they wanted to do when they got home was relax with their families, if it could even be called relaxing anymore. They were all overscheduled and burned out.

Josh *did* have free time. When Sasha was at Kimmy's, he could eat whatever he wanted, watch whatever he wanted on TV, and do whatever he wanted without consulting anyone. For the first few months, it had felt like a weight had been lifted. No more tension between him and Kimmy. No more arguments with their voices low so Sasha wouldn't realize her parents' marriage was disintegrating right before her eyes. No more worrying about the mood Kimmy would be in when she got home from work. No more competing with her phone for attention. No more moving about the house

111

like roommates.

But the problem with having time to fill was that he had no idea how he *wanted* to fill it. The last time he'd been single, he was eighteen years old.

"Get on some apps," Jordan said.

He groaned. Everyone was always going on about the apps. Justin had *met* Amber on an app, and now look at them. All Josh knew was that they came with a whole new set of rules he wasn't familiar with.

"You don't have to marry any of these women. Just see if there's one out there who wants to catch a movie sometime or meet up for a drink. Plus, you have needs, right?" His brother laughed like that was hysterically funny.

Sure, he had needs. But that didn't mean he wanted to rush right out and find a woman to sleep with. That was another difference between eighteen and thirty-seven. He could delay gratification for a much longer period of time and not combust in a hormonal explosion because he wasn't having sex.

"I changed my mind. James is my favorite brother."

"I'm sorry, man. That wasn't funny."

"No biggie," Josh said.

"Shit. I'm out of whiskey. I'll be back,"

Jordan said, patting him on the shoulder as he took off to refill his drink.

Josh's phone vibrated with an incoming text.

Your goofball dog wanted to say goodnight, it said. There was a picture of Norton under the covers of a bed, Layla's he presumed, and the dog's head was on her pillow. This was not staged. I found him like this when I came into the room. No need to respond. I just wanted to let you know that everything is going fine, and Norton appears to be "settling in" quite well. Hope you're enjoying your week-end.

Josh texted her back right away. I'd say he's settling in fine. Don't get any ideas about stealing my dog. I know where you live. He found himself staring at the screen, hoping she'd send another text. He smiled when she did.

You've uncovered my evil plan. She sent another photo. This time, Norton was wearing a cowboy hat. He wished she had sent a picture of herself next to the dog, but something told him she wouldn't have been comfortable doing that. He wasn't sure about her yet. He definitely found her attractive, and she couldn't have been nicer.

But what was her story? What did she want?

What did he want?

He sent another text: I know one thing for sure. Norton's got a new favorite dog sitter. Thanks again. I'll be over to pick him up in the afternoon tomorrow. No later than four.

Again, he waited for her response. Sounds good. See you tomorrow was all it said.

CHAPTER 15

LAYLA

On Sunday, while she was drinking her second cup of coffee, Norton at her side, Layla set down her coffee cup and reached for her phone. She googled Josh Summers, but the only thing that came up was a listing for his electrician services. He had a five-star rating on Google, it seemed. But he didn't appear to be on social media, and neither was she. Layla had deleted her Facebook account months ago. It had seemed easier to delete it when she left Liam rather than change her marital status and deal with the avalanche of well-meaning but mostly nosy inquiries.

After lunch, Layla took Norton for a walk, and when they got back the dog followed her down to her basement studio and flopped down on the rug. She plugged the guitar into her amp and tuned it a bit until it sounded exactly the way she wanted it to.

"This is gonna get really loud," she said to the dog. But he appeared to have already fallen asleep, and when the first thirty seconds of her playing didn't rouse him, she let it rip.

By the final months of 2007, Storm Warning had added more original material to their sets. Their fans knew they would still hear their favorites, still be able to jam out to the songs they'd grown up hearing on FM radio. But they had begun to embrace the original songs and started requesting them between sets when the band was taking a break. It was that original material intended for their first CD that Layla always thought of as the soundtrack to the time when Liam started pursuing her in earnest.

They were still playing at Connie's almost every weekend and Suzanne was still a regular fixture. Layla hadn't noticed her sitting on Liam's lap again, but she was often on the stool next to him. By then, Liam's time in the bar always included a conversation with Layla. Several, in fact. He'd inserted himself into her world so slowly, so gradually, that it felt like he'd always been there. What began as a friendship had intensified into something romantic without her being fully aware that it was happening.

Liam was excellent at anticipating what someone might want and then using it to his advantage by providing it. There were more bottles of beer handed to her when her throat felt the driest and most raw. There was the time a drunk and belligerent guy got way too handsy with Layla when posing next to her for a picture and Liam stepped in and diffused it effortlessly, without even raising his voice. Layla had had a splitting headache that night. She was hot, tired, sweaty, and starving and she did not have the energy to deal with a drunk fan. Liam simply made the problem disappear, and when she tried to find him ten minutes later to say thank you, she wasn't quick enough and spotted him walking out the door with Suzanne. When she saw him the following week, she made sure to go up to him first thing and tell him how much she'd appreciated his help. He was starting to interest her by then, and she found herself seeking him out in the crowd as she sang. There were times it might have seemed to the audience like Layla was singing directly to Liam, because she was. And Liam would sit there on his barstool ignoring whatever group of friends he'd come with as if Layla were the only thing worth watching in the bar.

The first time Layla hung out with Liam after a show was because he'd had the forethought to duck out during the band's last song and pick up a gourmet pizza from the restaurant up the street that catered to the late-night crowd.

Instead of bringing her a beer, he waited until the crowd standing in line for pictures had all moved on. He walked up to Layla, the pizza balanced on his palm, and said, "I need someone to help me eat this. Know anyone who's hungry?"

He was going to get kicked out of the bar any minute, because people were supposed to be heading for the door, not arriving with dinner. But the owner of Connie's didn't mind if the band hung around for a while and had a beer or two while they were packing up. The perk was also extended to anyone who might be dating a band member.

"I'm starving," she said as he opened the box. She selected a piece from the side with pepperoni; the other side had sausage.

Kevin, the band member Layla was closest to and had slept with a few times back in college until they decided it was a terrible idea, walked by, a pair of drumsticks sticking out of his back pocket. "Only one of your groupies would bring pizza," he said, helping himself to a slice before continuing out the door.

"I am not one of your groupies," Liam said.

Layla grinned, her own slice halfway to her

mouth. "If you say so."

He smiled. "I do. And by the way, we're on our first date right now."

She choked on her pizza. "We're definitely not."

"Sure we are. It's the type of date you go on when the girl you'd like to take somewhere is busy until two A.M. every weekend."

"How can this be a date when you're already dating someone?"

"Who am I dating?" he asked with genuine confusion.

"Suzanne. You know, the girl I went to school with and have known practically my whole life."

"Trust me, I am not dating Suzanne."

"She said you were that night I stopped to talk to you all." And Layla had watched him leave with Suzanne the other night, not that you needed to be dating someone to take them home with you.

"We went out a few times. That's it. I'm not interested in her."

"You're free to date whoever you want," Layla said.

"I want to date you. I'm trying to do that right now."

"The pizza is really good," she said.

"That's all I get, huh?" He smiled and opened the box. "Have another slice."

She liked Liam. She wasn't exactly sure why at that point, but she did. Maybe it was because he acted like a gentleman and he didn't smother her, and he understood that the music was important to her and was willing to work around it. Lots of guys had tried to persuade Layla to go back to their places after the show, but that was always about their needs. None of them had ever thought to bring her a pizza to satisfy one of hers.

"When you closed the third set with that original ballad. Did you write that?" he asked.

"Kevin did. I don't write. I just play and sing."

"I liked the way you guys opened the second set with 'Magic Man.' You were made to sing that song. It's seriously hot. I didn't even realize how much I liked it until I heard you sing it. Why don't you play more Heart covers?"

"Because someone else needs a turn to sing. And I'm going to blow out my vocal cords trying to emulate Ann Wilson, who, by the way, is an actual rock goddess."

"So are you," he said.

"You can stop now. No need for flattery."

"It's the truth," he said.

As they talked and ate, it stunned Layla that Liam knew the order of every song in every set and seemed truly invested in the band from an entertainment angle.

"Do you have any musical abilities?" she

asked. "Is this the part where you tell me you're a closet musician secretly angling to join the band?"

"I can't play anything, and trust me, you don't want to hear my singing voice."

"Then why?" she asked.

"Why what?"

"Why are you here every weekend?"

"Because I cannot get enough of watching you on that stage. Hearing you sing."

Layla smiled.

"Shit. You know what I sound like?" he said.

"I do, but I wasn't going to point it out." The pizza was almost gone, and Layla yawned. She was full and happy, and her bed would feel so good tonight.

"Fine. I'll admit it. I'm one of your groupies. I like the way you sing. I like the way you look when you sing. I want to know you better."

"I play guitar, but I think you might just be a player."

He tilted his head, looked her in the eye, and held her gaze. "You've been singing to me, Layla. I like it when you do that. And I like you. A lot. Give me a chance to show you how good we can be together."

He fell harder and sooner than she did. She wasn't sure about him yet, but she chose to believe that he was telling her the truth that night. In time, he would tell her he loved her and list all the things he loved about her, and she believed those things, too. Liam was a salesman through and through, and one of the things Layla was most ashamed about was that he'd sold her on himself and made her believe he supported her dreams as much as she supported his. She paid the full asking price for something she found herself wishing she could return later, but by the time she figured it out, it was way past way too late.

Norton was still sawing logs on the floor when Layla took a break, gulping from the water bottle she'd brought down to the basement. She'd worked up quite a sweat and had stripped down to the thin tank top she wore under her flannel shirt. She'd slowly worked her way through her favorite covers, but there were many more and her throat would need a break long before she ran out of songs to play.

CHAPTER 16

JOSH

Josh pulled into the parking lot of Kimmy's condo and shut off his truck. "I want to go to Miss Layla's with you to pick up Norton," Sasha said as he walked her in. "I missed him."

"I know, but your mom missed you too. Norton will be waiting for you in a few days."

He kissed her good-bye, and then Kimmy opened the door and enveloped Sasha in a tight squeeze. Josh drove home and took his overnight bag into the house and grabbed a toolbox before getting back into his truck for the short drive to Layla's. He'd texted her before he pulled out of the parking lot of Kimmy's condo, but she hadn't responded. No one answered when he rang her doorbell, so he walked around to the backyard and came through the gate. She wasn't on the deck, either, but he heard music coming from somewhere — Heart's "Magic Man," to be exact — so he assumed she was there.

He followed the sound to a basement window where it grew louder. He peered inside the window and what he saw surprised him. Layla wasn't listening to music — she was the source of it. The glass muted the sound a bit, but her voice was incredible.

She was wearing faded jeans, and there was a long-sleeved shirt that looked like she'd flung it to the floor when she got too warm. All she had on above the waist now was a thin tank top. She was singing into a microphone and the cords of her neck and the muscles in her forearms flexed from the exertion of playing and singing.

He tapped on the window.

She couldn't hear him; she didn't see him.

It was clearly a private moment and he should have looked away, but he couldn't.

And anyway, he didn't want to.

Shy, quiet Layla had been replaced by a woman who looked as if she was starring in her own music video. Her expression changed with the lyrics, and it was like watching someone tell a story. Her hair clung to her damp neck. He wasn't close enough to confirm it, but he imagined a rivulet of sweat running from her neck straight down into the front of that tank top.

It wasn't that Layla wasn't attractive, because she was. But it was understated, as if she wasn't trying to draw attention to the way she looked. Her strawberry-blond hair was usually in a ponytail or tucked behind her ears. He couldn't remember what color her eyes were, because he'd never paid that much attention, and they were often hidden behind the sunglasses she wore for morning drop-off. She wasn't tall or short or big or small. It was almost as if she didn't want to stand out in any way. That didn't quite make sense to Josh, but there was something about Layla that he couldn't get a handle on.

Maybe that's because you don't really know her, he told himself. He'd only seen what she'd allowed him to see, and right now he had a feeling that he was seeing more of who she really was. Right then, she looked like she was on fire, as if her joy had lit her from behind in vibrant oranges and fiery reds.

It was a long song, but he wished it were longer.

He waited until she played the final notes. The sound ceased, and he watched for a few more seconds as she inhaled deeply, her

125

chest rising and falling. She looked spent.

He should have stood up and hurried around to the front of the house to ring the bell again. She'd probably hear it now. But a split second before he tore himself away from the window, Layla's head whipped up toward him, and the look on her face was sheer panic.

He wished he didn't look like such a creepy stalker. They stared at each other for what felt like hours but was, in fact, only seconds. She scooped her shirt up off the floor and pointed a finger toward the ceiling to let him know she was heading upstairs. Josh walked around to the front of the house, and the minute Layla opened the door he said, "I am so sorry. I was not trying to be creepy or spy on you or whatever. I tried knocking on the door. I knocked on the window, too, but you couldn't hear me."

She finished shrugging into her shirt and buttoned it quickly. "It's not your fault. I knew you were coming. I just . . . I lost track of time." She looked mortified, but for the life of him, he couldn't understand why. He was the one who should be mortified, and he was.

Norton registered Josh's arrival and was about to knock him off his feet. "Come on in," Layla said. She shut the door so the dog wouldn't escape into the street.

He gestured toward the toolbox in his hand. "If you can open the garage door so I can get to the breaker box, I'll look at that light. Then we'll get out of your hair."

"Sure," she said.

It didn't take him long to figure out what was wrong with the light and fix it. He turned the breaker back on, knocked on the door, and asked Layla to turn on the switch. She smiled when she saw the outdoor light glowing bright. "Thanks," she said. "I can finally cross that off my to-do list. It's been on there quite a while."

"No problem."

Layla disappeared into the kitchen and returned with Norton's bowls, food, and leash. He reached for the leash and attached it to Norton's collar.

"You said you didn't sing," he blurted. "You can *clearly* sing. Your voice is unbelievable." The lame adjective didn't do it justice, but it was all he could come up with. Later, when he replayed it in his mind, he would think of better words, like "commanding," "mesmerizing," "passionate."

"I meant I only sing for myself. I don't sing for anyone else. Not now."

"Did you used to?"

"Yes."

127

He waited patiently, not saying anything, hoping she'd elaborate. It was none of his business, but she'd piqued his curiosity in a big way. He wanted to know more about past Layla. Hell, he'd like to know more about present Layla, too.

"I used to be in a band," she said. "We called ourselves Storm Warning."

"Why didn't you say something before?" As far as he knew, she just liked to play guitar. For a music teacher, that was a perfectly understandable hobby. But what he had just witnessed was a skill level way beyond a casual hobby.

"Because it was a lifetime ago." But a lifetime where maybe she thrived, he thought.

"When?" he asked.

"The band got together in college. I was about twenty-two when we started booking paid gigs. We played for a few years."

"Are they still around?"

"Not really. By the end of 2008, everyone had kind of gone their separate ways."

He filtered through the timeline in his brain. The reason he had never seen her play, the reason he didn't know anything about the band and had never even heard of it, was because that was during the time when he and Kimmy were in a very different place in their lives. The difficult-but-finally-starting-to-make-something-of-themselves years, as he sometimes thought of them. They had not been in a position to go anywhere, much less go out and watch live bands.

He pressed two twenties and a ten into her hand. "No, I don't need any money," she said. "And you fixed the light."

"Just take it," he said. "It would have cost more than that to board him."

"Thank you." Layla crouched down and ruffled Norton's fur. "Bye, Norton. Thanks for hanging out with me this weekend."

"Again, I'm really sorry." He felt like he'd never be able to apologize enough for the invasion of her privacy.

"Nothing to apologize for. I was in the zone and should have looked at my watch. That happens to me sometimes when I play."

"It was pretty amazing."

She looked at him with a half smile, but she didn't say anything, lost in thought as if what she remembered was amazing indeed.

CHAPTER 17

LAYLA

"How was the dog sitting?" Tonya asked.

"It was good. He's a sweet dog. I don't think he can hear very well, though."

"Ask Josh if you can borrow it sometime and then take it to a dog park. I've heard that's a wonderful way to meet men. Very wholesome."

"I don't hate that idea, but I'd need to do it quick. The weather's about to turn." The wind was blowing hard and carried the distinct smell of snow. Layla shivered. Morning bus duty would be downright miserable a month from now, and they were getting an early taste of it.

"Take it to PetSmart. I've heard there are loads of men just wandering the aisles with their dogs, looking for babes like you."

"Or maybe just dog food. Also, you sure have heard a lot about where to meet men," Layla teased.

"Just tryin' to help a friend," she said. "How was Josh?"

"He stayed and had a glass of wine when he dropped off Norton."

Tonya held up a finger. "We'll return to that first part in a second. But the dog's name is Norton? Like the antivirus?"

"Yes, but no. He was named by someone who was not familiar with today's technology."

"Okay, on to the good stuff. You had drinks together," she said. "How did that go? Do you think he might be interested?"

"I don't think interest had anything to do with it. And we did not have drinks together. I asked if he wanted a glass of wine and he said his ex-wife didn't drink so he didn't much either but that it sounded good. I poured one for him and we chatted and after he finished it, he went home. He's a nice guy."

"Do you think there could be something there?"

"I think I'm the dog sitter. That's all I can tell you for now. One *tiny* little thing did happen, though."

"Oh my God, what?" Tonya asked. "Did you lose the dog for a while or something?"

"No, nothing like that. Josh busted me rocking out in my basement when he came

131

to pick up Norton. I was in all my guitar glory and singing at the top of my lungs."

"What song?"

" 'Magic Man.' I was feeling very Ann Wilson." Layla told Tonya all about it and described how awkward it had felt to look up and see Josh at the window.

"You were doing something you loved in the privacy of your own home. You can't possibly be embarrassed by your musical talent."

"I'm not. But playing is a way for me to let out all my pent-up energy and these stupid emotions I'm working through that have nowhere to go. It's my creative outlet. It's just for me. I play like nobody's watching because *literally,* nobody is watching. Until now."

"I think you might be overreacting just a tad. It's not like you were playing naked, right?"

"No! Why would I be playing naked?"

"I don't know. Why are you so freaked out about him seeing you play?"

"I guess I don't want him to think I fancy myself as some kind of . . ." *Rock star.* "I don't know."

There was something she'd never told anyone, and it involved the verbal wound Liam had inflicted the first time the gloves had really come off in their marriage. Layla hated that she couldn't get past it, but wounds had a way of lingering long after the dagger had been thrown.

"I bet Josh was impressed," Tonya said.

"He was very complimentary." But Liam had been impressed once, too.

Annie walked her boys inside the building and joined Layla and Tonya. "What are we talking about this morning?"

"Our creative outlets," Tonya said.

"I've seen the inside of your house, Tonya," Annie said. "I know what yours is."

Tonya smiled. "Yes, it's colorful and I've been known to stencil a thing or two. Some women like to browse clothing stores; I've never met a paint sample I didn't want to bring home and slap on something. However, and I'm only admitting it out loud because I've just given Layla a pep talk about being true to oneself, and, well, this might shock you girls, but I don't take those exercise classes at five A.M. for my health." Tonya had been attending classes at Dance Ignite for almost as long as Layla had known her.

"I, too, have a secret past," she said. "I was head of the drill team in high school and I can bust a move like nobody's business. I am the *star* of the five A.M. class. I'd like to think that if I ever auditioned for the Timberwolves Dancers, I could hold my own. If they had another team made up of gals in their thirties, that is."

"I think that is so cool!" Layla said.

"I'll need to see those dance moves the next time we have a girls' night out," Annie said. "Wait, you said you *also* had a secret past. That means Layla does too. Spill, Layla."

"I used to be the lead singer in a moderately successful cover band. I've started singing and playing guitar again. For me."

"What?" Annie yelled.

Layla laughed. "Don't make it weird."

"Why would I make it weird?" Annie asked. "I think it's really cool. So, you played in bars and stuff?"

"Yep. And then I came to my senses and joined the rest of the grownups in the real world."

"Did you know she used to be in a band?" Annie asked Tonya.

"Yes, but she doesn't like to talk about it."

"It was a long time ago," Layla said.

"Wow. I feel like I don't know you two at all."

"What about you, Annie?" Layla asked. "What's your superpower?"

"Ha," she said. "I have three boys. My

superpower is keeping everyone alive and not losing my goddamned mind in the process. I do get up an hour before everyone else so I can have my coffee in peace. I like to open Pinterest and design rooms full of white furniture that no one can sit on but me. All the décor is feminine and highly breakable. Nothing is durable or meant to withstand any kind of beating, unlike the furniture in my own house. The rooms I've designed would rival those of an interior decorator, or at least an aspiring one. It's just for fun. And I know a lot about astrology." Annie tacked that sentence on at the end, as if she were trying it on for size. Saying it out loud to see what they might say.

"Astrology?" Layla asked. "Like Mercury retrograde and stuff?"

"That's part of it." Annie looked away and down at the ground a little. "I saw my horoscope one day. I can't even remember now where I read it. Maybe a magazine or something when I was waiting in a doctor's office with one of the boys. And that day's prediction seemed to fit what was happening in my life so closely it was almost scary. So then I started looking into it a little, you know, just sort of learning about it. And then I started reading more about it in the morning when I was by myself and I just, um." Her voice cracked a little then and Tonya and Layla did not say a word.

"I love my boys and I worry about them so much. And my dad was showing signs of early Alzheimer's and I had a questionable lump in my left boob that turned out to be nothing, but I just needed something to hold on to. It just kind of got bigger from there because it helps me make sense of the world."

Tonya reached out a hand and laid it on Annie's arm. "I understand."

"I do too," Layla said. And boy, did she. Layla thought that for the first time since she met Annie, she was finally seeing a side that not many people had or would, and it gave her such a feeling of belonging. It made Layla realize that sharing some of her struggles with other women had unburdened her a little, and maybe she could help unburden other women in return.

"Thank you," Annie said. "I've never said a word to Ed about this. I always close my browser when he comes into the room so that he won't see the astrology sites. Doctors are very pro-science and I am too. But I can look at something from two different mindsets. I know a lot about astrology. Probably enough to pull both of your charts and give you an idea about what's heading your way."

"As tempting as it would be to hear some good news after the shit year I've had so far," Layla said, "I'll have to pass. If there's something coming that's going to knock me off my axis again, I don't want to know about it because I will not be able to handle it. I cannot handle any more right now."

"Something tells me you could," Tonya said.

"I think so too," Annie said. "Maybe it doesn't seem as obvious to you because it's happening on the inside, but I can see something starting to happen on the outside too, Layla. Whatever is coming, you will get through it. We all will."

"Can I offer you some advice, Annie?" Layla said. "You don't have to take it and we don't ever have to have this conversation again."

"Of course," Annie said.

"Tell Ed about the astrology. Tell him what you just told us. Because as women, when we start hiding our truth from other people, especially the people who should be aware of it the most, that's when we give them the power to diminish it. Ed doesn't have to share your enthusiasm. He doesn't have to like it or believe in it. But he needs to know that it's important to you and that it's something you're going to keep doing."

Annie took a deep breath and nodded. The bell rang. "I better go," she said. "Good talk, girls."

Good talk, indeed.

CHAPTER 18

LAYLA

Layla swung by the guitar shop after school. Brian smiled when she walked in and approached her immediately. "Hey. How's it going, Layla? What's it going to be today? Picks? Strings?"

"Hi," Layla said. Brian was always so cheerful and easy to talk to. Maybe because they had so much in common and never ran out of musical topics. "I do need some picks, actually. And a footrest."

"How's the studio coming along?"

"It's getting there." She'd paid a contractor to hang drywall and then painted the walls a soft gray. The flooring had been installed and now it looked like a real room. She was thinking about putting a small couch down there, so she'd have somewhere to sit with her journal or glass of wine if she felt like listening to music instead of making it. It was quickly becoming one of her

139

favorite rooms in the house.

She'd also ordered some curtains for the window after the embarrassing episode with Josh. She'd lose some of the natural light, but it was a small price to pay for her privacy. She could only imagine what he must have thought. Did he think she had aspirations of someday being more than an elementary school music teacher and was secretly practicing in the basement, so she'd be ready for her big break? It was too humiliating to think about it.

"So, I ran into someone who knew you back in the day."

"Really? Who?"

"A guy named Nolan who used to play at one of the same dive bars I used to. He was telling me about a friend of his who used to play in a local band called Storm Warning. We got to talking and he started telling me about the band's lead singer. A girl named Layla who used to, and I quote, 'Bring the goddamned house down.' You should have said something." He was looking at her so admiringly.

"We had a good run for a local band. It was a long time ago."

"I spent most of the nineties and two-thousands in Minneapolis trying to break in. Finally realized it was never going to

140

happen and moved back home. Opened this shop. I missed your heyday."

Layla flushed. "I don't know if I'd call it a heyday, but we had some very loyal support from the locals."

"Did you ever try to expand?"

"We got as far as Edina," she said. "And that didn't even work out."

"The music business is not for the faint of heart, that's for damn sure."

"No, it is not," Layla said. "So, what was the name of your band?"

"Didn't have one. I was strictly solo. I write too."

"Ever sold anything?"

"Nope. But not for lack of trying."

"You're still one step ahead of me. I don't write."

"Not interested in that side of it?"

She shrugged. "I guess I just didn't have anything to say." Layla had never minded playing someone else's songs. All she needed was a spotlight and an audience.

"I would have loved to sell something, but it just never happened. You know what they say. Those who can break in, do. Those who can't move back to their hometown and open a guitar shop."

Layla smiled and pointed at herself. "Elementary school music teacher. But I didn't have to move back because I never left."

"Ah," he said. "Well, I bet you're a good music teacher."

"I try to be."

"We should play together sometime."

"Maybe," she said. "Right now, I'm just tinkering. Getting my feet wet again. I'm really enjoying playing for myself."

"I get it. Let me know if you change your mind. Maybe we could find a place in town that wouldn't mind giving two former musicians a chance to relive their glory days. I bet they'd even throw in a few bucks if we entertained their clientele."

"I'll keep it in mind," she said.

He rang up her purchases, and on the way home Layla couldn't stop thinking about how it would feel to perform again and that maybe her insistence that she only wanted to play for herself was complete and total bullshit. The one thing she did know was that if she were to perform again, there would not be a man waiting in the audience this time around.

Liam slowly won Layla over. Gone were the grand gestures of cold beers on the back of her neck and pizza boxes balanced on his palm. Those had been used to get her attention and now that he had it, he shifted gears. He was always polite and attentive, but he also gave her plenty of freedom. She didn't feel like he was waiting in the wings to claim her, which was good, because it would have only sent her running. They still had plenty of conversations between the band's sets, but there were also nights that Liam's favorite barstool remained empty and Layla wondered where he was.

She thought maybe he'd changed his mind about wanting to date her, but one night after they finished playing, he asked her to go to a diner that was open twenty-four hours and she said yes. They talked until 5:00 A.M. and he was humble and gracious and funny and kind. As he spoke, she realized he was finally showing her the stripped-down, more authentic version of himself. He talked less about his job and more about wanting to succeed in life so that his mom and dad would be proud of him. That was something Layla could relate to, because she feared she was letting her own parents down by continuing to chase the rock-and-roll dreams she wasn't ready to let go of. The attraction she felt toward Liam and the common ground they shared seemed like a stable foundation on which to build a relationship, and together they began laying the bricks. Liam might have set the hook early on with his pursuit of her, but Layla reeled herself right on in.

They'd been dating for about six months when the band received the inquiry from the booker in Edina. Storm Warning was attracting bigger and bigger crowds at Connie's and the bouncers had to regularly turn people away at the door or risk violating the fire code by letting anyone else inside. Layla got the sense that they were about to explode in popularity, and the thought of that thrilled her almost as much as performing did. It was time to take it to the next level, and while Edina was no Minneapolis, it was a good place to start.

Liam was the first person she wanted to share the good news with. His face lit up when he opened the door to his apartment, and she blurted it out before he'd even shut the door behind her. "That's awesome," he said. "Is this the first time that's happened?"

"Yes. Scotty's spent hours cold-calling and emailing different clubs trying to get us on the bill. Before they'll agree to book us, they want to know that we can bring in the crowds, which isn't as easy when you're not a local band. It's kind of a chicken-egg situation. The more we play a venue, the more we become known. But we can't become known until we play enough shows. But get this, the booker actu-

144

ally reached out to Scotty. He said he'd heard about us and wanted to come and watch a few sets for himself."

"I'm really happy for you. Let's go out tonight and celebrate. Anywhere you want to go."

Liam loved to wine and dine her. She was more accustomed to the drive-through at McDonald's, and she felt so grown-up when she and Liam would arrive at a restaurant and the hostess would confirm the reservation Liam had made and lead them to their cozy table for two. Though she often tried to pick up the check if she thought she had enough in her bank account to cover it, he never let her.

The first time she'd spent the night with him, he'd picked her up and tucked her into the passenger seat of a gleaming black sedan that still had that new-car smell. Then he'd taken her out for dinner and to a movie, and when they got back to his place, he'd parked the car in its underground space at the luxury apartment building where he lived.

"This is really nice," Layla said when he opened the door and ushered her inside. "The budgets of starving artists who are still trying to make it don't really allow for this level of housing."

It was furnished with top-of-the-line everything. He also had a closet full of suits and always dressed just a little better than everyone else. His grooming was impeccable, and she'd never seen him overdue for a haircut or with stubble on his face. There were no beer-can pyramids anywhere and he had plenty of toilet paper.

Liam had been in an especially expansive mood for the last couple of months, because once he'd completed his training at work, he'd hit the ground running, positioning himself as the clear front-runner of the inside-sales training class. He'd shown her a few of his commission checks, and Layla had been surprised by the amounts. No wonder he could live so lavishly. Her own tastes weren't quite so extravagant, but it was nice to date someone who had his shit together and that was something that Layla really liked about him. Sometimes, it seemed that while Liam had actually crossed over and become a grown-up, Layla was still trying to get there. He'd broken free from the pack in the race to successful adulthood, but Layla was closer to last place and in danger of being lapped. Nothing seemed to be happening with her music, which made her feel stuck. Most of the time, she lived paycheck to paycheck, and even those didn't come in with any guaranteed regularity. She was starting to worry that maybe she should have taken her friends' and family's well-meaning advice and done something with her life.

The band put considerable thought into the sets they played for the booker, showcasing a little bit of everything they had to offer. After the bar closed for the evening, the booker — a guy named Seth — had wanted to do shots of sambuca. Therefore, they all did shots of sambuca.

Liam picked her up at the bar at three in the morning, brought her home, and poured her into his bed. Around noon the next day, he ran out for pancakes and sausages from Layla's favorite breakfast spot and brought them to her along with a big glass of ice water and a bottle of Motrin.

"You must have an epic hangover," he said.

"I'm never drinking again," Layla said. And to add insult to injury, when the band finally convinced the booker they couldn't drink any more, he told them he didn't think they were a good fit for the club's image, and Layla was still bristling about it.

"There's nothing wrong with our image," she said to Liam as he spread the food out on the bed and stretched out beside her with his own Styrofoam container. She stole a piece of his bacon. "I've been to that club and their image is overpriced drinks, a restrictive dress code, and an inflated sense of their own importance. At one point the booker asked if I only wore jeans when I performed. Scotty told him I often wore skirts and I had to go along with it."

It wasn't that Layla didn't understand image. It was just that she had a hard time understanding why it should be given so much importance. Shouldn't the music be their focus? The guys in the band weren't going to suddenly start wearing sport coats with their jeans. Loafers instead of tennis shoes. So why should she have to glam it up? Layla had her own sense of style and she didn't want to be tied to any particular look. She wanted something to start happening for the band, but what they'd be wearing when it did was the furthest thing from her mind.

"Also, what kind of maniac does more than one shot of sambuca?" Layla muttered as she took a bite of her pancakes. She paused because she feared she might see them in reverse, but she managed through sheer will to hold the food down and felt marginally better after she finished her breakfast. She reached for the Motrin and swallowed four capsules, draining her entire water glass in the process.

"That seems like a lot to take at one time, honey," Liam said.

"It's fine," Layla said. "I mean, I think it is."

And then Liam pulled her into his arms for a nice long cuddle, which was exactly what she wanted, because she had no intention of getting out of bed for the rest of the day.

And then Liam pulled her into his arms for a nice long cuddle, which was exactly what she wanted, because she had no intention of getting out of bed for the rest of the day.

Chapter 19

Josh

Josh opened the app on his phone and started swiping. His brother had been texting him every day for a week asking if he'd "gotten back out there yet," and Josh said yes, mostly so he'd shut up. Then, curiosity had gotten the better of him. Dating now seemed a lot like window-shopping, and he could do it from the comfort of his own living room. A small part of him *did* wish for someone to spend time with, to see a movie or grab a drink like his brother said. Something casual. Some adult conversation.

A brunette with pretty eyes and a nice smile caught his eye. She was a nurse, and her bio said she liked dogs and tacos and movies. When did women start loving tacos so much? He swiped right, and by the end of the evening he'd swiped on five or six profiles. Several of the women sent friendly messages, and by the end of the week he had dates set up with three of them. Maybe one of them was looking for the same thing he was, and maybe one of them would be willing to take things slow.

Dating in the modern world blew Josh's mind, and not in a good way. The nurse who liked dogs was even prettier in person, and Josh relaxed a bit, settling in for a pleasant hour or two of drinks and getting to know her a little. Her name was Jen, and it turned out that her brother was friends with Josh's oldest brother. She was articulate and the conversation flowed. Maybe his brother was right. Maybe this was just what he needed.

"What about kids?" she asked.

"I like them. I have a daughter and she's my world."

"Do you want more?"

"If it happens someday, sure. I'd love more kids."

"How soon do you see yourself getting married again?" she asked.

He let out a chuckle. "I was barely out of high school when I did it the first time. I don't know that I'll ever want to get married again," he said, and watched her face deflate.

As soon as they graduated, he and Kimmy

spent all their free time together and had sex every chance they could get. In her bed if her mom was at work, in the back seat of Josh's car if she wasn't, and one night, when his parents were out of town, they spent an entire night together under the covers of his double bed after Kimmy told her mom she was spending the night at Angie's.

Josh spent his days pouring concrete. It was backbreaking work, but Kimmy said that his back and shoulder muscles felt bigger under her fingertips and that his dark tan made him look even cuter.

Kimmy had found a job selling children's clothing at the mall. For the first time in her life, she had real money to spend, and she could spend it on whatever she wanted. She was able to walk right into her favorite shoe store on her lunch break and buy two pairs of shoes, she told Josh. At one time! She had forgotten about her goal of buying a car. It didn't seem as important now that Josh drove her everywhere or let her use his car.

Evenings were spent in Mikey's garage or in someone's backyard now that a few of their friends had started moving out of their parents' houses and into the crappy rentals that were all their low budgets allowed. Josh's parents still held out hope that Josh would go to school somewhere, anywhere, and said they'd pay for an apartment if he would just enroll.

"I can't do it, Kimmy," he said one night when they were sneaking a quickie in Josh's bedroom while his parents were out to dinner. "There is no way I'm going to take another English or math class or whatever I'd have to take to go along with the stuff that might actually interest me. School of any kind sounds awful." Josh was always moving, always finding a project to fill his time when he wasn't working. He liked tinkering in his parents' garage, and he loved tools of any kind.

By fall, they were in the kind of ridiculous, all-consuming love they were certain no one besides them had ever experienced. Josh chafed at the rules his parents set forth. At eighteen, he no longer had a curfew and could come and go as he pleased. But they'd laid down the law about him paying rent. It wasn't that they needed the money, but they told him if he didn't want to go to college, he'd need to start living like an adult and that included paying his own way.

Josh had a stubborn and headstrong side, and when he put his mind to something, good luck to anyone who thought they could change it. It was one of the things Kimmy said she liked most about him. Nothing bad would ever happen to her as long as Josh was in charge. For the first time in Kimmy's life, she had someone she could really count on, and her loyalty to Josh ran as deep as an ocean trench. She had found her soul mate, her hero. If she stumbled, he would always be there to catch her. Kimmy made Josh feel ten feet tall, and he liked that feeling.

"If I have to pay rent, it's going to be for the place of my choosing," he told Kimmy that night after he'd picked her up and they'd blown off steam by throwing back a few beers in Mikey's garage. "Let's get our own place," he said.

Kimmy had been in midswallow. She set the beer can down on the garage floor and looked at Josh, a big smile on her face. No one had ever committed to her like that. There would be no more sneaking around. No more wishing they didn't have to say good-bye at the end of the night. It would be their place.

The start of their life together.

Josh didn't give much thought to how they'd pay for the roof they'd be solely responsible for putting over their heads. Between the two of them, they'd have plenty of money. Maybe not enough to buy two pairs of shoes at once, but enough to get by. At that moment, nothing mattered but Kimmy and how much he loved her.

"You're whipped, man," Mikey yelled.

He looked into Kimmy's eyes. "Marry me,"

he said. "Be my wife."

"Really?" she said.

"Really."

"Yes," she said, jumping into his arms. "Yes, yes, yes!"

Their friends cheered them on with the youthful enthusiasm found only in those at the foothills of their adult life, before the arduous climb toward a nine-to-five. Before mortgages and 401(k)s and babies, when life was still mostly unencumbered. It was partying and believing that your friends were the most important thing in your life. It was sleeping until noon on the weekend. It was doing whatever the hell you wanted in the present because the future seemed so far away. And so he and Kimmy made one of the most momentous decisions of their young lives with the fearless optimism of two people who didn't know what they didn't know.

"So, that's it?" the disappointed woman sitting across from Josh asked. "You're only interested in dating. No hope of a long-term commitment?" It was as if Josh had announced he'd rather chop off his finger than walk down the aisle again.

"You're the first woman I've set up a date with," he said. "My divorce isn't even final yet. I'm not trying to hide that or anything.

The marriage is over. I'm just waiting on the paperwork."

"Then why are you doing this?"

This? Josh thought. *You mean going out for a couple of drinks?* Because it seemed like maybe she meant, *Why are you wasting my time?*

"I just thought it would be nice to meet someone who might want to catch a movie sometime. Or meet for drinks. Maybe dinner. I'm sorry if I misled you."

She recovered quickly. "Oh, yeah. Me too. I was just curious."

"I was with my ex-wife for nineteen years." It blew his mind sometimes that he'd spent more than half of his entire life with Kimmy.

"I get it. You've done all of this already." She picked up her glass and drained it. "It's just that I'll be thirty-five in a few months and, well, I go to a lot of wedding and baby showers." She squared her shoulders in a way that told him there would probably not be any movie dates in their future.

The second woman Josh met for drinks — coffee late on a Saturday afternoon — was a tall blonde who was working on her Ph.D. in biostatistics at the University of Minnesota. She spent most of her time in Minneapolis.

"I'm looking for something long-distance.

156

I'm really committed to my studies right now, but I still need an emotional connection. I want someone I can count on to be there at the end of the day," she said. "I can text, email, Skype, whatever. That's not a problem."

"I'm not really a phone or email person," Josh said. "I'm actually looking to get out of the house a little more."

"Good to know," she said, and Josh could almost see the word "next" hovering in a little thought bubble above her head.

He felt like he'd fallen into some twisted modern-day version of "Goldilocks and the Three Bears." This porridge wants a timeline for commitment. This porridge wants a commitment but doesn't require your physical presence. Maybe the last bowl of porridge would be a match?

The third woman was cheerful and bouncy, with blond hair that had pink and green streaks on the ends. She showed up for their smoothie date wearing her workout clothes and said she was on her way to the gym. He liked that she wasn't decked out in a full face of makeup and that her hair was up in a ponytail. She seemed very down-to-earth, with a natural kind of beauty that appealed to him.

"So, you like smoothies too," she said after

they ordered and took their drinks to a corner table.

"They're okay, I guess." He felt indifferent toward smoothies and would never seek one out on his own, but she'd suggested the location and he'd been fine with it.

She took a sip of her smoothie. "These are kind of crap. I know of a much better smoothie," she said, leaning toward him. "A real protein-packed, antioxidant-rich superfood. With hemp oil. I don't start my day without one."

"You must really like smoothies."

"I do, but I also wanted to meet you here, so you'd have something to compare to our smoothies."

"Your smoothies? You mean the kind you have every morning?"

"Yes. I'm a personal trainer, but I'm also fiercely dedicated to sharing this wonderful product with everyone I can. It's life-changing."

What exactly is happening, he thought.

"I'll send you the product info. What's your email address?"

"Can't you just tell me while we're sitting here across from each other?"

"No. That's not how it works. But trust me when I say this is the opportunity of a lifetime. We've recently added CBD to our smoothies. The whole CBD product line is about to explode. Most of us will be able to retire in less than five years." Josh didn't know if the smoothies were responsible for her glowing skin and natural beauty and he didn't care to stick around to find out. She'd started to go a little crazy in the eyes and he didn't need any of that.

He stood up. "Well, I need to get going. Good luck with the smoothies."

She pushed her chair back with a scrape and scrambled to catch up with him. "I still need your email address."

"No, you don't," he said, and kept on walking.

When he got home, he kicked off his shoes, flopped down on the couch, and texted his brother. Online dating is a raging dumpster fire.

His brother responded, It's a numbers game. You need to keep at it for a while. Our very own brother met his wife this way. Don't give up!

Josh deleted the app. He didn't know if he ever wanted to get married again, and he could watch movies at home.

CHAPTER 20

LAYLA

The kindergarten class's music program fell the week before school broke for the Thanksgiving holiday. The performances were staggered, with each grade getting their own night to showcase what they'd learned. The kindergartners were always a bit of a wild card; all Layla could do was brace herself for the unexpected.

She was especially apprehensive because she'd wanted to try something new this year and she'd taught them the Beatles' "Let It Be." The abbreviated version she arranged was adorably sweet, and she'd also be accompanying them on acoustic guitar. If they could remember all the words and get through it without anyone tumbling off the risers, she knew the parents would love it.

Dressed to impress, the kids ran around backstage like they'd eaten nothing but sugar for dinner. Layla tried desperately to corral them before they started sweating or ripped their clothes. She clapped her hands five times rapidly in succession — the signal to pay attention and listen — and they stopped what they were doing and clapped back in the same pattern. Once they were quiet and she had their attention, she asked them to sit down so they could warm up. They collapsed into a haphazard circle on the carpet, and Layla took them through their vocal exercises.

When it was time to line up, Layla gave them a last-minute pep talk. "I know you'll do a wonderful job," she said. "Remember not to lock your knees. And I know you'll want to wave at your families, but try not to do that, okay? They'll be waiting for you afterward." Telling them not to wave was futile, because they'd do it anyway, but at least she tried.

They missed the intro. She had hoped they wouldn't, but it happened almost every time in class unless she sang along, and adding stage fright to the mix hadn't helped. Layla had prepared for this, and she played it off like the delay was intentional and strummed the intro again.

They missed it again.

She strummed it a third time and began

to sing. The kids immediately followed her lead, and their voices sounded every bit as sweet as they had in class. Layla tried to keep her voice low, because the parents hadn't come to listen to the teacher sing, but she and the kids had a sort of rustic-sounding harmony that sounded pleasing to her ear and like they'd totally planned it that way. When the last notes faded away, a deafening applause filled the auditorium. The kids broke protocol and waved at their parents, smiling and jumping up and down, high on the enthusiasm from their families.

They filed from the risers and headed back to the music room, where Layla congratulated them on a wonderful performance. Their sugar high had been eclipsed by their performance high, and they went back to running around the room as, one by one, their parents came to collect them.

Layla was still flying high herself and couldn't believe that — other than the missed intro — the music program had gone off without a hitch. Last year, one of her students threw up midsong and another knocked himself out when he fainted and tumbled from the top riser down three rows, his head hitting the floor with a rather gruesome-sounding thud.

Josh and Kimberly arrived to claim Sasha,

who was standing right next to Layla twirling in a circle, watching the pleats of her dress fan out. She'd sleep hard tonight, Layla thought.

"This is our first experience with a music program, and I wanted to tell you how wonderful it was," Kimberly gushed. "And you have a fantastic voice. You must sing often."

Layla and Josh exchanged a quick glance. It was almost involuntary on her part, but her head turned toward him instinctively, and all she could think about was him watching her through the basement window. It was something she'd thought about a lot lately. "Sometimes, yes."

"The program was absolutely precious," Kimberly said.

"Thank you," Layla said.

Kimberly took Sasha by the hand. "Let's go, Sasha. Time to get you home for bed."

Josh looked at Layla. "It was really great."

"Thanks," Layla said. "The kids worked very hard."

"I'll see you tomorrow," he said, and the smile he gave her seemed like it was just for her and had nothing to do with the fact that she was Sasha's music teacher.

What she felt then took her by surprise. After Liam, she wouldn't have thought she

163

was capable of feeling it again, but she did. The first flutters of interest for a man. She thought back to when she'd met him and Kimberly the first time, when the Alanis Morissette lyrics had popped into her head.

Kimberly was still beautiful, but it turned out that she wasn't Josh's wife.

CHAPTER 21

JOSH

Josh and Kimmy had struggled when it came time to figure out Thanksgiving. "I'm going to Angie's this year," Kimmy had said when she returned Josh's phone call. He'd left her a voice mail saying he wanted to get a plan in place for the holiday. "Her parents decided to go on a cruise, so she's doing a Friendsgiving this year and I want Sasha to be there with me."

"What time?" Josh asked.

"Noon." Kimmy knew that was exactly when his family sat down to Thanksgiving dinner, because she'd been sitting down with them since 1999. Josh and Kimmy had decided to go with the flow when it came to the holidays, and Josh now regretted that they hadn't put something more official in place, because clearly, one of them was going to be disappointed.

"I really don't want my daughter to not

be with me on this holiday," Josh said.

"I feel exactly the same way," Kimmy said. "But it's not like I'm taking her to a random group of people. Angie's her godmother."

"That's not the point," Josh said.

"Then what is?" she said, and an uncomfortable silence followed. She broke it by saying, "What if Sasha and I start at Angie's and then I bring her over to your parents' house around four o'clock since she'll be switching to your house that night anyway? And then next year she can start with you and eat dinner at noon and then you can bring her to me when you're done?"

"That's fine," he said. He agreed because he didn't want to make a big deal out of it and at least he would have his daughter for part of the holiday and the two days following it.

"Okay," she said.

"How do you think Sasha's gonna feel when we tell her there will be two Thanksgivings this year?" Josh asked.

"I think it'll go over about as well as it did when we told her we aren't going to *The Grinch* as a family. She doesn't understand, Josh."

"Of course she doesn't," he said. "You're not telling me anything new here. I'm capable of understanding this without it being explained to me."

"I'm sorry," Kimmy said. He could hear the wobble in her voice and he immediately softened.

"I'm sorry too," he said. He was the one who asked the question. It was just hard when the person you always discussed the problems with was not the one you could discuss them with going forward, even if they were half the reason there was a problem in the first place. "We'll figure it out."

"I know we will," she said, because they always had.

His parents had given up on trying to convince them to slow down and give it some more time, and Josh's mom seemed especially resigned to the fact that her baby was getting married when he was still just a baby himself, at least in her eyes. Josh and Kimmy had planned to go to City Hall, but in the end his parents convinced them to get married in the backyard with a casual reception for friends and family afterward. Josh liked that because it felt like maybe his parents were at least warming to the idea, and Kimmy liked it because she wanted her mother to be there.

He'd let Kimmy take the car and he'd gotten a ride to work with a coworker so that Kimmy could move some of their things into the house they'd rented. It was a total shithole, but they'd discovered the hard way that no one wanted to rent a nice property to a couple of eighteen-year-old kids with nonexistent credit and not a lot of money for rent. They were also crushed when they'd discovered just how little disposable income they'd have after they paid that rent each month. They were lucky that Josh's car had been a gift from his parents, but some back-of-the-napkin math made it clear that after they paid the rent, utilities and gas and food would swallow up most of what was left of their paychecks.

Though Josh's parents were not in favor of them marrying so young, it didn't stop his mom from offering her wedding gown to Kimmy. She had only sons, no daughters, and when she'd offered it, Kimmy had burst into tears and accepted immediately.

Kimmy loved Josh's mom. She told Josh that the last thing she wanted was for either of his parents to be angry with her, to blame her for Josh not going to school. "They don't think I'm pregnant, do they?" Kimmy asked after Josh told her he'd broken the news to them.

"No, because I told them you weren't the minute they asked me, which was about thirty seconds after I told them we were getting married. I've never seen my mom look so relieved."

"Do they think I talked you into it?"

"No."

Kimmy's mom hadn't seemed to care when Kimmy told her she and Josh were getting married and moving in together. "Guess I can't stop you now that you're eighteen," she'd said.

"I thought maybe she'd have more to say about it," Kimmy said when Josh came to pick her up. She'd stared out the passenger-side window of his car as she told him that the only other thing her mom had said was "When do you think you'll have your stuff out? I might want to move into an apartment or something now that I won't need so much room."

He'd reached over and squeezed her shoulder. "You're my family now," he said, and Kimmy had cried so hard in his arms that it was fifteen minutes before he'd been able to pull out of the driveway.

Kimmy's mother had snorted when Kimmy brought the white dress home, assuming correctly that her daughter's virginity was no longer intact. But later that night Kimmy went to the kitchen for a drink of water and when she passed by the dining room where she'd hung the dress, she saw her mother inspecting it, running her hand lightly over the sleeves as if wishing she'd had the chance to wear one herself. She'd been holding a lit cigarette at the time, and Kimmy held her breath until her mother left the room.

Then Kimmy took the dress back to Josh's house and asked his mother to keep it there until the wedding. She told Josh's mom it was because she didn't want it to smell like smoke, but she told Josh she was terrified it might go up in flames, which seemed like a really bad omen and a horrific way to start a marriage that no one besides her and Josh really seemed to believe in in the first place.

On Tuesday, the last day of school before Thanksgiving break, Josh stopped to talk to Layla after he walked Sasha into the building. It was freezing and he felt bad that she had to stand outside and endure the winter temperatures, but she was wearing a different coat — royal blue — and that made it easier for his eyes to lock on her now. Maybe the coat was warmer than her old one.

"Sasha is still talking about the music program," Josh said. "I made a Beatles playlist and she loves it when 'Let It Be' comes on."

"You're starting her early," Layla said. "Good. I like that."

"She also said she's asking Santa for a guitar." He hoped mentioning the guitar did not make Layla think about the day he saw her playing at home, but it probably did. *Awesome, Josh. Remind her of that time you creeped on her like some weird Peeping Tom.*

"Let me know if you want me to teach her how to play it."

"I will," he said. "Big plans for Thanksgiving?"

"My folks live here in town, so I'll be spending the day with them. How about you?"

"Little trickier for me this year. Trying to split the day so that Sasha's mom and I can both celebrate with her, but I think we figured it out." His parents had decided to move Thanksgiving dinner to six o'clock because two of his brothers had a conflict with the regular time, so the problem had solved itself.

The week after Thanksgiving, Josh and Kimmy were both planning to take Sasha to see *The Grinch* — Kimmy on opening night and Josh two days later for the Sunday matinee. They would each buy her some sort of movie tie-in merchandise. Sasha would get popcorn at both showings and she would begin to realize that being a child of divorced parents meant two of everything.

171

He was already dreading what he and Kimmy might encounter for the Christmas holidays. Santa was a very big deal to Sasha, and he knew she was going to have questions. They still had some time to come up with a story about why Santa was visiting both houses.

"I'd be happy to watch Norton again if you've got any travel plans during the holiday season," Layla said. "I've got a long stretch off from school for winter break, and my parents live here, so I'll be around."

"That would be great, actually, if you're sure you don't mind. I'm planning on being gone for a week."

Layla smiled. "I don't mind at all. I liked having him around."

Kimmy was taking Sasha to the Mall of America to visit the American Girl doll store, and then Josh was taking her to Colorado to introduce her to the slopes in Breckenridge. Two of his brothers and their families went every year, and it was something he and Kimmy had talked about but had never actually gotten around to doing. The cabin his brothers had rented was big enough to hold everyone. If Sasha hated skiing, there would be hot chocolate in the lodge and sledding with her cousins. They were going to fly out on the twenty-ninth and would return on New Year's Day. Sasha couldn't stop talking about it. And then, after Josh dropped Sasha off at Kimmy's, he was going to hop on another plane and meet his brother James in Vegas for a three-day getaway full of gambling, drinking, and whatever else they felt like. Josh had been to Vegas several times in the past — bachelor parties and once with Kimmy for a close friend's wedding when she was pregnant with Sasha — but it had been a while. It would really help having the option to drop Norton off at Layla's, where he knew the dog would be comfortable.

A bell rang in the distance and he said, "I better get going. Have a good day. Stay warm."

"Thanks," she said. "You too."

CHAPTER 22

LAYLA

Thanksgiving passed uneventfully for Layla. She enjoyed spending time with her family, especially when she thought about last year and how Liam had bragged to her dad and brother about how well he was doing at work, which had made Layla cringe. Did he think they'd forgotten about all the other jobs he'd had and the peaks and valleys of his career? Did he think her family was that clueless or that she never confided in them?

This year, Layla laughed a lot more. Her siblings and their families went home after they finished dessert, but Layla stuck around long after the time Liam would have wanted them to leave. She got comfy on the couch, and even though she was thirty-five, she felt a bit like a college student who'd come home for the holiday break as her mother showered her with attention and offered another glass of wine, a different piece of pie. During commercials, her dad asked her how her studio was coming along, and she lit up when she told him it was done and that he needed to come over and see it. She got choked up thinking about how much she loved her parents and the role they had played in her life. Layla felt so much lighter sitting on that couch, and by the time she left to go back to her own house, maybe even a tiny bit hopeful.

By Saturday, her festive holiday mood had deflated considerably. She cleaned rooms that weren't dirty, streamed a new comedy that failed to elicit a single laugh, and wished desperately that she had someone to talk to. Mostly, she felt like crying. It happened sometimes, usually on the heels of something good like Thanksgiving. It was as if her life had become a roller coaster and it had recently crested a giant hill and had nowhere to go but down for a while before gathering enough steam to climb again. The only solution she'd found when she felt this way was to leave the house and find something to take her mind off it until she felt better.

Layla went to a bookstore and browsed the new releases, buying the ones she'd been looking forward to the most. She stopped at

Target and bought a few of the household items she was low on. While she was inside, snow had started falling, and as she carried her bags to the car she decided to splurge and treat herself to a steaming cup of fancy coffee. At the coffee shop, once she'd paid for her drink, she took it to a cluster of chairs in front of the fireplace. She took a sip and opened her new book, and it was so cozy she couldn't think of anyplace she'd rather be at that moment.

Layla, whose back had been to the counter, might not have noticed Suzanne at all, but she wanted to throw away her empty coffee cup and when she stood up to look for the garbage can, she spotted a familiar blond head. Suzanne was wearing a fluffy white turtleneck sweater with winter-white jeans and camel-colored over-the-knee boots. She was also wearing a camel-colored wool fedora. Her daughter, who looked about five, was dressed almost identically, right down to the hat, although her boots were, thankfully, a more appropriate length and stopped at the knee. Her toddler son was wearing a white sweater — *white!* — and red pants and a camel-colored newsboy cap.

Too much, too much, too much, Layla thought.

It was like they'd come to the coffee shop for a photo shoot, but the table was covered with things that would ruin all that white in a heartbeat, so maybe not a photo shoot. Maybe that's just how they dressed for a casual Saturday coffee shop outing. Then Layla remembered something Liam had said about Suzanne having a fashion blog and how she had hundreds of thousands of followers on social media.

Suzanne's eyes grew big and round when they locked with Layla's. She started frantically trying to gather up the drinks and cookies on the table, and when that didn't work she tried to convince her kids to leave the treats behind in an effort to get them out the door as quickly as possible. They wanted nothing to do with that plan and refused to hold on to their mother's outstretched hands. Suzanne looked terrified while simultaneously appearing as if she would burst into tears at any moment. Layla walked toward them, intending to say that they should stay and that she was on her way out, but Suzanne panicked. She reached out and picked up the younger child, knocking his sister's hot chocolate off the table and onto the floor in the process. It was so pathetic Layla almost felt sorry for her, and she definitely felt sorry for the children, who had undoubtedly been looking forward to their treats.

"Are you kidding me?" Layla said. "*You're* the one running away?"

The little girl started crying. "We will get more," Suzanne yelled, pulling on her hand and hurrying her toward the door. Heads turned, and Layla was left standing there to deal with the scrutiny.

If the coffee shop hadn't been so crowded and if there hadn't been children present, Layla didn't know if she could have restrained herself the way she did. She wanted to tell Suzanne to grow a pair. To stop acting like a big scaredy-cat at the first hint of conflict and confrontation. To deal with the consequences of her actions like a grown-up.

Running into Suzanne empowered her. Liam might've torn her down brick by brick, but she took pride in the fact that she was rebuilding her foundation from the ground up, and this time around, she would be made of much stronger stuff. She threw away her coffee cup, walked out the door, and got into her car.

She no longer felt like crying. Maybe it wasn't such a cliché after all, because whatever didn't kill you certainly *did* make you stronger.

The lights were still on at the guitar shop when Layla drove by. It was 3:57 P.M., and she thought it closed at four on Saturdays. She pulled in anyway. She was full of righteous indignation and she wanted to take it out on a guitar. But she was low on guitar strings and maybe Brian wouldn't care that she was dashing in at the last minute.

The bell tinkled when she walked in, and Brian looked up. Layla could see the irritation on his face. He'd probably been manning the store by himself all day and was ready to go home and enjoy his Saturday night. But he smiled as soon as he realized it was Layla.

"I'm so sorry. I just need some strings and then I'll dash back out the door. And if you don't have time, I'll come back tomorrow."

"If it was anyone else, I'd care," he said, walking toward the door to flip the sign over to the CLOSED side and lock up. "But I'm happy to help you out. You're my best customer."

"I wonder if I should be worried about that," Layla said, smiling back at him.

"I'm the one who should be worried. It

means I don't have very many customers."

Layla selected her strings and brought them up to the counter. "I appreciate this, Brian. I really, really need to play."

He rang up her purchase. "Feel like jamming? It's okay if you don't have time or don't want to. It's a standing offer."

Suddenly, jamming with Brian was exactly what she wanted to do. "Actually, I do feel like it."

He pointed to a row of guitars and then toward an amp. "Pick one out and plug it in."

They played for two solid hours and fell into the kind of easy rhythm musicians were sometimes lucky enough to experience. It helped that they both knew the songs and weren't fumbling their way through the arrangements. He'd play a few opening chords and she'd join in as soon as she recognized it. Then she'd play a few chords and he'd jump in, and it wasn't long before they were trying to stump each other as their song choices grew more obscure. She could play anything, and so could he. He brought a microphone into the mix and Layla discovered that Brian was no slouch in the singing department, either. After that, they shared a microphone and they didn't stop until they'd sung every song in their shared

repertoire. Her alto blended well with his deep voice, and she could go up the range if needed. The result was a soothing harmony that reminded her of the way she and her fellow band member Rick had sounded when they sang together.

"My friend was right. You can definitely bring the house down," he said.

"So can you." Together, they'd be a force to reckon with. She put the guitar back on its stand. "I didn't realize how much I wanted to play with someone else," Layla said. "I've just been playing alone, but God, this felt good."

Imagine how good it would feel to play for a crowd.

He glanced at his watch. "Felt good for me too. I lost all track of time. Will there be anyone sending out a search party for you? Husband or boyfriend filing a missing person report?"

"Oh, no. I'm single. Divorced," she clarified now that she and Liam had signed the papers and it was final. It felt strange, like she was admitting she was tarnished goods and had been booted back to the singles table to try again.

Brian didn't wear a ring. He was nice and she found him attractive. They certainly had a lot in common and could probably talk about music for hours. She didn't feel the flutter the way she had with Josh, but she felt a strong urge for companionship, and the way they'd meshed so seamlessly appealed to her. Maybe she and Brian would be one of those made-for-each-other couples who started out as friends. Layla opened her mouth to ask him if he'd like to grab a drink or a bite to eat sometime, but then his cell phone pinged and before she could ask him, he looked down at it and said, "Sorry. That's my fiancée. I better grab it before she's the one who files the missing person report." He picked up his phone, punched a button, and then said, "Hey, sweetie. Sorry about that. I'll be home in fifteen minutes." He hung up the phone, and Layla's face was still warm with the embarrassment of her narrowly avoided proposition.

"I was single for a really long time," Brian said. "I always said I'd never get married. Swore it wasn't something I ever needed to do. Then I met Jeannie and a year later, I was down on one knee. I guess falling in love will do that to you."

"Yep. I do remember that part," Layla said.

She and Liam had been dating for about

182

fifteen months when he announced he was taking her to the Seychelles. Their friends were all vacationing in Mexico or the Bahamas. Turks and Caicos if they wanted to flaunt their travel budgets. That was exactly why those places wouldn't do. Liam had to show everyone that their vacation was bigger and better than theirs, and Layla spent an inordinate amount of time giving an impromptu geography lesson to everyone who asked her where exactly the islands were located. When she protested that she couldn't afford her share of a vacation like that, Liam said he didn't expect her to. "Can't a guy spoil the girl he loves by taking her someplace warm every once in a while?"

The bonuses had continued to roll in, and he looked so excited and so genuinely happy that he had the means to make this kind of grand gesture that all she said was "Of course he can."

Liam was surprised that she'd never vacationed internationally and even more surprised that she didn't have a passport. The Hilding family had always vacationed closer to home, and they usually arrived by car. Layla and her siblings had spent plenty of time fighting in the back seat as their parents introduced them to the Great Lakes, the Grand Canyon, and Washington, D.C.

Layla expedited her passport application, and she had a feeling Liam might propose to her on the trip. They'd been living together for over a year by then, and the love she felt for him was genuine. They were good together, and when it was just the two of them they never ran out of things to talk about. Liam was exuberant and fun-loving and there was nothing standoffish about him. Meeting new people was one of his favorite activities, and you could plunk him down in the middle of any social situation and he'd come away with five new acquaintances. He also bragged about his job a lot, and one night Layla grew frustrated. They'd had an argument in the car on the way home when she said, "People don't always want to hear about your job and how good you are at it. You can keep some of the details to yourself. It's really no one's business."

"If people want to ask me about my job, I'm going to tell them. I'm a salesman," he said. "Nothing wrong with selling them on myself, first. It's all about networking, Layla." She could hear the change in his tone, and she knew he was mad.

"I just meant that people might relate to you better if you came across a little humbler."

He'd looked over at her sitting in the passenger seat. "Humble? The way you're humble when you're strutting around onstage under a spotlight?"

"That's different," she said. "The crowd is there to see a performance."

"It's not that different, Layla."

"Yes, it is." It wasn't like she went around telling people how good she was. She performed and then she left it up to them to decide. "All I'm saying is that they'll like you anyway, regardless of your accomplishments."

But would they? She and Liam didn't get together with Christine and Noelle and their husbands anymore. They had at first, but lately her friends always seemed to be busy when she tried to make plans. It wasn't until much later that Layla could look back on that time through a different lens and realize that Liam was off-putting to a lot of people.

Liam did not propose to her in the Seychelles. He proposed to her in the airport as they were waiting to board their first flight. He actually raised his voice and asked the gate attendants if there was any way to delay boarding for just a couple of seconds because he had a question he needed to ask his girlfriend first. Everyone looked at him like he was annoying and delusional, but the question was all part of the performance. He asked again, loudly, and this time he caught the attention of the passengers clustered around the gate waiting to board. Then he took a knee right then and there and he whipped out a ring so big Layla felt certain she'd be mugged on the street while wearing it. The passengers cheered when he laid a big kiss on her after she said yes, and even the gate attendants smiled at him like okay, you got us good. The doors opened, everyone boarded, and Layla and Liam drank champagne in first class all the way to the Seychelles.

Despite Layla's ease at being onstage in front of a crowd, she would have preferred a proposal that was a bit more intimate and private. But she accepted the well-wishes of the first-class passengers who had observed the spectacle with a genuine smile on her face, and the Seychelles really was a breath-taking place to visit.

Layla put on her coat and picked up her bag of guitar strings. "Thanks again for staying late and for reminding me how much I love playing with other musicians."

"You're welcome. See you soon, Layla. Remember, you're my best customer."

Layla laughed and Brian unlocked the door. As she drove home, she felt a little like maybe the roller coaster had started chugging its way back up the hill again.

CHAPTER 23

JOSH

Josh took care of the dishes and the laundry. The weather forecast was calling for snow, so he made sure the snowblower was ready to go and he filled up the gas can and stashed it in the garage. He went to the hardware store for salt and emptied it into a five-gallon bucket and then sprinkled it on the front steps and sidewalks. He made potato soup, which really meant opening a packet and pouring the contents into a pot once the water started to boil. At four o'clock he ran out of things to do, so he sat down on the couch and turned on the TV, even though the football game wouldn't start for a few more hours. He might not have been interested in playing sports when he was younger, but he'd always enjoyed watching them, especially with his brothers.

The house was far too quiet without his daughter in it. Kimmy had called, and when she put Sasha on the phone she told Josh she was having a great time at the Mall of America. They'd already gone to the American Girl store and were headed to the amusement park to ride the carousel.

The last time they'd visited the mall, they'd gone as a family. But now vacations would be of the double variety, much like movies and Santa's visit, which had gone okay and was probably aided in part by the double number of presents. Sasha was with Kimmy on Christmas Eve, and then he'd picked her up on Christmas Day and they'd gone to his parents' house. He'd asked Kimmy if she wanted to join them, because no matter how he felt about the fracture of their relationship, he had a hard time picturing her sitting alone in her condo on Christmas Day. "I've got plans with Angie and her husband. They've invited me over to her parents' house. I told her she didn't have to invite me to everything, but she said it's very casual, more of a drop-in kind of thing. But thanks, Josh."

"Sure."

I'm your family now, he'd said to her once. But that wasn't true anymore, and family was something Kimmy had never really had much of in the first place.

It had been two years since their backyard wedding, and neither Josh nor Kimmy had much to show for what they'd been doing during all that time. They partied with their friends and kept working the menial jobs they'd settled into. Josh's concrete-pouring job had a lot of downtime, because there wasn't as much work in the colder months, and Kimmy was still working in retail. His parents were frustrated with his lack of ambition, but he'd never once asked them for help, so there wasn't much they could say.

The start of 2002 was especially tough. Josh was all but laid off for almost eight weeks, and Kimmy's shifts had dwindled to less than twenty-five hours per week, because the company she worked for had suffered a decline in their overall sales and was in danger of going under.

There was nothing to do that bleak dark winter but stay inside and party. Most weekend mornings, Josh and Kimmy would walk into their living room and be greeted by the sight of empty beer cans and at least one of their friends asleep on the couch.

They threw an epic party for St. Patrick's Day despite neither of them having any claim to an Irish heritage. They started early, and by six o'clock that night very few of the people crammed into their tiny living room were sober. One of their friends had gotten ahold of a bottle of absinthe and brought it to the party because it was green, and that decision would change the trajectory of both Josh's and Kimmy's lives.

"This is supposed to make you hallucinate," someone said.

"Nah, not really," someone countered. "But this will fuck you up, no doubt."

They all tried some. Josh seldom deviated from beer, but Kimmy didn't really like the taste and often drank the higher-octane cocktails, the brighter-colored, the better.

He should have known by then to keep a close eye on Kimmy, as he was usually the voice of reason when it came to partying, almost always managing to cut her off before anything terrible happened. Sure, they'd each had a few nights hugging a toilet or an entire day in bed recovering, but they were in their early twenties and almost everyone they knew drank a little too much, a little too often. They were young. It was fine.

Sometime around 3:00 A.M., Josh scanned the living room and realized Kimmy was missing. He'd started to sober up and all he wanted to do was crash. He went looking for Kimmy, checking first the bathroom and then their bedroom. She was lying on their bed fully dressed. Most of their guests had gone home by then, although a couple of people had passed out on their couch. He took off her shoes, but she didn't stir. He placed his hand on her shoulder to wake her and let her know he was shutting down the party, but when he glanced at her face his heart started to pound. Her skin looked weird, damp and mottled with a slightly blue tinge. He shook her harder. "Kimmy. Kimmy!"

He could not rouse her, and he panicked, yelling her name louder. His brain kicked in and he ran for the phone in the kitchen and dialed 911. His friend Tommy woke up and said, "What's going on?"

"Get over here and stay on the line until they get here." A lot of things went right that night because Tommy did what Josh asked, and Josh ran back into the bedroom seconds before Kimmy puked. He rolled her onto her side and gathered her in his arms so that her back was pressed up against him and her face was pointing toward the floor so she wouldn't choke. "It's okay, it's okay, it's okay," he said. "They're coming. It's okay."

They pumped her stomach at the hospital, and when they finally let Josh back into the room, the charcoal they'd used coated the outline of her lips like some ghoulish lipstick. She couldn't stop crying, and all Josh could do was hold her and tell her she was safe.

Josh didn't tell his parents what had happened, and he didn't really believe Kimmy when she said she would never drink again. Nevertheless, they took it easy for the next few weekends, but the pall lingered as the first few signs of spring arrived.

He got home from work one day to find the house empty. Kimmy had the day off, so he'd left her the car and bummed a ride with a coworker. She came home an hour later.

"Hey, where've you been?" Josh asked. Kimmy looked pale and kind of out of it.

"My mom called. Wanted me to stop by. Said she had something she needed to tell me." That was unusual, as Kimmy's mom rarely called her or even seemed like she wanted Kimmy in her life. "I thought . . . Well, I thought maybe she wanted to know how I was doing. How we were doing and everything."

"Yeah? What'd she say?"

"She's dying." Kimmy sank down into the cushions of the lumpy, shitty couch. "She has something called COPD. It's like a lung thing." Kimmy started crying and Josh gathered her into his arms. He had no clue what to say. Her shoulders shook and she cried for a long time.

"What do we need to do?"

"There's nothing we can do," Kimmy said. "She's going into hospice tomorrow. She said

192

she'll be lucky if she makes it to the end of the month."

But she wasn't lucky, and she died two and a half weeks later.

The family she'd worked for all those years buried her, and Josh felt a massive amount of relief, because there was no way they could have handled the expense themselves. And the bill for Kimmy's ambulance ride and emergency room visit had just landed in the mailbox, and the amount made him feel like he'd been slammed to the ground and the wind knocked out of him. Josh was still covered under his parents' policy, but Kimmy had no coverage at all. They could barely pay their rent, and their checking account was frequently overdrawn, resulting in service charges that put them further in the hole.

This was reality. A wake-up call for both of them. Josh stopped thinking about what he was missing out on and started thinking about what he needed to change in himself. It was time to stop playing house and start living like two adults who desperately needed to get their shit together.

It took a month of searching, but he lucked out when he found an electric company looking for apprentices. It would require buying some tools, and he had to swallow his pride and ask his parents to loan him the money.

They took it better than he thought they would and told him to consider it an investment in his future. He thanked them profusely, and though he should have felt good about taking such a positive step, he felt like shit. He worked out a payment plan with the hospital and tried not to think about the fact that it might be years before they could pay it off. It would protect their credit history, though, and that was more important.

Kimmy had not gone back on her word about not drinking again, and Josh was down to a beer or two after work, but their house still seemed to be where everyone congregated. He came home and told Kimmy there would be no more hosting their friends until two in the morning and no one passing out on their couch. He had to get up early and he didn't want to be dragging ass all day while he worked.

Kimmy agreed, although she didn't look excited about the lifeline Josh was grabbing for them. Her eyes looked vacant and her skin was an alarming sallow shade. She just lost her mom, he told himself. It didn't matter that they hadn't been close. It was the only parent Kimmy had ever known and now she truly had no one but Josh.

Now Kimmy didn't have Josh anymore,

194

either. But Kimmy was not that same girl. She was thirty-seven years old and very capable and she would always have Sasha and that made him feel a little better. And someday, Kimmy would meet a man and maybe she'd grow to love his family the way she'd loved Josh's.

Maybe Josh would meet someone, too.

Someday.

Norton, who had been following Josh around the house, settled in on the couch beside him and looked at him like, *Well, what are we going to do now?*

Josh reached out and scratched the dog behind his ears. "I'm not sure, buddy. Kinda sad, isn't it? Grown man who spent his day doing household chores and cooking." Josh sighed. "No, you know what? Not sad at all. It's relaxing. If I can't have my daughter, at least I've got sports and soup and you. No woman, though. That would be kind of nice. First snowstorm of the season. Maybe a little red wine. I don't think I'm supposed to be thinking about that yet. Might make me look like some sort of desperate player who can't be alone. I can be alone," he muttered, as if the notion that he couldn't was absurd. "Layla's alone. You know Layla, that nice lady who took care of you when we were out of town. She's gonna watch you

195

again while I'm gone. She said it was just her. That means she's single. Probably. Or maybe it just means no one lives there with her. She's pretty, too. She might have met someone since then. I don't know. I guess I could ask her."

Oh, my God, he thought. *I am talking to the dog.*

A text popped up on his phone from his brother Jordan. It's too loud at my house. Kids everywhere. Toys. Chaos. Sticky. Can I come over for the game?

Yep. I have soup and beer.

Be there in five.

Josh looked over at Norton. "I will take this to my grave. We never had this conversation."

Norton looked at Josh like he had no idea what he was saying but he was happy someone who cared was beside him.

Josh thought maybe that was all anyone wanted.

Josh double-checked that he and Sasha had everything they needed for Colorado and then put the suitcases in the car. He gathered up Norton's supplies, and the three of them drove to Layla's. "Hey," she said when she opened the door. She smiled and reached down to ruffle Norton's fur. "Come on in."

"Can you please send pictures of Norton like last time?" Sasha asked.

"Of course," Layla said. "I know you're going to miss him, but don't worry. I'll take good care of him."

"Any big plans?" Josh asked. "Still quite a bit of break left."

"You're looking at it," she said, pointing to the slippers on her feet and the mug of hot tea in her hand.

"Staying out of the cold, huh?"

"I might head out at some point to see a movie."

"With your boyfriend?" He'd been pre-occupied with setting down Norton's food and water bowls and didn't think about what he was asking before it came out of his mouth.

"No. I mean, I don't have a boyfriend. I meant one of my friends from work. Tonya. The teacher who's always with me in the morning."

"Oh, sure." He leaned down and scratched Norton's ears.

There was an awkward silence as they stood there while Sasha hugged Norton and told him not to be sad. Then Sasha said, "Let's go, Daddy," and they said their good-byes, and Josh was still thinking about Layla when they boarded the plane two hours later.

CHAPTER 24

LAYLA

It was the first truly cold and miserable evening of the season, with windchills around ten below and a thick blanket of snow on the ground. Layla had never been so happy to be inside the home she bought on her own, sitting on the couch she'd paid for, wearing her comfiest yoga pants and warmest socks, a dog curled up next to her. Dinner that night was a cup of tomato soup, a few crackers with cheese, and a Coke. Layla still cooked a few of her favorite recipes and stacked them in their glass containers in the freezer, but mostly she allowed herself the pleasure of eating intuitively, and now dinner was whatever the hell she felt like eating.

Layla did not miss having someone to cook for. Maybe it would have been different if she and Liam had cooked together side by side in the kitchen as they shared snippets of their day. But during their marriage Liam had just expected Layla to do it once she started working for the school because she got home so much earlier than he did. There were a lot of things Liam had enjoyed without having to put any of the effort toward them himself: shirts that got dropped off and magically returned from the cleaner's, appointments scheduled for oil changes and dentist visits, and a fridge and cupboards stocked full of groceries. Liam earned more money than her, and Layla had often felt like there was an unspoken expectation that she would manage the household, as if to offset the discrepancies in their financial contributions. From the moment she moved in with him, Layla was the one who made sure there was always toilet paper in the bathroom.

The news ended and *Wheel of Fortune* came on. Vanna White and Pat Sajak were still solving those puzzles. (How? Oh my God, how? And weren't they bored out of their minds?) One of the contestants, a woman who was a newlywed, gushed to Pat about her new husband and the honeymoon they had just returned from.

"Yeah, sure, it's all fun and games for a while," Layla shouted at the TV. The novelty of newlywed bliss would fade and real life, without its fairy-tale sheen, would take its place and there was a reason everyone said the first year of marriage was often the hardest.

They argued about the wedding budget right out of the gate. Liam was pushing hard for a splashy reception at a high-end hotel in downtown Rochester. "My parents are not going to pay for that," Layla said.

"Well, I don't want to cheap out on this."

"My family is not cheap," Layla said. "They're smart. They realize it doesn't make sense to blow a ton of money on a party that lasts one night. My dad even joked once that he'd give twenty grand to any kid who wanted to elope. We could fly somewhere warm, get married on a beach, and save whatever's left."

"I don't want to elope," Liam said. "People who elope are people who can't afford a wedding. Or they're pregnant. Or hiding something."

"That's not the only reason," Layla said. "Do you know how much it costs to throw a big lavish wedding? It's dumb to spend that much for one night."

He didn't say anything for a minute and neither did she. Finally, he looked at her, his face softening, and said, "I just want it to be nice. For us. Will you talk to your parents?

Just find out what they're willing to contribute, and I'll pay for the rest. I don't expect them to shoulder the cost of something they're not comfortable with. They're not obligated to pay for this."

Liam had left inside sales behind and was currently the highest-producing sales rep for Pfizer. His earnings seemed mind-blowing to Layla, but she worried that a lavish wedding would be less about them and more about showing everyone how well he was doing. And there was that slight, niggling guilt about not holding up her end of the partnership as she chased her dreams, waiting patiently for success that might never come.

The paychecks she received from the band barely contributed to their household income, but the fact that Liam made so much more than she did made her feel like she didn't have a voice when it came to how he wanted to spend it. She had recently heard about an opening for music teachers in their school district, and the guilt of not holding her own financially had started to gnaw at her. But the band was on the verge of breaking out, and she felt like she owed it to the rest of the members to stick around a little longer. And if she was being truthful with herself, she wanted them to succeed even more than they did. It kept her from falling asleep at night.

She would lie awake beside Liam thinking about all the exciting things that could happen — the record deals, the live shows. A tour. She dreamed of living her life onstage. She would turn her passion into a successful career, and she'd make good money, too. She didn't think a lot about how that would work — her on the road and Liam at home. Surely, they could figure out how to handle success for both of them? Those are the good kinds of problems to have, she told herself.

She did speak to her parents, and they were wonderful and offered the same amount they'd contributed for her siblings' weddings. The only time they'd raised an eyebrow was when Layla shared the details of it all. "I'd hate to see you go into debt for this," her dad said.

"Liam's paying for it with his commissions. He really wants to do it this way." Liam didn't seem to care what anyone thought about the lavish affair they were planning, and he would laugh right along with Layla when she called him a bridezilla.

"Well, you're both adults and it's your day" was all her dad said.

The plans moved forward as they finalized the menu and the bridesmaids' dresses. The cake and invitations. Layla and her mother went dress shopping, and the one she chose was far below what she would have paid if

Liam had been with them. The wedding might have been flashier than Layla wanted, but the dress was simple, elegant, and so completely Layla's style that she smiled whenever she thought about walking down the aisle in it. Sure, she and Liam had different tastes, but she loved him and planning the wedding hadn't dimmed her feelings in any way. Lots of her friends had reported arguments with their soon-to-be-spouses during the planning phase. There were disagreements over how much to spend, but it was a good lesson in learning how to compromise, Layla told herself. Although, how exactly Liam had compromised wasn't quite as evident as the many ways Layla had.

Layla came home from the hair salon a month before the wedding. Liam's eyes widened when he saw what she'd done. When she'd left for the appointment, her long messy hair had been its usual vibrant shade. She was mostly still alternating between pink and blue, with a deep violet thrown in occasionally for variety, and once platinum, although that had been a nightmare to maintain. Now it was the color she'd been born with, which was a faint strawberry blond. Layla thought her hair would look classic and romantic under her bridal headpiece, and that's exactly how she wanted to look on their big day.

"You look shocked," she said. "Call me old-fashioned, but I really didn't want neon hair for my wedding."

"I thought you said you were a blonde."

"I said I was a strawberry blonde."

"Are you going to make it blonder?"

"Why would I do that? Do you not like it? This is my natural hair color. I told you that a long time ago. You've seen old pictures of me," she said, as if she had to defend her hair color with a cold hard fact. "I would think that would have tipped you off."

"No, I love it," he said quickly. He had walked over and hugged her, squeezing her tight. "You're going to be a beautiful bride. I was just surprised. I'm glad you kept it long." She'd almost cut it to shoulder length but had kept the current length because her wedding hairstyle was an elaborate updo and she didn't want to cause problems for her hairdresser if she showed up with shorter hair.

But no matter how many times Liam assured her that he loved her hair, she knew deep down that he didn't. She liked to think she was confident enough not to care. When she was onstage with her bright hair and whatever makeup look she was going for at the time, she felt bulletproof. But standing in their living room, stripped of the eye-catching color he was used to, she realized she had just lost a little bit of that swagger.

Then Liam gave her his guest list, and when Layla skimmed it and saw that he wanted to invite Suzanne, she turned to him and said, "Why in the world would we invite Suzanne?"

"I ran into her the other day and she said she'd heard we were engaged. And then she asked when she should be watching the mailbox and I didn't know what to say so I told her end of April."

"Liam!"

"I'm sorry, but isn't she one of your oldest friends?"

"If by oldest you mean because I've known her since childhood, then yes. But not oldest as in dearest. We're not close anymore. And you dated her for a while. Should I invite my tenth-grade boyfriend? How about the guy I slept with for a couple of months in college?" She said it jokingly, but inside she was incredulous.

"It won't hurt anything. She probably just wanted to be included and might not even show."

Suzanne had always had a way of working herself into situations where her presence didn't seem necessary. She clung to their friendship in a way Layla had outgrown years ago. What was the point? Layla had reached an age where she valued friendships based on quality, not quantity, and she had never known someone who was so worried about missing out, even if she only halfheartedly wanted to be there in the first place.

But Suzanne did show, and Layla really didn't care, because she had so many other wonderful things capturing her attention on her wedding day. It was a beautiful ceremony and the reception was spectacular. She got caught up in the elegance and the splendor of the magical night, and she basked in the way Liam looked at her and how he'd stared into her eyes as he'd recited his vows. She had cried through hers, which had taken her by surprise. She was not highly emotional, but tears filled her eyes because she was just so happy.

They had both agreed that Storm Warning would play at the reception, but that Layla would obviously not be onstage with them. She wanted to dance and mingle, and this was one night she'd happily hang up her guitar. But she did have a surprise planned for Liam, and after the toasts Layla climbed onstage. Kevin handed her an acoustic guitar, and Layla sang a brand-new song that he'd written specifically, upon her request, for Layla to sing to her new husband. She loved the song. It was good, better than any of their current original songs, and the band would go on to sing it at their gigs, where it would become a fan favorite, and one day in the far future Kevin would sell it to an up-and-coming singer out of Nashville who would take it all the way to number six on the country charts. But back then, Layla just wanted to show how much Liam meant to her by singing the words to him in front of their friends and families.

Liam smiled at Layla adoringly as she sang, and he only took his eyes off her once, and only for a few seconds.

Layla's eyes followed to see what had caught his attention and it was Suzanne.

Now that Layla was thirty-five, her former girl-next-door cuteness had morphed into a delicate, fresh-faced elegance that caused her to be routinely carded for alcohol. Her face had matured in a way that allowed the delicateness to be replaced with a classic, more refined appearance. She had been using liberal amounts of sunscreen from an early age, and as a result she looked like a woman who took damn good care of herself.

She'd also settled on a look and a style that was all her own. She'd cut her hair in a shoulder-grazing bob and she leaned into the strawberry tones by adding more of them. At school, she often wore glasses instead of her contacts, and she owned several pairs, treating them as an accessory. When she wasn't at school, she often played up her eyes with mascara and winged her eyeliner simply because she liked the way it looked. Maybe someone who knew about such things would say she was trying to figure out who she was by way of choosing a persona. And maybe that was true. But all Layla knew was that she enjoyed being whoever she wanted to be with no one to please but herself.

The newlywed won the big prize on *Wheel of Fortune.* Layla drained the last of her can of Coke and then she burped, loudly. Norton looked at her like, *You are my kind of person.* Then she laughed and thought about how far she'd come and that maybe she had lots of things to be happy about.

CHAPTER 25

LAYLA

The first thing Layla saw when she opened her eyes on the morning of December 31 was Norton's face approximately six inches from her own. He'd been asleep in his dog bed on the floor when she'd shut off the lights and crawled under the covers, but he'd clearly had a change of heart about his sleeping preferences at some point. Either that, or he just had to pee and wanted her to wake up. She'd been sending pictures of Norton to Sasha and Josh at least once a day, so she grabbed her phone and snapped a quick picture, holding the phone above her and keeping the angle wide enough to show that Norton was practically sharing her pillow. She thought about adding a caption that said WE WOKE UP LIKE THIS but decided it was dumb. What if Josh thought she was trying to say she looked pretty first thing in the morning, without makeup? She did look good first thing in the morning, but that was beside the point. She cropped herself out of the picture, didn't include a caption but did include a smiley face, and sent it with a text that said, I think your dog prefers my pillow.

Layla let Norton out in the backyard and started the coffee. Her phone pinged an hour later and the text from Josh said, I'm not at all surprised.

She spent the remainder of the morning lounging on the couch with Norton. Her phone rang around noon, and the caller ID showed that it was coming from the guitar shop. "Hello," she said.

"Hey, it's Brian. I got your number from our customer database. I was wondering if you were busy tonight. I have a proposition for you."

"What might that be?" she answered in a cautious tone. She'd hear him out and then politely decline. Maybe Brian and his fiancée had a friend who needed a date to round out their foursome, and now that Layla had revealed her marital status and availability, he'd thought of her. Layla had already turned down several invitations for New Year's Eve because she didn't feel like third-wheeling her married friends' evenings and she was even less enthusiastic about a blind date. She'd planned to stay home and sit on the couch with takeout, some wine, and Norton.

"I have a friend," he said. *Here it comes,* she thought. "He was supposed to play at a bar tonight, but he ate something sketchy and is down for the count with a severe case of food poisoning."

Wait a minute. This didn't sound like a setup. It sounded like a gig.

"And he asked you to fill in for him?"

"Yep. And I'm asking you to sit in with me. Jeannie and I had plans to go to dinner and then join a group of our friends to listen to him play. He knew I was coming tonight and he's in dire straits because the owner is pissed about losing his New Year's Eve entertainment. Jeannie said she didn't care if I was sitting at the table or up on the stage as long as we were together. You interested?"

She felt it then, like a Pavlovian response, the urge to perform. To hear the applause. See the smiles on the faces of the crowd.

"Maybe," she said. "What kind of music?"

"Covers. Maybe not quite as rockin' as you might prefer, but pretty close to the songs we played together at the shop. I can text you my friend's set list."

"Yeah, send it over."

"Let me know if there's anything you can't

play or don't know the lyrics to."

"I'll take a look and get back to you within the hour."

"That'd be great. My friend is shitting himself right about now. In more ways than one."

But his friend didn't need to worry, because Layla sent a text to Brian twenty minutes later that said I'm in.

Before she left the house, she leaned down to talk to Norton. "I'm heading out for the evening. I know you're going to miss me, but if you take a nap maybe the time will go by faster. Then I'll come home, and you can sleep in my bed tonight."

At the bar, Brian introduced Layla to Jeannie and the rest of their friends who'd come to watch. They claimed the reserved table in front, and after the introductions had been made they gathered around it with their drinks waiting for the set to start.

"Did you invite anyone tonight?" Brian asked. "I mean, I gave you so much notice."

Layla laughed. "No. I'd already planned an exciting evening of sitting on the couch and turned everyone's invitations down weeks ago. They all have plans tonight. It's fine." Who the crowd was made up of was far less important to her than the simple fact that after all these years, there was a crowd to play for at all.

"You nervous?" he asked.

"Nope." Performing exhilarated her, and she could count on one hand the number of times she'd ever been nervous. And she had hours of recent basement-studio practice under her belt. She was more than ready to unleash it.

"Then let's do this," he said. They took the stage half an hour later and they moved fluidly through the set list, to deafening applause from not only the table of Brian's fiancée and friends, but the bar patrons themselves. It was a decent-sized crowd, a little older and more respectful than some of the audiences Layla had played for in the past. They sipped their wine and their whiskey and they watched attentively as Brian and Layla sang "Brown-Eyed Girl," "Mustang Sally," and "Fire and Rain." The older songs were always crowd favorites, but the set list also contained more recent songs from the Lumineers, Mumford & Sons, Sufjan Stevens, and Adele. They dusted off a few duets — "The Time of My Life" and "Leather and Lace" — that everyone seemed to enjoy. They played three forty-minute sets, and for Layla it felt like they'd flown by in seconds. Brian had asked if there were any songs she wanted to add to the set list, and she'd suggested a few, making sure he knew them, and he did.

At the end of the evening, she and Brian hugged, high-fived, and smiled like a couple of kids who'd been called up to the big leagues after patiently waiting their turn on the sidelines. Jeannie came up to them and threw her arms around Brian. He picked her up off the floor and they kissed. Layla stood awkwardly to the side as the others who had been sitting with Jeannie came up to offer handshakes and hugs. They were all so coupled up, and though Layla was bursting with excitement and happiness, she had no one there to share it with. This was the kind of thing you shared with a spouse or significant other. It was the kind of thing she'd have rushed home to share with Liam, if for some reason he hadn't been there to see it for himself.

"I'm not sure if we'll ever be asked back but only because my friend really likes this steady gig," Brian said.

"That's okay," she said. "I don't know if I'm ready for that, anyway." What Layla did know was that tonight's performance had been exactly what her creative soul needed. It had felt so good and it had been a long time since she felt those feelings. The sheer and utter bliss of doing what she loved in front of a crowd. Watching their faces. Seeing them smile and stop talking to each other and set down their drinks and *listen.*

She said her good-byes and then she drove home and got ready for bed. She patted the space beside her, and Norton jumped up and cuddled close, falling asleep instantly.

Layla was exhausted but couldn't fall asleep.

This was what the rest of her life could look like. Maybe a few more opportunities for creative expression and doing whatever else she wanted to do with her time. She saw nothing but freedom ahead of her, and she realized that Liam had given her the greatest gift by showing her that she wasn't shiny enough for him after all.

And lying there in the dark, still high on adrenaline, Layla decided not to regret the fact that what she hadn't realized all those years ago was that Liam was never going to be enough for her, either.

CHAPTER 26

LAYLA

On Saturday afternoon, Layla did, in fact, have plans to go to a movie with Tonya. Layla had already told her all about New Year's Eve and Tonya had seemed genuinely crushed that Layla hadn't invited her and her husband to come.

"But you had that party to go to. And you were meeting friends."

"We would have come," Tonya said. "We would have brought everyone with us."

"Next time for sure," Layla promised.

Before she left the house, Layla crouched down to give Norton a treat. He scarfed it down and then he panted and pushed his head into her chest. She put her arms around him and gave him a hug, and she didn't feel the least bit foolish about it, either.

Layla and Tonya found their seats and sat down with their popcorn, waiting for the lights to dim. "How's the dog sitting going?"

"Good. It's hard to leave him at home. He looks so sad."

"Where did you say Josh was again?"

"He started out in Colorado, but he and Sasha flew home and then he went to Vegas. Bachelor party. Probably drowning in women and whiskey by now. He'll be home tomorrow." Layla told Tonya how she'd been sending photos of the dog every day.

"So, you're texting with him regularly?"

"Just so Sasha could see pictures of her dog." Unlike the last time she'd watched the dog, Josh's responses to her texts hadn't involved much more than a short comment or a simple thank-you. "I'm not sending them anymore now that Sasha isn't with him. Also, I mentioned I might be seeing a movie and he asked if I was going with a boyfriend. I told him I didn't have a boyfriend and was going out with you, as usual."

"And? What did he do with that magical slam-dunk opening?"

"Nothing. He did nothing with it. Total crickets. Maybe he's got a girlfriend or something."

"Would you have said yes if he'd asked you out?"

"I don't know. I feel like I'm ready for something casual. Or ready-ish. But it's a moot point because he didn't ask."

"Or maybe he *doesn't* have a girlfriend but thinks there's a policy about asking his daughter's teacher out on a date or something." There was no such policy, but dating the parent of a student did require some degree of discretion, at least while Layla was at school.

"Maybe he's not interested."

"Or . . . ," Tonya said, drawing the word out. "Maybe he is interested but is worried about the awkwardness of seeing you every morning if you turn him down."

Layla reached for Tonya's box of M&M's and dumped half of them in their shared tub of popcorn. "We can hypothesize all day, my friend. But only Josh knows the answer to this one."

"He seems like a great guy," Tonya said.

Layla dumped the rest of the M&M's into the popcorn and said, "They all do at first."

Norton was waiting at the door when she came back. Maybe Josh *did* have a girlfriend. Maybe he had zero interest in Layla and that's why he hadn't taken the opening. Maybe Layla wasn't even sure she wanted him to. But what she hadn't admitted to

Tonya — what she could barely admit to herself — was that something inside her was waking up and that something was the part of her that wasn't necessarily ready for a romantic relationship but still craved human companionship. Josh seemed like a perfectly viable choice, because he wasn't a stranger she met on a dating app and he could relate to her situation, and she to his. He was nice and, if pressed, she would admit that he was not hard to look at, not at all. But as she'd already said, she knew nothing about his current situation, so there was no need to hypothesize about his availability or interest in her. Then Layla remembered something Tonya had once said, and she grabbed Norton's leash. "Hey, buddy. Wanna go to PetSmart?"

The parking lot was awfully crowded for a Saturday night, and Norton turned into a total maniac the minute they set foot inside the store. "Whoa, whoa, whoa," Layla yelled, struggling to contain the big goofy dog as they made their way through aisles crowded with customers. "Shit," she muttered. Maybe this place was for women who had small, well-behaved dogs. It wasn't that Norton was especially naughty; Layla just got the impression he hadn't spent a lot of time around other dogs and didn't play well with others. He calmed down after about ten minutes of wandering the aisles and sniffing every single dog he encountered, none of whom were there with a nice man in his mid-to-late thirties.

"Norton!" she yelled when the dog noticed a cat someone had brought in on a leash. Norton put his nose so far up the cat's butt that Layla apologized profusely to its owner.

"Norton," an excited voice yelled from the next aisle over. Layla was still trying to figure out why the voice sounded so familiar when Sasha rounded the corner, Kimberly right behind her. "Miss Layla! Miss Layla." Sasha threw her arms around Norton. "Hi buddy hi buddy hi buddy."

"Hi," Layla said to Kimberly, who could not have looked more confused.

"Hi. Is this my husband's dog? I mean . . ." She let the sentence trail off as if she hadn't gotten used to saying "ex."

"It is. I'm dog sitting."

"You're watching Josh's dog?"

"Sasha asked me one day at school if I liked dogs, which turned into me watching Norton. I think it embarrassed Josh a little bit that she asked, but I told him it was no big deal."

"I didn't realize you saw Josh that often."

"I see him every day," Layla said. "The fine arts teachers handle the morning drop-off." *Stop talking, Layla. Just stop talking.*

"Oh, I didn't know about the morning. I've only done the afternoon pickup. So, Sasha asked you to watch the dog?"

"Yes, but I live alone, and I don't have any kids or pets of my own to juggle. It's no trouble, really. And he's a great dog."

"So, you're single?" Kimberly asked.

"Yes." Layla couldn't quite discern how this revelation made Kimberly feel, but it did look a little like the wheels were turning in her brain. "How were your holidays?" Layla asked, mostly to change the subject.

"Fine, fine," Kimberly said, waving her hand in the air as if Christmas and the arrival of the new year weren't important.

"Do you have a pet?" Layla asked.

"We're getting another hamster," Kimberly said.

"Oh, fun," Layla said.

Kimberly smiled brightly. "We don't have a pet at my house and Sasha thought we needed one so it will be with me all the time. I can't compete with a dog, but I'm not home a lot during the day and when Sasha isn't with me, I tend to work extra hours so I thought this would be a good compromise."

222

Oof, Layla thought. A dog would always trump a hamster. "I think that's wonderful. It's obvious that Sasha really likes animals."

"Well," Kimberly said. "I'll let you get back to it. I'm guessing Josh will pick up the dog tomorrow night when he gets back?"

"Yep, that's the plan."

Sasha gave Norton a few more kisses and grabbed big handfuls of his fur and buried her face in them. "Bye Norton. I will see you tomorrow."

"C'mon, buddy," Layla said, giving a gentle tug on the leash. "Let's get out of here."

CHAPTER 27

LAYLA

Josh texted Layla to let her know that his plane had landed and that he'd be over to pick up Norton as soon as he got home. An hour earlier she'd been lounging on the couch in a pair of sweats and her favorite stretched-out-but-too-cozy-to-get-rid-of sweater. She'd changed into a pair of jeans and a much nicer sweater and she'd run a flat iron through her hair and applied lipstick.

"Hi," Layla said when he arrived forty-five minutes later. "How was your trip?"

"Good, but I'm always happy to be home. Especially after a trip to Vegas."

Layla laughed. "I get it. Norton's asleep in the basement. I put a dog bed down there and he seems to like it." Josh followed her downstairs. She hadn't planned to show him her basement sanctuary, but it wasn't like he didn't already know about it, and that

224

was where Norton was anyway.

"Wow," Josh said when they entered the room. "This is quite a setup."

"It's something," she said with a laugh. It had changed a lot since the day he saw her playing. She'd bought a couch and a large rug. There were two end tables with a lamp on each one to bring more light into the room. She hadn't put anything on the walls yet, but she'd been narrowing down a few choices she'd found online.

Norton was still curled up in the dog bed in the corner. "You'd think the volume level would bother him," Layla said. "But if I'm down here playing, he's with me."

"I think he's almost fully deaf now. I noticed the other day that he didn't come when I called. As soon as I made visual contact, he charged at me like he thought I'd disappeared or something."

"Well, that would explain it." Layla looked over at Norton. The dog opened one sleepy eye and bounded out of the bed. "Is that something to be worried about?"

"He's almost thirteen." Josh crouched down to accept Norton's enthusiastic welcome, ruffling his fur as he said, "Hey, boy. You happy to see me? I missed you."

"I knew he was a senior dog, but I didn't realize he was that old." Norton looked so happy. Layla wished he were staying another night, but Josh undoubtedly missed him more than Layla would. "We took a little field trip to PetSmart. He seemed to really like that."

"Yeah, I heard about that. Sasha was thrilled to run into you and Norton."

"I thought he'd enjoy getting out of the house." No need for Layla to mention that she'd utilized him purely for wingman duties. And she'd bought him some treats while they were there, so the outing had probably been a win from Norton's standpoint. It was Layla who'd failed spectacularly.

"Thanks for sending all the pictures. Sorry I didn't respond as much. Sasha likes to play on my phone. She and her cousins kept swiping them when we were at the condo. Playing some game, I guess."

He said it in such a way that she understood what he was really saying. *Oh, you didn't want your daughter to accidently see the texts you're exchanging with her music teacher. In case those texts took a flirty turn, maybe?* "No problem," she said.

"Ready for school tomorrow?"

"I am, actually. Going a little stir-crazy." She'd been home alone in an empty house a few days too long. If it weren't for Nor-

226

ton, she'd probably have been climbing the walls by then. "It'll be nice to have someone to talk to. Humans, that is."

"So, what you're saying is you're having lots of conversations with my dog."

"More than I'm comfortable admitting."

"If it makes you feel any better, I, too, have been known to have conversations with Norton. I wouldn't admit that to anyone else, but it seems we're both doing it so why hide it."

"He's a great listener," she said.

"You ready to go home, buddy?" Norton looked like he could take it or leave it. Why not? His two most recent caregivers were in the same room. Josh took another look at the microphone and the guitars in their stands. "You must have been a real force to be reckoned with back in the day."

I was, she thought. But it wasn't enough.

Layla and Liam had just celebrated their first wedding anniversary when a scout from Minneapolis showed up at Connie's one night and quietly, unobtrusively, watched the band's first and second sets. Not even Scotty had known he was coming, which pissed him off when he found out about it after the fact. But as she would soon find out, this wasn't really about Storm Warning; it was about Layla.

She never did find out how the scout, whose name was Michael, had gotten her number, but he called her four days later and left a message on the answering machine. She'd been standing right next to it when the call came in, and if her hands hadn't been full of the mail she'd grabbed on her way in, she'd have answered it. But instead she stood beside the phone listening to the message as it came through. She dropped the mail right before it ended, picked up the phone, and said, "Hey, it's Layla. I just walked in the door."

Layla drove to Minneapolis to meet with Michael two days later. They convened at a nondescript office building that looked a lot less rock-and-roll and a lot more corporate than she'd anticipated. The scout also looked like nothing Layla had expected him to. He was dressed casually, his handshake was firm, and his eyes were kind.

That was her first mistaken assumption.

They shook hands and then he introduced her to the other man who'd accompanied him into the room. "This is Neal." Layla would describe Neal's eyes as calculating. He looked her up and down as if cataloguing her physical characteristics, which was exactly what he was doing.

Layla slid a CD in a plastic case across the table. "We don't have a demo yet. This is just something we recorded live one night. And I can sing anything you want."

Neal held up his hands as if he thought she might belt out a tune right there in her seat. "Michael has heard you sing. You've got a great voice."

"Thanks," she said, and she waited to hear what he would say, because why in the hell was she even here?

"You guys would do fine playing Steve Miller covers for the college crowds, but your original stuff isn't going to fly; it's not distinct enough. There's no hook."

Layla wanted to point out that they rarely played Steve Miller Band covers and their fan base was not composed entirely of college students, but that wasn't the point, so she didn't. "I can't really help with the original part. I don't write. I just perform."

"You've actually got a really great stage presence. When you're singing and playing it really electrifies your look. It elevates it. You could do something with that. The others can't because they don't have it, but you could."

So, the fact that she didn't write her own music didn't matter at all. And thank goodness for the spotlight, because apparently she leveled up when she was under it. She'd probably be at the mercy of a producer who planned to take this lump of female unformed clay and turn it into a pop singer. They'd tell her what to wear, how to look, and they'd wrap it in a sparkly bow like it was a gift and wasn't she lucky? Would she be required to dye her hair? Wear contacts that punched up the blue in her eyes. Implants? The list of ways Layla's current look wouldn't fly was probably a mile long. Would she be expected to dance on-stage? That wasn't as bad as hearing that her physical attributes were such a disappoint-ment, but it would be problematic because she wasn't a great dancer. The thought of standing on a stage doing choreographed moves while wearing a headset was too ridiculous to contemplate.

"I guess I'd have to think about that. I was really hoping there might be something for us as a band."

"I don't see that happening," Neal said. It was the kind of news he probably delivered once a week and he had probably forgotten how soul-crushing it felt to the recipient. Or he knew exactly and didn't care. The music industry wasn't for the faint of heart, and she liked to think she was realistic enough to understand that. In Rochester, the band was at the top of the food chain and she was its star attraction. In Minneapolis, she was just another cute girl with a guitar who could be molded into something better.

Little fish, big pond.

Had she really expected to leave the meeting with a recording deal? In her wildest fantasies, maybe. But at the very least she'd preemptively been thinking about how she'd announce the fantastic news to Liam, to the band. That she'd made some inroads and they were finally going to inch forward and become something more than a bar band. There was also a hollow feeling in the pit of her stomach, a very conflicted sensation when she thought about what might happen if she decided to grab the opportunity and leave the others behind. Wasn't this exactly what she wanted? To be onstage singing to a crowd? Hearing the applause? Seeing the looks on their faces? Fame and fortune and everything that came with it? She dyed her hair all the time. Colored contacts weren't so bad. She'd draw the line at implants, but maybe the other things wouldn't be a deal breaker.

She'd promised Michael and Neal that she'd think about it, so maybe she'd take a week or so and really contemplate the crossroads she found herself at.

When she got home, she called Scotty and asked him to meet her for a drink. She told him everything, because she wanted to head off the possibility of the news somehow getting back to him or the band and she wanted to make sure he heard it directly from her.

"He's right, you know," Scotty said. "You guys just aren't there yet with the original stuff. Don't get me wrong, you're getting there. You need more songs like the one you sang at your wedding. That was good. Crowds love that shit."

"What about the things he said about me?" She had a hard time looking Scotty in the eye when she asked it.

"All true," Scotty said. "Pop stars are not born; they're made in a studio." Layla didn't think that was one hundred percent accurate. Plenty of female singers had made it big on their own merits — Ann and Nancy Wilson came to mind. But that was in the seventies, and the turn of the century had brought disruptive changes to the entertainment industry. Things were different now.

"There are lots of things the band can do that we haven't even tried yet," she told Scotty.

"Yeah, and they'll either work, or they won't," he said, always the pragmatist. "Only time will tell."

The sound of Norton whining in protest when Josh tried to coax him from his warm dog bed startled her. "I'm sorry," Layla said. "I got lost in a memory there for a minute."

"Thinking about the glory days?" Josh asked as he leaned down to pick up the bed that Norton had reluctantly vacated.

"Yeah, something like that."

CHAPTER 28

LAYLA

Layla and Tonya were standing at the curb the next morning trying not to freeze. Layla wouldn't have minded being able to feel her extremities, but she was happy to get back into a routine and it would have been futile to complain. "So, I took your advice and Norton and I went to PetSmart."

"And you struck up a conversation with a nice man and you're meeting him for a drink this weekend?"

"Or, I ran into Josh's soon-to-be-ex-wife, who was there with his daughter buying a hamster."

"Wow, spectacular fail. How'd that go?"

"Well, for starters, she didn't realize that Josh and I interact on an almost daily basis. It felt like I was in the wrong, somehow." Layla recounted the conversation for Tonya. "It was a little weird."

"Maybe she's not over him."

Layla shrugged. "I don't know. Maybe she's still getting used to the fact that they're free to talk to other people if they feel like it. Personally, I couldn't care less who Liam is talking to. I don't want to know anything about what he's up to. They have a child together, though, so they still have to talk to each other." Thank God she and Liam had never procreated. That was about the only smart thing Layla had done.

Annie's arrival cut their conversation short. They'd already watched her wrangle her boys into the building, which had looked like herding a tribe of feral cats. They'd been more unruly than usual, and Annie had had her hands full making sure they stayed in the crosswalk. She'd almost dropped her travel mug of coffee when one of the youngest darted in front of her, nearly tripping her. Now she approached Layla and Tonya with a triumphant smile on her face. "I want you both to know that I'd take a bullet for my kids, but holy fuck that break nearly killed me. Was it longer than usual this year? I think it was. It had to be."

"Good morning to you, too," Layla said.

"Good morning. I hope you both had a wonderful holiday." Annie looked at the drop-off line and shook her head. "I see that the time away from school has caused a regression in whatever car-line skills the parents had managed to amass. Good luck today. If all these kids are anything like mine, you'll need something to look forward to when you peel out of the parking lot this afternoon."

"Already booked a massage," Tonya said.

"Pedicure appointment ten minutes after I'm off work," Layla said. Josh had just pulled into the parking lot. She felt as giddy as a middle-schooler and she didn't care. She watched them approach and told herself to act normal, natural.

"Miss Layla," Sasha said. "My hamster died."

Already? "Oh, no," Layla said. "I'm so sorry."

"Yeah. My mom said we can get another one."

"Good morning," Josh said. "I hope you're both staying warm."

Layla could no longer feel her toes. "It's not that bad," she said.

"Did I leave Norton's treats at your house?"

"Yep," Layla said. "I saw them sitting on the counter right after you left."

"I'll stop by and get them sometime this week," he said.

"Okay," she said.

He looked like he might want to say something else, but then Sasha said, "Dad, I'm cold."

"Have a good day," Josh said, but he mostly looked at Layla when he said it.

"You too," they answered.

CHAPTER 29

JOSH

Josh called Layla after he finished eating dinner on Thursday night. Sasha had been with him from Monday night through Thursday morning, but she was back at Kimmy's and Josh had a free evening. "Hey, it's Josh. Are you busy tonight? I thought I'd stop by and pick up Norton's treats." He was glad he'd forgotten them there, because it gave him a reason to call her. "It's okay if you have plans. Norton has plenty of treats at home. He'll survive."

"No, I don't have plans," she said. "Come on over."

"Be there in five," he said.

"Come on in," she said when she opened the door. "The treats are on the counter." He followed her into the kitchen. There was a puzzle on the table and a half-full glass of wine next to a big pile of pieces. From the box, he could see that the puzzle was a pencil collage and that each pencil was a different size and color. "That's quite a puzzle."

"It's definitely ambitious. I thought it would give me something to do in the evening now that it's so cold."

"I didn't even think about a puzzle. I mostly just wander the house, give up, and turn on the TV." He pointed at one of the pieces. "That one goes on the edge."

"Oh, you're right." She picked up the piece and set it in place. There was an awkward pause, and he was trying to figure out what he wanted to say next when she said, "Do you want to work on it with me? If you're not busy, I mean."

"Sure," he said.

"Wine?" Layla asked, motioning toward her glass.

"That would be great."

"Red okay?"

"Whatever you're drinking is fine." She poured him a glass. "Boy, you're not messin' around, are you?" Josh asked when he sat down at the kitchen table and surveyed the pieces. Another glance at the box told him there were a thousand of them.

"Nope," she said, handing him a glass of wine and sitting down across from him.

"Thanks," he said, then took a sip of the

wine and set the glass down far away from his elbows and the puzzle.

Layla searched the puzzle pieces, picked one up, and put it in its place. "I've been trying to find that one for the last fifteen minutes," she said, giving Josh a satisfied smile. She had her glasses on and her hair in a ponytail and he had always liked that look on a woman.

They spent the next half hour making good progress on the puzzle while exchanging small talk about the holidays and the weather. They worked together to find tricky pieces that had stumped them both. Though his relaxed state was partly due to the wine, it was also brought on by the soothing yet cerebral act of figuring out the puzzle pieces and working them into place. It was easy sitting across from Layla. Nothing about it felt forced.

"You said you didn't have a boyfriend." He'd taken note of that, but it wasn't something he was going to ask her about in front of Sasha. He'd tucked the information away and he'd been thinking about it. "Did there used to be one?"

"There was a husband, actually. We split up last March. The divorce is final now. Glad to have that part behind me."

"I bet. Mine's in the works but it's not

final yet," he said. He'd asked Kimmy again about the paperwork and been happy to hear that at least she'd filed it and would let Josh know when she needed his signature.

"Kimberly told me you were separated when I met all of you at back-to-school night."

"Really? I didn't know that."

"Do you have a girlfriend?" She was focusing awfully hard on looking for a place to put her puzzle piece.

"No, but I have a dog. I did manage to get one of those."

"Then you're definitely on the right track," she said.

"A dog seemed like something I could figure out. Romantic relationships seem a little trickier. There's probably a whole set of rules for dating after a divorce that I know nothing about."

"Oh, there's all kinds of rules," Layla said. "If you read as many women's magazines as I do, you would know that." He liked that she said it in a teasing way.

"I prefer to fumble my way through it cluelessly, apparently. Help a guy out."

"First of all, you should be taking time for yourself." Layla made little air quotes around the last four words.

"I am definitely taking time for myself."

"You should pursue a hobby."

"Like playing guitar?"

"Exactly."

"I'm no expert, but something tells me you're a little past the hobby level."

She smiled. "Well, you've seen my basement."

"I have hobbies. I've recently taken up boxing, so I guess I can put a check mark next to that one." He'd grown up with three older brothers, so he knew how to throw a punch and how to take one. But he needed something to do on the nights Sasha was at Kimmy's, to give him some semblance of routine. At thirty-seven, he relished the structure and discipline he'd fought so hard against at eighteen, and he needed an outlet and a way to blow off steam. Boxing was the only activity that sounded interesting to him. He'd gone to a class on a whim and he'd been boxing ever since. He showed up, he hit a bag, he felt better, he went home.

"You really need to get to know yourself and what it is you want." She was becoming more animated as they went along, and it was adorable.

"That's a little trickier," he said, but he didn't elaborate. He was still trying to figure that out.

"What all those articles failed to mention

242

was how *boring* it would be," Layla said. "I like my independence. I like it a lot. But sometimes I feel like I'm stuck in some sort of purgatory full of thousand-piece jigsaw puzzles that you have to spend time in before they let you out."

"Maybe it's better than the alternative. I knew a guy who met a woman a week after he split from his wife. And I don't mean divorced from his wife. I mean he moved out and a week later he had a new girlfriend. Now they're engaged and she's already pregnant and he's miserable and I'm not going to kick him when he's down, but what did he expect?"

"That sounds incredibly shortsighted on his part. Maybe those magazine articles know what they're talking about after all."

"And don't forget about online dating," Josh said. "That is a *whole other thing.*"

"I made it as far as downloading the app one night."

"My brother insisted that I at least try it. It was like being on a bizarre job interview. Also, I hated it. And I don't think I'm supposed to be using an app considering I'm not officially divorced yet."

"I don't get the impression that online dating is highly regulated."

"I wouldn't know. Online dating didn't

even exist the last time I was single, which was, admittedly, a long time ago."

"But it's worked for so many people," Layla exclaimed.

"Everyone knows someone who found the love of their life by online dating," Josh said with equal fervor.

"I think I'll pass," Layla said.

"What else am I supposed to know?" he asked.

"If you're lucky enough to click with someone, you're not supposed to talk about what went wrong in your marriage, at least not at first. You're just supposed to say it didn't work out."

"So, don't meet someone before you've taken up a hobby and figured out what you want, don't tell them anything about your life and what went wrong in your relationship, and once that's behind you it's okay to start looking for your next relationship."

"And don't forget that second marriages are statistically proven to fail at an even higher rate than the first," Layla said.

"I get the feeling our views are not of the glass-half-full variety."

"Which is probably the reason we're still in purgatory." She placed another puzzle piece in its place. "It's nice to have somebody to talk to about it."

"I agree," Josh said. "People mean well when they offer advice, but unless they've been through it, they really can't weigh in. I mostly feel like they're just happy not to be in my shoes."

Josh was a little bit curious about what had gone wrong in Layla's marriage, but he couldn't exactly say, *So, were you the problem or was he?* And that wouldn't be fair, anyway, because if there was one thing he'd acknowledged it was that every relationship took two people to succeed and two to fail.

"Supposedly, you need to spend half of the total time you spent with someone getting over them," Layla said.

"That means I'll need about ten years. Awesome. I'll be almost forty-eight before I get back out there."

"I'll only be forty. But this is also a stupid rule. I mean, no one wants to jump in too soon, but that rule is ridiculous and arbitrary."

"Surely, there's a happy medium," he said. "Something to tide us over while we're waiting."

"I think it's called friends with benefits. Which is not for me, by the way."

"It's not for me, either." The one thing he and Kimmy had been short on for the last few years was an intimate connection.

Friends with benefits didn't sound so hot to him. Why even bother? "So, friends without benefits?"

"I think that's just called being friends," Layla said.

"Maybe there's something in between that and friends with benefits." There had to be, because he never thought about what it would be like to kiss his friends the way he was wondering what it would be like to kiss Layla.

"Friends with . . . potential? Is that an actual thing?"

"Works for me. Normally, I would just ask a woman out, but the rules . . ." They could joke all they wanted, but there was some truth to those rules. And he wasn't in a hurry. Companionship was one thing. Falling in love was another. But committing to someone for the long haul. He wasn't ready for that yet. "We could be friends with potential. What do you think?"

"Hmm, I don't know. I mean, you're so unattractive. It would be sort of torturous for me."

That made him laugh, because it was not at all what he'd thought she was about to say. "And you're my daughter's teacher."

"That's not really a problem as long as we keep it on the down-low because the moms in the drop-off line would not be able to *deal*. I have a feeling you're the subject of a lot of romantic speculation."

A few of the moms had already struck up a conversation with him if they happened to be walking back to the parking lot at the same time he was. There was one in particular who he could almost swear arrived exactly when he did every day and parked right next to him. She was attractive and couldn't be nicer, but he wasn't interested in any of the moms. But he'd be lying if he couldn't admit, at least to himself, that it was nice to know he was wanted by *someone.*

"This is something I missed," he said when they took a break and Layla refilled their wineglasses.

"Puzzles?" she asked.

"No. Just something to do with someone else." Kimmy was always on her phone, and Josh knew that if he went and found something of his own to do, it would only make the divide between them bigger. Like he'd be waving the white flag and admitting that the only shared interest they had by then was Sasha. "My ex-wife and I weren't doing much together toward the end." And when they *were* together, without Sasha, things were pretty contentious, which was putting it nicely.

"What did you used to do together?" Layla asked.

"When we were younger, we figured out life together. We were barely out of high school when we got married, so we learned how to support and take care of ourselves. We figured out how to run a household and pay bills and we relied on each other."

"Wow. That's really young."

"I didn't know what I wanted to do with my life, and she was the only thing I was certain about. In hindsight, it was not my best decision, but I just couldn't see it at the time."

"How long you been here?" his boss asked when Josh was three weeks into the job. Josh had already checked over the tools and supplies they'd need and was sitting next to the van drinking a Coke.

"Twenty minutes or so." He turned his head slightly so his boss wouldn't see the stupid-looking grin on his face. Why had he waited so long to do this? Why hadn't he realized how much better life could be if you could find work you enjoyed? He was twenty-one by then, and he was finally starting to feel like an adult who could make something of himself and not an idiot kid with no direction, no clue.

The only downside of Josh's new outlook was that the higher he soared the lower Kimmy sank. She had been calling in sick to work a lot, and sometimes when Josh got home at the end of the day, she'd still be in bed, asleep. He knew she was depressed and he had no idea how to help her, so he did the only thing he knew how to do and that was to keep going to work and doing whatever he could to cheer her up. He brought home pizzas for dinner and he stopped at the mall one payday and bought her a pink sweater because it reminded him of the one she'd been wearing in detention. He expected her eyes to light up, to show some kind of spark, because it had been a long time since there'd been enough disposable income to spend on new clothes for either of them. But all she said was "Thanks, Josh," and then she stuffed the sweater back into the bag and fell asleep again.

Kimmy had told Josh that getting her stomach pumped had been traumatic and she never wanted to drink again. She'd made good on that promise and was clear about what she didn't want, but what she struggled with was deciding what she did want. It was like she was stuck in neutral and had no clue how to shift her life into gear. Josh couldn't do it for her; he was too busy celebrating the fact that he'd been able to do it for himself and wasn't really in any position to figure it out for her.

She lost her job a month later. They fired her for not showing up, and after that she didn't bother getting out of bed at all.

Josh put one of the trickier puzzle pieces into place. "Once we got a handle on things and got a little older, we had more time to pursue our own interests. And then we had Sasha and we poured everything into her. Toward the end, it was like we'd forgotten all about *us*. We never did stuff like this anymore." He gestured toward the puzzle. "We stopped doing things together."

"We always did what Liam wanted to do because everything was always tied in with his job. We went to the parties, the functions. Liam spent most weekends on the golf course courting more business. He always acted like it was a hardship to socialize with my coworkers because he had nothing to gain from it. Liam didn't really like being at home. He had the biggest fear of missing out of anyone I've ever known. It was go, go, go, all the time. He never turned it off. It was like he was always looking for the thing that would finally make him happy. I'm not sure he even knew what that was.

He only knew he had to keep looking."

"We're breaking the rules right now, aren't we?" he asked. But he was only teasing, and he wasn't sure he really cared about the rules.

Maybe she didn't care either, because all she said was "Sometimes rules are over-rated."

It occurred to him that maybe you had to go through some big things in life in order to appreciate the smaller stuff, like a glass or two of good red wine on a cold night and the pretty woman sitting across from you who was concentrating on finding her next puzzle piece.

At nine he stood up and stretched. They'd made good progress on the puzzle, but there were still a lot of pieces scattered on the table. At least another two to three evenings' worth, he thought. "I'll be happy to keep working on it with you," he said. "If you want company, that is. I feel like I'm in-vested now."

"I would," she said.

She handed him the plastic container filled with dog treats. "Don't forget these," she said.

He took them from her. "Thanks. See you in the morning, Layla."

He thought about her as he drove home.

They might have been two people who were mature enough to have a direct, adult conversation with each other about what they were looking for and what they wanted. But they were also two lonely people who were about to discover the answer to the question of what exactly it meant to be friends with the potential for something more.

CHAPTER 30

LAYLA

By the time they finished the puzzle — which had taken them two more nights over the next week, and another bottle of wine, which Josh brought over — they'd become even more comfortable with each other. There was a formalness to their communication that had slowly faded away, and with it the tension you felt when you started spending time with someone new whom you also found attractive. She found him attractive, at least. She wasn't sure what he thought of her. They talked about their days — Josh's job, Layla's students. Nothing too heavy or that could be considered oversharing. *I want to keep spending time with him,* Layla thought the night they placed the final puzzle piece and high-fived each other.

The second thing was that they were also texting each other. It started as a way to confirm when Josh was free to work on the puzzle again and had morphed into general chitchat. At lunchtime, when Layla checked her phone, there was often a message from Josh asking how her day was going. Not every day, which might have been too much for her, but enough that seeing his name when she checked her phone always put a little spark in her step. Layla had picked up on the custody schedule Josh and Kimmy followed, and Josh usually sent a message on his last day with Sasha asking if Layla was free the following evening, when Sasha would be at her mom's. Layla started to anticipate those messages, and it made her happy when he asked if she was available.

Layla felt comfortable initiating text messages of her own: How was work? Tell Norton I bought some more of those treats he likes.

There hadn't been another puzzle, but Josh had called around six o'clock on a Thursday night and when Layla answered he said, "Hey, I know it's late notice, but I just found out the brewpub in our neighborhood has a trivia night. I thought if you were bored and felt like getting out of the house, we could check it out."

"Sure," she said.

They'd sipped craft beers and shouted their answers, coming in a respectable fourth. They had each driven their own car, and their goodbye consisted of Josh making sure Layla got into hers safely before pulling out of the parking lot right behind her and heading home.

Nothing romantic had occurred between them, but Josh had placed his hand on her lower back as they were leaving the brewpub because a group of college-aged drunk guys were all trying to fit through the door at the same time Josh and Layla were trying to walk out of it. He'd moved his hand from her lower back to her hip and gently moved her out of their way. The feel of his touch had electrified her and made her hyperaware of how long it had been since she'd been touched by another human, and she was still thinking about it when she pulled into her driveway.

If he ever kissed her, it was quite possible she might burst into flames.

CHAPTER 31

LAYLA

Layla stomped her feet, trying to return the blood flow to them. Her royal-blue parka was made of down and was the best purchase she'd ever made, but her boots weren't living up to their promise. *Warm down to zero degrees, my ass,* she thought.

Josh and Sasha were hurrying into the building as quickly as possible. As they passed by, Josh said, "Hope you weren't too tired this morning."

Layla grinned at him. "That's what I get for leaving the house on a school night. I'll manage."

"Tonya," Annie said after they disappeared into the building. "What just happened here?"

"I'm as confused as you are. Layla?" Tonya said. "Care to fill us in?"

"We went to trivia night." She told them about her evening and the things she and

Josh had discussed.

"So, what exactly is unfolding?" Annie asked, clapping her hands together and smiling. "I thought you were doing puzzles at home. Now you're out and about together? Are the two of you dating now?"

"We are not dating."

Annie's forehead crinkled in confusion. "Friends with benefits?"

"What? No. Neither of us are interested in that. It's more like . . . . friends with potential."

"Are you actually calling it that? Like out loud and everything?" Annie asked.

"What does that even mean?" Tonya asked, laughing.

"I don't know," Layla said. "Stop laughing."

"I'm sorry," Tonya said.

"Me too," Annie echoed.

"We're both in dating purgatory and we'd both like someone to spend time with. For companionship. It's not a big deal. Easy come, easy go. That's my motto for romance going forward."

"But this whackadoodle friends-with-potential label means you're open to being more than friends, right?" Tonya asked.

"I'm not not open."

Tonya patted Layla's arm. "I think you

can just say you're open."

Josh came out of the building, and as he walked by he gave her a little wave. Her eyes followed him until he reached his truck and climbed inside. "I don't know," Layla said. "I mean, sure. I'm as interested in him as I would be in anyone at this stage. I know it's funny to you two, but once you've been in my shoes, you become a lot more cautious. The thought of making another mistake makes you second-guess every decision you've ever made. At least for me it does. One of the things I like about Josh is that he knows exactly what I mean by that."

"I'm sorry," Tonya said. "I wasn't thinking about that part. A new romance would be great, but I just want to see you with a smile on your face again."

"Me too," Annie said.

"No apology needed. I know you're excited for me to meet someone. I like spending time with Josh because we share some common ground. I don't have to explain the stage I'm at in my life because he's in it too."

"There's nothing wrong with being friends first and taking things slow," Tonya said. Annie reached out and squeezed Layla's arm in agreement.

"We had fun and it's been a while since

my life wasn't a total shit show. I forgot how much I liked having fun. Talking to him felt good," Layla said. "I'm looking forward to doing it again, although if something disastrous happens between us I'm warning you both right now that the morning drop-off is going to get *really* awkward."

"I don't think anything disastrous will happen," Tonya said.

Layla laughed. "Oh, it could. But I hope not."

CHAPTER 32

LAYLA

One night, instead of sending him a text, Layla called Josh. "Hey, I'm about to put a lasagna in the oven and I'll have way too much. Do you want to join me for dinner?"

"Absolutely. The sandwich I was contemplating sounds even less appetizing now."

"Come on over," she said.

He arrived with Norton in tow. Layla bent down to pet him and ruffle his fur, and then he ambled over to the new dog bed in the corner and sniffed it.

"Aw, look, Norty, that sweet pet sitter of yours bought you a bed." Josh had brought Norton with him on previous visits and she thought the bed might come in handy.

"It was nothing." She opened the refrigerator and pretended to move a few things around so that the cool air could remove the warmth from her cheeks.

Norton gave the bed another sniff and

then flopped down on it.

"He says thanks," Josh said. "How was school?"

"It was good." Layla busied herself with slicing the fresh mozzarella. "Sasha actually said something in class a couple of days ago, and I wanted to ask if there was any truth to it."

"What was it?" Josh asked.

"She said, 'My mommy and daddy are getting back together.' " Layla explained to Josh that they'd been having circle time at the end of class and she'd asked the kids to quickly say something about how their week was going.

Josh looked like Layla had just driven a stake through his heart. "Oh, man," he said.

"I know. I'm sorry."

"I'm not sure why she said that. There's no basis for it. I'm still waiting on paperwork, but otherwise, nothing has changed. Kimmy and I are not getting back together."

"It's really none of my business," she said.

He leaned back against the counter, studying her. "You don't think so?"

They were grown adults and Layla would be damned if she was going to start mincing words now. Never again would she shy away from asking — or answering — the hard questions. They could pretend all they

261

wanted, but whatever dance they were doing was picking up steam and Layla didn't feel like having the rug pulled out from under her again.

"Maybe it is my business," she said, and they shared a look.

She finished prepping the lasagna five minutes later, and after sliding it into the oven, she set the timer. "We've got thirty to forty-five minutes to kill. I guess I could have waited to call you until it was done."

"I'm glad you didn't because I probably would have eaten my sad-single-dad sandwich by then. I've got an idea, but you might not be up for it."

"What is it?" she asked, leaning up against the counter. Her heartbeat pinged wildly around in her chest, which it had started doing quite a bit anytime Josh was near. The tension that had been building felt like a drug that Layla wanted a bigger hit of every time she and Josh got together.

"I didn't have a chance to walk Norton yet and since it's not brutally cold — 'brutally' being a relative term — I thought we could take him for a walk."

"I'd be up for a walk," she said. She looked at the timer on the stove. "We've got twenty-eight minutes until I need to check it."

262

"Norton can poop way faster than that."
Layla laughed. "Yes, I know."

The late January air was bitingly cold but no, not brutal, not to Layla anyway and obviously not to Josh. They were seasoned Minnesotans used to spending time outdoors in temperatures that others would find uncomfortable. The sidewalks were mostly clear of snow, but what was left didn't seem to bother Norton's paws. She liked being outside and had often taken walks in the winter, but it wasn't the same when there was no longer anyone waiting at home to talk to when you came in, ready for human interaction again. Now, going on a walk just felt like more of the solitude she already had an abundance of at home. She had forgotten how much a person could thrive when they balanced their alone time with quality companionship, especially if it was someone who seemed caring and not so self-centered. You could enjoy it without regard for rules or timelines or anything other than the natural organic feeling of spending time with someone who genuinely wanted to be there with you. No agenda, no ulterior motives.

"How long were you in the band?" Josh asked.

"About three years, give or take. We had a good run, but in the end, we came up short on what we needed to take it to the next level."

"So, you decided to stop playing and become a music teacher?"

"No, I gave it up to become a music teacher." She realized a split second too late that she sounded every bit as angry as she had felt when Liam urged her to take the job. But she'd just discovered the state of their finances and there was no way she could continue chasing some pipe dream. Besides, the band had reached the end of the line. She'd tried her hardest and she'd failed, and she probably wouldn't ever get a shot at it again.

"You need to think about cutting a demo," Scotty said.

Layla's disappointment about what had happened with the scout from Minneapolis ran deep, but there was more than one way to achieve their goals and making a demo would mean she'd never have to tell the band that she'd considered throwing them under the bus and going on without them.

Lately, she had gotten the feeling that they were starting to be eclipsed by other local bands who had stronger original material.

Storm Warning had grown stale, and it was hard to stay on top when there was someone hungrier, someone willing to work even harder, nipping at your heels. Being the underdog who succeeds was ten times more satisfying than being the top dogs fighting to hold on to their spot. One was exhilarating and hopeful; the other, agonizing and stressful.

A demo was necessary.

A demo would only do good things for them.

But a demo meant paying for studio time, and since anything they earned went right back to the band members so they could afford to eat, a demo would require a cash investment, in equal amounts, from all of them. They took a vote and it was unanimous.

"The timing couldn't be better," Scotty said. Connie's, which had been their bread and butter for so long, was currently closed due to a fire that had smoldered in the kitchen after hours. A passerby out for an early-morning walk called the fire department, which put out the blaze quickly but left the establishment with significant water damage. They'd be closed for at least a month, but that also meant that Storm Warning wouldn't be playing there for a while, which would cut into everyone's income. The band hadn't exactly endeared themselves to other bars in the area, preferring to keep their cozy gig at Connie's instead of branching out to play other venues. They'd have to scramble for bookings, so maybe using the downtime to record a demo was exactly what they needed.

That night, Layla told Liam about the demo while they were eating dinner. She felt a little weird about it, because it was the first time she really thought about the fact that she'd willingly given up all financial control to him, and that she was clueless about the state of their finances. She rarely spent money on herself and she deposited every penny she earned into their joint bank account. The band needed a little more time to make something happen, and Liam was generous to a fault. Certainly, he would understand. It wasn't like she was asking for money to go shopping. This would be an investment in her future.

Liam set down his fork when she told him about the demo and about the band pitching in. He took a drink of water and fiddled with his napkin. "Ordinarily I would have no problem with that at all. We're just a little short on cash right now and there's a credit card balance I need to take care of first." Liam had recently switched jobs. He had moved from pharmaceuticals to medical devices, but there had been a lag between starting the new job and receiving his first commission check. It was fine, he'd told her. Nothing to worry about, so she didn't.

"We don't have five hundred dollars?" she asked. That was all she'd asked for and it seemed like someone who earned as much as Liam should have more than that in the bank. It was her account, too, though, and shouldn't she know how much was in it? "I didn't know we were carrying a balance on our credit card."

Liam pinched the bridge of his nose like she was making this so hard on him with her incessant questions. "We have plenty. I said you didn't need to worry about it."

"I do have to worry about it," Layla said. "We're married."

"What I meant was, I'll take care of it," Liam said.

But Layla couldn't help with a demo because making a demo took money and they didn't have it to spare. She applied for a job with the school district, and when they offered it to her, she didn't hesitate before accepting. She also put up an ad so she could start giving music lessons again, and it didn't take long before she had a full roster of kids that she taught how to play guitar three nights a week.

She did all of this because when Liam finally handed over the credit card statement and she saw the total, it appeared they owed Visa the staggering sum of forty-two thousand dollars.

Considering their lavish wedding, she was lucky it wasn't higher.

It took him six months, but he did take care of the balance and he replenished their savings account, too. That was the thing about Liam. He worked harder to correct his mistakes than he ever did to avoid them in the first place. It was almost as if he enjoyed the challenge. He never held it over her. He never once said I told you so. And he always came through.

"Can I take the leash for a while?" Layla asked. Josh had removed his glove to get a better grip and his fingers had to be freezing.

"Sure, but only because I need my fingers to do my job." She took off her glove and their fingers brushed as he handed her the leash.

"Leaving Storm Warning was the right decision, really," Layla said. "And I do love my job. I love the kids and how open they are to learning about music. And now I get to play again, for me. Maybe someday for others again." She told Josh about playing with Brian on New Year's Eve.

"What happened with the band?"

268

"It fizzled out. We had these big plans to record a demo, but that didn't work out. Then our bassist took a full-time job so he could pay his bills. Kevin, our drummer, wanted to focus more on songwriting. Sam got married. We called it a break, but it was really the end."

"Did you ever play together again?"

"No. I watched Rick play one night at a country club my ex-husband wanted us to join." She would never forget what had happened that night. The things she'd discovered. How she would always think of that night as the catalyst for the end.

"You must miss it."

"I miss the way it made me feel," she said. "Have you ever been driving in your car alone and it's a beautiful day and you're in a really good mood and the sun is shining and you've got the sunroof open and you're on your way to do something that you've been looking forward to?"

"Sure," he said.

"And then a song comes on the radio and it's one of your favorites and you sing along and you don't care how loud you're singing or if the car next to you notices your little concert for one?"

"I may have done that once or twice."

"That's what performing feels like for me.

And if doing it in the car feels good, doing it up onstage with an audience feels indescribably good. And I didn't really like that I had to stop doing it."

"Then why did you?"

"Because it was time to be a grown-up." Layla's house was in sight when the alarm went off on her phone. "The lasagna's ready," she said. "Let's eat."

CHAPTER 33

JOSH

On Friday, Josh swung by the grocery store on his way home. He consulted the list he'd typed into his phone after googling "easy dinners for beginners" and started gathering the ingredients for chicken and snap pea stir-fry. "Excuse me," he said to the woman who was putting bell peppers into a produce bag. "Scallions?"

She smiled at Josh like *isn't he clueless* and said, "Green onions. They're next to the cucumbers."

"Thanks."

He'd texted Layla around lunchtime yesterday and asked if she had plans for the evening, and she'd responded with Nothing yet.

How about dinner at my place?
I'd like that.

He liked it, too.

Layla wasn't always available, though. Sometimes, when he texted her to see if she was free, she'd write back that she already had plans. He found himself feeling more let down by that than he'd expected to.

When Sasha was with Kimmy, he liked to spend one night alone enjoying the solitude. He spent another with a friend or one of his brothers. But that left another night wide open, and the thought of spending it with someone like Layla felt increasingly appealing. She was easygoing and didn't take herself too seriously. There was nothing pretentious about her and he'd never heard her gossip or speak unkindly about anyone. She was independent and she had her shit together and there wasn't a single thing he didn't like about her.

"So, quick disclosure," he said when she arrived at his house on Friday night. "Dinner isn't quite ready yet."

"That's okay. I can wait."

"Additional disclosure. It hasn't actually been started. I need your help because I'm nowhere near the cooking-for-other-people stage yet. I cook for Sasha, but chicken nuggets and buttered noodles are all she'll eat and that's a menu I can handle. I think I can level up with a little help."

"What's in it for me?" she asked. "I can't just give away all my culinary knowledge."

"Cheesecake that I picked up at the bakery counter."

"You drive a hard bargain, but cheesecake is one of my favorite desserts. Okay, what are we making?"

"Chicken and snap pea stir-fry."

"Sounds good," she said as he began pulling ingredients from the fridge. He didn't have exactly the right frying pan, but she dug around in the cupboard and found one that would work. He took on the role of sous-chef as she explained each step, and soon the kitchen filled with the smell of sizzling chicken and garlic and rice vinegar.

"You never cooked with your ex-wife?"

"She didn't cook, either. She took up baking a few years ago, but we ate a lot of fast food when we were younger and made it about as far as sandwiches and frozen pizza. We tried harder when Sasha came along, but mostly we just ended up making two meals. We learned how to do a lot of things together, but cooking wasn't one of them."

Back then, they'd had much bigger problems to solve than what they were going to eat for dinner.

A few months after Kimmy lost her job, Josh

came home from work expecting to see his wife under the covers, the house a mess, and nothing for dinner because if he didn't go through the McDonald's drive-through on his way home there would be nothing for them to eat. Their financial situation had improved immensely, and that allowed some of the anxiety and stress to dissipate, but he had no idea how to help Kimmy. He'd finally spoken to his parents about it and their concern only added to his. "You've got to get her some help," his mom said. "This can't go on. Do you think she's in danger of harming herself?"

That had scared Josh more than anything ever had, including the night they pumped her stomach. It hadn't occurred to him that she might be so depressed that she'd consider something like that. He had insurance now, good insurance, and he made a call at work and found out there were options — inpatient, outpatient, counseling, and medication.

But when he got home that night, Kimmy was not under the covers. She was sitting on the couch with her hair combed and a weird look on her face. Not weird bad, just different. "What's wrong?" he asked, his heart sinking. He didn't think he could handle any more bad news.

"Nothing. I just wanted to talk to you about something."

"Sure," he said, sitting down beside her.

"Someone rang the doorbell today. I wasn't going to answer it, but I was up and on my way to the bathroom and I just . . . I don't know. I felt like answering it. It was a woman and she wanted to talk to me about the election." Kimmy looked down at her lap and then back up at Josh. "I didn't know what she was talking about."

It was 2004 and John Kerry was up against George Bush and gunning for the presidency. Josh wasn't the most political guy, but he did know that. The number of calls they received and the messages on their answering machine made it hard to ignore. At the time, politics were far from his mind. He had a job and a wife who seemed to be fading right in front of him and his plate was too full for much more.

"What did she want?" Josh asked.

"She wanted to know if I was registered to vote. I said no. She wanted to know if she could help me with that. And you, too. I said yes because it seemed like the right thing to say. We're old enough. We should vote," she said.

"Yes, absolutely." His parents had always voted, and he remembered them casting their ballots in 2000. Registering to vote would feel so grown-up and different from anything they had done together at that point in their lives.

Each step forward erased one of the missteps they'd had, and Josh was fully on board. He would have been on board with anything that got his wife out of bed.

"She asked if maybe I'd want to volunteer for the Kerry campaign."

"What did you tell her?"

"I said I wasn't working and that I thought maybe that was something I could do. I know I need to get another job, but maybe I could find something part-time until I felt a little better. And I'd like to volunteer. I need to be a part of something."

"I get it, Kimmy. I do. And I think you should do it."

So, she did, and he noticed a change in her immediately. Gone were the days of lying in bed all day; Kimmy was up early, and she smiled more often, and Josh took pride in the fact that they were finally nailing this thing called life.

They couldn't afford cable back then, but they started watching the TV show *Lost,* and settling in on the couch together every Wednesday night with a bowl of popcorn at the end of a long workday felt good and right and grown-up. In time, the feeling of being disconnected from Kimmy started to lift and he was glad he'd never confided in anyone just how hopeless he'd felt and how frustrated he'd been. How utterly terrified that he might lose her. He almost felt ashamed when he thought about it. This was marriage. This was honoring your commitments and getting through the rough patches.

Kimmy did find a part-time job at the mall, this time at a Pottery Barn. Slowly, she brought home things she'd purchased with her employee discount and their place started looking less like a frat house and more like an actual home. She had immersed herself in the campaign, and though Kerry didn't win, she spent hours learning everything she could about how the government worked. They were twenty-three by then, and when she asked Josh what he thought about her enrolling in college, he was all for it, although it would strain the finances he'd worked so hard to improve. He was starting to get a taste of what his income would be like in a few years, but he wasn't quite there yet. But they could swing it and it was a good investment in their future, and this was so much better than the dark days when she could hardly get out of bed.

Kimmy kept her Pottery Barn job and went to school at night. When she was at work, Josh took on extra jobs because there was no reason for him to sit home alone in an empty house. They bought their first home and moved out of the crappy rental, and late at night, even though they were both exhausted, they were never too tired to reach for each other in bed. And afterward they would lie in each other's arms, and one night, as the sweat cooled their naked skin, Kimmy said, "It's just like that song, Josh. Our future is so bright we should be wearing shades."

He'd laughed and he'd kissed her, and he'd agreed.

His single coworkers headed out to the bars three to four nights a week. And when they weren't at the bars, they were at the college football game or a concert or flying off to Vegas for the weekend. The few times he did go out with his coworkers for a drink, businessmen in suits threw mild looks of disdain their way, which made Josh laugh to himself. He and the other electricians might have been wearing uniforms with their names stitched on the front, but their wallets were bulging and none of them had had to pay six figures for their education.

More importantly, he was happier with his career choice than he'd ever dreamed he could be.

Kimmy was halfway through her junior year of college by then and she'd started coming into her own. His memories of her dark days and the lean times had faded and left him with the kind of longing he didn't understand. He didn't really want to go to the bars or the football games or Vegas. But what he sometimes wanted was the option to do those things without having to consider another person. He began to idealize the freedom that his single coworkers had when it came to making decisions, even if he didn't really mind that he and Kimmy made their decisions together. The juxtaposition confused him. Josh seemed happy on the outside, but every now and then he'd think about the seeds he hadn't sown. The itch he'd never scratched. He'd begun to feel something when he thought of his relationship with Kimmy, and the word that kept popping into his head was "trapped." But that wasn't fair, because no one had trapped Josh into getting married. He'd done that all on his own, and he loved his wife. Maybe this was just another one of those rough patches and in time whatever he was feeling would go away.

It hadn't gone away, not completely, but Josh beamed with pride when Kimmy walked across the stage and accepted her diploma for the political science degree she earned a month shy of her twenty-ninth birthday. Two years after that, he came home from work one night and Kimmy laid a positive pregnancy test in his palm. A child was something they both wanted very much, so he put the thoughts he'd had out of his head for good and he never looked back.

"Josh," Layla said.

"What? Sorry. Did you say something?"

"I asked if you could add the onions you just chopped."

"Did you know these are called scallions?" he asked as he scraped them off the cutting board and into the pan.

"Yes." She tried to hide her smile. "I did know that."

"Of course you did." He poked her in the ribs, teasing and tickling her and making her squeal. "You've probably never had to ask random strangers for help in the grocery store," he said.

"Can't say that I have," she said, and she didn't look like she minded the tickling at all. "And now you know. For next time."

They ate dinner side by side on the couch, plates in their laps. When they were finished, Josh took the plates into the kitchen and then he said, "Do you want to stay and watch a movie?"

She held his gaze for what seemed like a minute but was probably only a few seconds and then she said, "Yes."

Later, when he thought about that night, he couldn't remember what they'd even watched. He could recall that he'd let her choose and that she'd chosen a comedy. "I can't watch horror movies," she'd said. "And I don't like anything with violence. I can't handle guns and knives."

So, they'd watched a comedy and they'd stayed in the same spots on the couch that they'd been in all night. There was no sharing a blanket, no cuddling, no woman's head resting in his lap as he played with her hair. But he wanted all those things and he didn't think it would be long before he would ask Layla if she might want them, too.

It also seemed like both yesterday and forever ago that he'd been sitting on another couch with another woman, who, at the time, he couldn't fathom no longer being married to.

CHAPTER 34

LAYLA

Layla and Brian were messing around at the guitar shop after hours. They'd been refining their sets — adding songs and deleting others — but mostly they were playing for the sheer enjoyment of it.

"How do you feel about listening to something I wrote?" Brian asked.

"I'd love to. What's it called?"

Layla took off her guitar and Brian settled onto his stool and began to strum. " 'Thankful,' " he said.

I thought we'd have forever
Not an expiration date
The time I'd invested
Now straight down the drain
I wallowed and raged needing someone
    to blame
Hurt and broken I lashed out
Couldn't even say her name

It's hard to let go when you've done all
the work
So much time and effort and none of the
perks
It's old news
Bad news
Nothing meant to last
Get back in the game
Bring the lessons you learned from the
pain
They said don't long for what broke you
It's in the rear view
Let go of the old
Make room for the new
I only half listened to their stupid advice
Because everyone knows lightning never
strikes twice
Be thankful it ended
It's not what fate intended
Let it crumble
Let it shatter
Years from now it won't matter
Make your peace
Draw your line
Hold firm for next time
She's out there waiting
Go and find her
So I guess the advice they gave me was
true
Felt that spark again the night I met you

Picked myself up
Started living
And it happened by chance
It's true life's a journey
It's true life's a dance
Onward into the night
The love I found with you is the love that
    was right

"You wrote that?" Layla asked when he was finished. It wasn't ground-breaking material and artists had been mining lost love since the dawn of time, but the arrangement and the lyrics worked together in a way that caught Layla's interest right out of the gate. The quicker tempo made the song sound uplifting instead of maudlin or sad, and she instantly wanted to listen to it again.

"Wrote it fifteen years ago. Tried for a couple of years to sell it. I was going through a box of old crap the other day and came across it."

"Former girlfriend?"

"Lana Hines. Ha! I can say her name now with no problem. Spent seven years with her. Lived together for five of them. Man, she stomped on my heart the day she told me she'd given me all she could, but that it wasn't working for her anymore. Then she moved to Vegas. It was a dark time for me, and I thought I'd never get past it. Seems stupid now, but it didn't at the time. I wrote the song because everyone kept telling me that someday I'd see the heartache in a different light because my soul mate was still out there somewhere. Blah, blah, blah. It all sounded like platitudes to me, but the lyrics poured out one night and I told myself there was nothing wrong with working through my feelings with a song. I started to feel better after that. Started dating again. A few years later, I met Jeannie. And I am incredibly thankful she's who I ended up with, so maybe it wasn't bullshit after all. I played it for her, and she loved it. She wants me to sing it to her at our wedding reception."

Been there, done that, Layla thought.

"It's beautiful," Layla said. "It starts out like a break-up song, but it's really a love song." Layla especially liked the part about not clinging to the past and trusting that there was someone better on the horizon.

Brian handed her the sheet music. "Why don't we play it together, but you sing lead this time? Switch the lyrics to the female point of view."

"It's your song. I can take backup."

"Your voice is better. And I think maybe you can tap into the emotions right now more than I can."

"I can try," she said. But was Josh the person she would be thankful for years down the line? Committing to someone again and going through it all for the second time seemed like a monumental decision she wasn't quite ready to make. But the more time she spent with Josh, the more she realized their lives were becoming intertwined.

They tweaked the song and played it so many times that Layla would hear it on an endless loop in her head until she went to bed that night. It was hopeful despite the raw lyrics about how much it hurt to lose someone you loved. The underlying message was simple yet profound, but the song was catchy as hell. "This is really good, Brian," she said. "Like, add-it-to-your-playlist-and-sing-along-in-the-car good. What are you going to do with it?"

"How do you feel about recording it with me?"

"Like a demo? Are you going to try selling it again?"

"I thought I'd go in a different direction this time. How do you feel about us uploading it?"

"For people to stream?"

"Yeah. I mean, we'll have to use a third party for uploading, but I've checked into it. I found one that's like twenty bucks a year for unlimited uploads. We can make all the music we want."

"Ten bucks apiece. Those are my kind of operating costs."

"Mine too," Brian said. "We've got nothing to lose. It's not like we need the blessing of a record label to get airplay. Not in 2019."

He made an excellent point. The music industry had undergone a significant metamorphosis since the last time Layla had entertained aspirations of breaking in. But if anything, the listeners had so many choices there was no guarantee they'd get airplay even if they uploaded the most fantastic song to ever hit the airwaves. The competition was still every bit as fierce. Maybe more so.

Then again, this could be the do-over Layla had been pining for since Storm Warning broke up. And she didn't need to kick in five hundred dollars this time around.

"I say let's go for it," Layla said.

Brian smiled, nodded. "You ready now? My laptop has all the software we need for recording."

"It's a whole new world, isn't it?" Layla

said. "I'm all warmed up. This seems like as good a time as any."

CHAPTER 35

LAYLA

Layla called Josh one night after dinner. "Are you busy on Saturday afternoon?"

"Nope," he said. "Sasha will be with her mom. What's up?"

"I found a guitar on Craigslist and I'd like to look at it, but I also don't want to get murdered or thrown in the trunk of a car or planted in somebody's backyard. The price sounds a little too good to be true. Call me skeptical."

"That was a very colorful description of what can happen when you buy something on Craigslist. But your caution is understandable," he said. "Sure, I can go with you."

"Thanks. How does noon sound?"

"Noon works. I'll see you then."

If things worked out with the guitar, she would now own three. She needed to stop buying them, but guitars were to Layla what shoes were to most women. She could never have too many and they'd last a lot longer than shoes and would never go out of style.

The purchases were made even sweeter by the fact that she absolutely, positively had enough money to buy them.

Layla stopped at the mall on her way home from school. She and Liam were joining her family on Sunday for her mother's birthday, and Layla wanted to pick up her gift. It had been a while since she'd gone shopping, because she was teaching so many lessons in the evening that she barely had time to feed herself between the time she left school and when the lessons started. Last year, when Liam had received a bonus even bigger than the last one, they'd had one of their worst fights after he announced that they should go somewhere warm for a week to escape the god-awful cold snap that had blanketed most of Minnesota.

"I can't just take off for a week," Layla said. "I don't get very many personal days at school and I have lessons to give every night."

"Why don't you just quit?"

"My job?" she asked. "Why would I do that?" Did he really think her financial contribution to the marriage was so insignificant that she should just throw it away so they could spend a week on the beach?

"You can take a week off from school. What are they going to do? Fire you?"

"Well, I did sign a contract."

"At least give up those lessons," he said. Liam hated that she still gave the lessons. He couldn't understand why she did it, because they "didn't need the money." But to Layla, the lessons — and her job — represented much more than the income Liam thought was too meager to mean anything. He'd conveniently forgotten the buffer Layla's income had provided when he was between jobs or had overspent, which was something that seemed to be happening more often. Then, once he'd landed on his feet, he'd ramp up his spending once again like the lean time had never happened.

"I'm not giving up the lessons," Layla said.

Layla browsed the racks of sweaters until she found a soft burgundy one in her mother's size. She selected a scarf to go with it and asked for a gift box and gift receipt. On her way out she checked out her favorite department store and, on a whim, she bought some new clothes for work. She had been slowly building her business-casual wardrobe since she started teaching, and she needed to add a few pieces to it. The saleslady rang up her purchases and then leaned toward Layla slightly and said, "That card doesn't seem to have gone through. Do you have another?"

Layla's forehead crinkled. The card had worked for the sweater. "Can you try it again? I don't know why it didn't work." The saleslady tried it again, and it was declined again. Layla had first given her a debit card, but this time she pulled out her credit card, and it was declined, too. Her face grew warm, because there were a few people behind her in line. She dug in her wallet and came up with the credit card she used to use before Liam gave her the platinum card. She had no idea if it would still work, but the saleslady looked at her and gave her a commiserating smile and said, "There we go. Okay, I'll just wrap these up and you'll be on your way." Layla didn't realize that she'd been holding her breath until she tried to speak and didn't have enough air in her lungs to form words. She opted to nod instead, and as soon as the items were ready, she scurried from the store, full of questions. Full of worry.

Liam's face fell when she walked through the door holding the shopping bags. "Did you go shopping?" he asked.

"Why didn't either of my cards work?"

"It's nothing," he said. "My bonus is late. They were supposed to deposit them last Friday and we're all still waiting. Some sort of payroll glitch, they said. I'm going to pay everything off and then we'll be caught up from when I was out of work. I was going to surprise you and then we had this glitch. The deposit is supposed to be hitting our accounts by the end of the day tomorrow."

Jesus. How much did we owe this time? she thought.

And why wasn't she paying closer attention? She had grown complacent again because everything had seemed to run smoothly over the years, even with his gaps in employment, and she'd had no reason to doubt that Liam was managing their finances the way he was supposed to. How many times had they teetered on the edge of a debit or credit card being declined? If she hadn't gone to the mall on her way home, she wouldn't even have known there was cause for concern.

She wanted to believe every word that had just come out of his mouth. She decided that she wouldn't think about it until the next day to see if the money did make it into their accounts. And the next day the money was there just like he said it would be. "I wasn't lying about it," he said when she told him she'd checked.

"I know," she said. But the truth didn't change the fact that she and Liam were not at all compatible when it came to money and that incompatibility had slowly seeped its way into every crevice, every aspect of their marriage until the good parts of Liam that Layla had always loved were now being eclipsed by the fear and stress and anxiety she felt when Liam dragged her through the same issue over and over again.

That was around the time she started checking their bank balance every day. She knew the password to their online account because she'd been the one to set it up back when she never thought she'd have to worry about this kind of thing. Pay attention? Yes. But worry? No. It wasn't as easy to be judgmental or to monitor someone who outearned her by such a large margin.

Though she kept their intermittent financial troubles to herself, Liam's need to always have the best of everything — the luxury cars, the electronics, the latest gadget, the tailored wardrobe — had not gone unnoticed by anyone in Layla's family.

"Champagne tastes on a beer budget," her brother had once said to Liam after he'd bragged about something in front of her family while he was in between jobs. Liam had laughed like it was funny, but he'd been quick to put her brother in his place by stating loudly that their budget was also champagne because the next new job was already in the works. And this one would pay even better than the last!

Layla had cringed.

And certainly, if Liam did in fact have that champagne taste, then he would always make sure he had the budget to back it up, right? And most of the time he did.

Most of the time.

When she and Liam had been married for seven years, her parents asked her to come over for dinner. "We'd like you to come alone," they said. "It's a private family matter."

Layla had driven to their house worrying about what they might tell her. Was someone sick? Was there a job loss? Layla's thoughts raced as she imagined the potential scenarios.

They'd sat down at the kitchen table and her parents had laid it out for her. They'd decided to do some estate planning, and every January for the next several years they were going to be gifting some money to Layla and her siblings. "We'd rather give it to you now," her dad said.

Layla had been stunned.

"I don't know what to say," she said. Her parents, who had worked all their lives to provide a good home for her and her brother and sister, had somehow found the capacity to save and gift despite what looked to an outsider like very modest means.

"There are tax benefits for doing it this way," her dad said. "Your mom and I are getting older and it makes sense."

"Thank you," she said. "I just . . . thank you."

"Can I make a suggestion?" her dad said.

"Of course," she said.

"This is a gift and we can't tell you what to do with it. If we wanted to put strings on it your mom and I wouldn't have decided to give it to you in the first place. But maybe you could set yours aside, open an account with just your name on it somewhere. Then when you needed it or if there was something you've always wanted to do for yourself, it would be waiting there for you."

She tried her best not to cry and failed. She nodded, and her dad reached across the table and squeezed her hand.

Two years later, Liam decided they should buy a new house.

Chapter 36

LAYLA

Josh arrived five minutes early on Saturday. "Maybe we should come up with a code word," Layla said. "For our protection." Josh was tall and he had the kind of body that looked strong and capable and like it had been built by physical work. Plus, he did that boxing thing a few nights a week and she'd had a daydream or two where she imagined him boxing without a shirt on. His hands were rough, and he had an interesting scar on his palm that Layla had asked him about the second night they worked on the puzzle together. He told her he'd brushed a live wire when he was an apprentice and had never made that mistake again.

"A code word," Josh said.

"In case it seems super sketchy or like something that might get us both killed."

"There's that imagination again."

"I do tend toward worst-case scenarios." That was what happened after years of Liam knocking her off her axis. Springing his latest news on her, news that never seemed to be all that positive and was often some sort of setback in the making.

"Well, then, I guess we'll need a safe word."

Layla laughed. "I said *code* word. That's different than a safe word. And our code word is Gibson."

"Gibson. Got it," he said.

They needn't have worried. The seller turned out to be a man in his late seventies who was selling the belongings of his son who had died the year before in a terrible auto accident. The guitar was in wonderful shape and Layla bought it on the spot with the cash she'd withdrawn from the bank on her way home from school on Friday. Maybe someday she would learn that not everything in life was a shit show, and sometimes things worked out exactly the way she hoped they would.

The man seemed lonely, and Josh sat patiently as Layla listened to him reminisce about his son and how much music and the guitar had meant to him.

"Is it okay if I use your restroom?" Josh asked about twenty minutes later.

"It's right down the hall," the man said.

Layla had not let go of the guitar. The mother-of-pearl inlay shimmered in the afternoon sunlight that streamed in through the living room window. Josh came back from the bathroom, but he didn't sit back down on the couch next to Layla. He pulled his keys from his pocket and gave them a little jingle. "Okay," he said. "We should probably get going." His words sounded clipped, and maybe she and the man had been reminiscing longer than she thought.

"Thank you so much," Layla said to the man.

"It was my pleasure, dear. Maybe you can come back again sometime." His eyes shined with unshed tears, and when he reached out and clasped her hands in his Layla swallowed the lump in her throat. He was kind and he'd suffered a horrible loss, and now she was going to waltz right out of there with a guitar that he could have gotten a lot more money for. At least she could take comfort in the fact that she and Josh might have been the only bright spot in an otherwise long and lonely day.

"I'm sorry about that," Layla said when they got back in Josh's truck. "I probably got carried away. I can talk guitars for a long time, and I'm sure you were bored. He was

299

just so nice, and he seemed lonely."

"No need to apologize. You were fine. It's just that when I walked down the hall to the bathroom, the door to one of the bedrooms was wide open, and something caught my eye. I took a quick look."

"What was it?" she said as he backed out of the driveway, her curiosity rising.

"Just an entire wall covered in knives."

Layla's eyes grew big. "What do you mean knives?"

Josh handed her his phone. "Here. I snapped a quick picture for you."

She looked at the picture. Not just knives. Swords, daggers, a twelve-inch butcher knife. A serrated one with a curve at the end. Fifty at least on one wall alone. There was a neatly made bed and a nightstand beside it with a perfectly normal lamp on top. The juxtaposition only made the knives creepier.

"That's a whole lotta knives, Layla."

"Gibson. Gibson!" she yelled, half serious but half laughing because they weren't in any danger now, but it blew her mind how wrong she might have been about the lonely old man.

"People collect all kinds of things," Josh said. "And he certainly wasn't trying to hide it."

"Or he starts in that room and has a more private and secluded one in the basement." Layla exhaled and it was a mixture of incredulity and relief. She turned to Josh. "Do I strike you as a gullible person?"

"No. Not at all."

"I bought that whole thing. Not just the guitar, but him as a person. I'd never be so careless as to show up alone and I had no intention of going back. But I bought it, Josh. The tears. The story."

"To be fair, what you bought might be the truth. He might just be an old man who's lonely and grieving his son."

"Or I'm simply the worst judge of character."

"Sounds like you just want to believe the best in people," he said.

"I'm definitely feeling less guilty about that great price."

"There you go. Silver lining," he said. "You hungry? I meant to eat lunch before I came over, but I didn't."

"Starving," she said. It was almost two thirty by then. She hadn't eaten lunch either, because she'd eaten a late breakfast, but now her stomach rumbled.

"How about Mexican?" he asked, pointing to a restaurant up ahead on the right.

"Perfect," she said.

Once inside, they sat down at a table and attacked the basket of chips and salsa as soon as the waitress had taken their order.

"How's your song doing?" Josh asked.

Brian had handled everything to do with uploading their musical masterpiece, which they had jokingly started to call their MM. He'd figured out the album art and the metadata and a whole bunch of other details that Layla had no interest in, but that Brian seemed to love. He'd also set up their social media accounts, and they were planning on doing some live performances on Facebook and Instagram. Neither of them had thought it necessary to come up with a band name, since it was just the two of them, so they were calling themselves Brian and Layla. Brian had asked her if she wanted her name first and said he didn't care either way, but Brian and Layla rolled off the tongue a little easier and he was the songwriter. It wasn't the most dynamic name for a duo, but their expectations were so low that neither of them cared. They just wanted to release the song and see if they might find a listener or two in the vast sea of streaming music choices.

Low expectations notwithstanding, once the song was "out there" they metaphorically held their breath waiting to see what would happen, which so far was a big fat nothing. Layla could almost hear their song hitting the ground with a loud thud.

"We've had a few downloads," Layla said. She and Brian could pretty much trace them back to their family members and the friends who knew about the availability of their song and where to find it, but it was still thrilling. "It's just the passion project of a couple of independent artists, but it scratched an itch for both of us."

"One of those downloads was mine. I listen to it a lot. I'm a serious fan," Josh said.

Layla laughed. "You and like eleven others."

"It's pretty cool, though. It's a great song. You and Brian should be proud." They *were* proud, and Brian had a few more songs they planned to perform and upload.

When the check came, she tried to grab it, but he was too quick.

"I wanted to pay," she said. "It's the least I could do after you took time out of your day to accompany me to the knife house."

"Is that what we're calling it now?"

"That's what I'm calling it now."

"I've got it," he said, handing the bill and his credit card to the waitress.

On the way home, Layla was hoping he

might suggest extending their afternoon together into the evening, and she could think of nothing she'd enjoy more than hanging out with him. They could watch a movie again. Take Norton for a walk. But when he pulled into her driveway and put the truck in park, he said, "I've got plans with my brothers tonight. Hockey game."

"That sounds fun."

"What are you up to? Any plans?"

She patted the guitar case on her lap. "I'm going to disappear into the basement and play this guitar until my fingers bleed," she said.

"I imagine you're pretty excited to play it." He turned his body toward her and rested his arm along the top of her seat.

"I am."

He asked her a few questions about her guitars, and she answered them and then asked him about his brothers, and all the while the truck ran, and the heater blew out warm air. At one point, he turned it down a little so they wouldn't overheat. As they talked, Layla found herself sinking back into her seat, her head inches from his arm, as comfortable as if they were sitting in his living room, or hers. Every time she thought they were wrapping it up, one of them would say something else and her body would relax and sink into her seat again.

"I should probably go inside now," she said, finally. He shrugged one shoulder and tilted his head slightly as if to say, *I don't know. I kind of like having you in my truck.* "Thanks again. Have fun at the hockey game."

"I'll text you when I get home to let you know which one of my brothers overserved himself."

She laughed. "I'll be standing by for that info."

He studied her face for a few seconds, and she would have loved to be able to read his mind. As she walked inside, she smiled to herself, because Josh had looked an awful lot like he might be thinking about kissing her, and that was almost as intoxicating to her as the kiss itself would be.

CHAPTER 37

JOSH

On Monday, Josh texted Layla to ask if she'd be available on Saturday. He'd been thinking about her off and on since the minute she'd gotten out of his truck with her new guitar. She was the first person he thought of when he had free time to spend with someone, and he was trying not to look too far ahead and just enjoy the companionship that the budding relationship provided. He was no longer deluding himself into thinking they were just friends, because any casual observer could take one look at them together and call bullshit on that. There were too many looks shared between them. A little too much casual touching.

Layla had texted Josh back a couple of hours later to say that she was available. He hadn't elaborated on what they'd be doing, but he showed up at her house on Saturday night with Norton and wine and Chinese

306

takeout from her favorite place — which he was now fully aware of along with her preferred meal (sesame chicken and an egg roll), her favorite wine (pinot noir for now, but when summer finally rolled around she would switch to rosé), and her favorite candy for watching movies (Cinnamon Fire Jolly Ranchers, but if she had popcorn she wanted it mixed with M&M's).

"Ooooh, takeout and wine," she said when she opened the door. "I wondered what was on the agenda."

He unpacked the food and opened the wine, pouring a glass for each of them. He knew which wineglasses were her favorite and he knew which cupboard she kept them in.

Layla knew a lot about him, too. She knew that sometimes, instead of wine, he wanted a Hendrick's gin and tonic or a craft beer. He preferred pot stickers over egg rolls with his beef and broccoli, and he was severely allergic to shellfish. He was baffled by anyone who wore socks to bed, which she had vehemently defended as completely normal and in her case necessary. "I can't help it that my feet are like little blocks of ice," she'd said. Most of these getting-to-know-each-other-better revelations took place on the phone. In addition to the daytime texting, there were actual conversations at night. Josh usually hated talking on the phone, but he could spend an hour chatting with Layla after Sasha was in bed.

"Takeout, wine, and a concert," he clarified.

Her forehead creased. "Who's playing?"

"You," he said.

Her eyes grew wide. "Excuse me?"

"I was really hoping you'd be in the mood for a basement concert for one," he said. "I thought maybe I could sit on your couch instead of watching you through the window like some neighborhood weirdo."

"You're the reason I bought the curtains."

He laughed. "I said I was sorry."

She took a drink of her wine and then they carried their plates to the kitchen table and sat down. "Yes, I will play for you," she said. "But mostly because you brought wine and one of my favorite meals."

"Mostly? What's the rest of the reason?"

"I just feel like playing."

After they finished eating, Josh topped off their wine and they headed down to the basement, Norton in tow.

"What can you play?" he asked.

"I can play everything," she said as if it were just that easy for her. Maybe it was.

"How about starting with 'Let It Be'?" He sat down on the couch. Norton jumped up next to him and laid his head on Josh's leg.

"Sure. But it won't be the same without the kids."

"Try and muddle through."

She grabbed an acoustic guitar and settled herself on the stool in the center of the room. She sounded incredible, that was a given, but there was something so intimately sexy about a woman singing a song just for him and he found it as alluring as foreplay.

"That was really good," he said when she finished. "You don't need those kids." He hesitated for a moment, but then he decided to say what he'd been thinking. "Did you and your ex-husband ever talk about having a child?"

"Yes."

"Was that something you wanted?"

"I had reservations, but Liam wanted one."

She picked up the guitar again and started strumming. He requested several songs — all of which she could play — and then she ended the private set with "Ironic" by Alanis Morissette. It made her laugh for some reason.

He met the end of each song with his hearty applause. "Are you tired of my voice

309

yet?" she asked.

He shook his head. "Nope. I could sit on this couch for hours listening to you play. But you don't have to keep playing if you don't want to. This concert has been well worth the price of admission."

"Gotten your money's worth, have you?" she teased.

"And then some," he said.

"Is this the part where you tell me you've got a great voice and you'd like to join in, and we absolutely smash a duet?" she asked.

"Sorry to disappoint you, but I am mediocre at best when it comes to singing."

She traded the acoustic for the Craigslist guitar and plugged it into an amp. "I'll play one more, and I'm going to turn this down so your eardrums won't bleed," she said. Layla had mentioned that she hadn't been so kind to her own ears in the past and would probably need hearing aids in her old age.

She played the opening notes of "Magic Man" and he cheered. There was something almost animalistic about the way she sang the song. And a woman playing electric guitar and singing to you was just straight-up sexy, no two ways about it.

"This concludes the concert for one," she said as she set the guitar back in its stand.

She switched on some music, leaving it low in the background, and sat down beside him on the couch. She was flushed and breathing a little heavy and so utterly desirable to him that he wasn't sure he could resist her for much longer.

And no real reason that he should.

"That was absolutely fantastic. Thank you," he said.

"Anytime." It had been a good long while since a woman had looked at Josh the way Layla was looking at him. He liked that she was one hundred percent present and focused, because he knew what it felt like when the woman beside you was more interested in strangers on the internet than she was in you.

It wasn't fair of him to compare the two scenarios. He and Kimmy had been together for years; he and Layla were still on their best behavior. There were no distractions, no pressing concerns or decisions they had to make together.

There was just wine and music and the growing thrill of physical attraction.

Layla took a sip of her wine and sank further back into the cushions of the couch. "Comfortable?" he asked.

"Very. Playing relaxes me. Or maybe it's just the wine. What about you? Are you

311

comfortable?"

Norton's big head was pressing down on his leg and Josh was pretty sure Norton had slobbered on him at some point because there was a spot on his jeans that felt a little damp, but all he said was "Definitely comfortable."

Something needed to happen. Either he took this to the next level and hoped it was received in a positive way or he needed to interrupt the moment by going upstairs to refill their wine or pretend that Norton needed to pee.

He chose not to go upstairs, and his hand was halfway to her face so he could bring her mouth to his when his phone rang. He hesitated for a split second and then pulled it out of his pocket and glanced at the display.

Layla might have been the one he talked to on the phone voluntarily, but Kimmy was the one whose calls he would always take, because she only called when they had something immediate to hash out that was too long to go into over text, or there was a problem with Sasha.

"Hey, is everything okay?" he asked.

"Sasha is really sick. I can't get her fever down and she's screaming in pain and I'm really scared. There are no urgent care clinics open so I'm taking her to the ER."

"Meet you there," Josh said, and he filled Layla in on their way upstairs, asking her if she could keep Norton overnight if it came to that.

"Of course," she said. "Go."

Josh burst through the sliding doors of the emergency room and searched for Kimmy. After inquiring at the front desk, he learned they'd been taken back to triage, so he followed the signs and joined them. Kimmy was sitting on the side of the hospital bed, Sasha in her arms, and both of them were crying. Kimmy's tears fell silently so as not to alarm Sasha, whose head was pressed against her mother's chest. Sasha's whole body shook with the force of her discomfort, and he'd heard her wailing before he'd even reached the room.

"What's happening?" Josh asked above the noise of Sasha's crying.

"The nurse has been in," Kimmy said. "They swabbed her throat for strep and now she won't stop crying."

"Here, I can take her," Josh said.

Kimmy handed her over and Josh stroked Sasha's head. Her cries intensified and he could feel the heat coming off her body. Where was the nurse? Where was the doctor? Where was someone who knew what the hell they were doing, because he and Kimmy certainly didn't.

Sasha had been sick before, but never like this. He stood in the middle of the room swaying from side to side the way he used to when she was a baby and couldn't settle. A harried doctor joined them a few minutes later, and after a quick introduction, he looked in Sasha's ears and down her throat. "Both of her ears are infected, and the rapid test was positive for strep. We'll get her a dose of pain meds and write you a prescription for an antibiotic. She'll be feeling much better in a couple of days."

"Thank you so much," Kimmy said. She looked like she wanted to hug the doctor. Josh knew that she'd been mentally rifling through the possible worst-case scenarios, and though he hated that Sasha was sick, he was relieved that they'd received a diagnosis. Nothing would be worse than a doctor coming up empty-handed and telling them they'd need to move on to more invasive and uncomfortable testing.

There was a pharmacy in the hospital, and they sat down on a bench to wait for the prescription to be filled. The Motrin the nurse had given Sasha started to kick in and she stopped crying. "Can I take her?"

Kimmy asked.

"Of course." He tried to hand her back, but Sasha wrapped one arm around Kimmy's neck and kept the other one tight around Josh's so that she was half lying on both of them. Josh didn't mind and it didn't appear that Kimmy did, either. He could smell his soon-to-be-ex-wife's perfume and her shampoo, and he could picture clear as day the glass bottle on the dresser and the plastic one in the shower. Josh stretched out his arm along the back of Kimmy's chair to get more comfortable, and Kimmy shifted slightly, trying to do the same. The only one who was comfortable was Sasha. Kimmy's head ended up halfway on his chest, and he put his other arm around Sasha so she wouldn't slide off his lap. As he held and comforted two of the most important women in his life, a fierce sense of longing for what he no longer had hit Josh like a tidal wave.

A nurse walked by and she gave them a smile and Josh could almost picture the thought bubble over her head that said, *Look at that lovely family.*

And if there was a thought bubble above Josh's head, it might have said *It was* and *Maybe we threw it away too easily and too soon.*

CHAPTER 38

LAYLA

Layla attempted to quell the butterflies in her stomach as she waited for Josh to arrive. Sasha had made a full recovery from the illness that had sent Josh and Kimberly racing to the emergency room, and it had been over a week since they'd seen each other. She was almost certain Josh had been about to kiss her that night, and she would have welcomed it. She wanted to be with him, and she could sense that he wanted that, too.

Maybe it was too soon for them to get involved with each other.

Maybe it wasn't.

She'd taken a little extra care with her appearance. She was wearing jeans, but they were her nicest pair and they looked good with the heeled booties she'd chosen in lieu of the stylish winter boots she usually wore this time of year. She'd ditched her glasses, winged her eyeliner, and traded her cardigan for a formfitting top.

Maybe Josh was thinking about that kind of thing, too, because when he arrived, they both tried to act like it was totally normal that he was wearing a sweater and a wool coat instead of his usual sweatshirt and Patagonia jacket.

"Ready?" he said.

"Ready." Suddenly, she worried about tripping over her words or, worse, literally tripping due to choosing fashion over function. She had already wiped out in front of him once on a hidden patch of ice when they'd taken Norton for a quick walk. She'd fallen right on her ass and they'd laughed so hard she almost peed. But that was before the almost-kiss, and she really didn't want to fall again.

She needn't have worried, because the driveway was clear, and she made it to the passenger side of his truck without incident.

"Sasha's still feeling okay?"

"She's great," he said. "She had a rough couple of days until the antibiotic kicked in all the way, but she's fine now."

"Good." As they buckled up, Layla asked, "So, where are we heading?"

"I thought we'd just get something to eat. I was going a little stir-crazy after being home a lot this past week. Wanted to get out of the house. What do you think?"

"Sounds good to me."

They went to an Italian restaurant they'd both eaten at before and enjoyed. Any awkwardness she'd felt upon Josh's arrival dissipated as they fell back into their normal, relaxed groove and flowing conversation. Maybe he hadn't really been about to kiss her, she thought. Or maybe he had but the interruption and the time apart had cooled the way he'd felt that night. At the very least, it might have given him pause, and she understood that.

They'd each had a glass of wine with dinner, and afterward Josh suggested dessert or a drink at a place he liked that she'd never been to. She said yes right away, because she was having too much fun to even think about going home yet. There was nothing fun about realizing your marriage needed to end, and there was certainly nothing fun about moving ahead with ending it. For so long, Layla had doubted she would ever have fun again. And here she was, almost a year later, having the time of her life on a date with a man who might or might not be thinking about kissing her at the end of it.

The only spot available at the restaurant

was in the expansive bar area, which was in a completely different room than the restaurant's dinner tables. There was a tiny nook in the corner just big enough for two leather club chairs, and they grabbed them before anyone else spotted them. There was a fancy bourbon cocktail on the drink menu that Josh had tried before. "It counts as both a drink *and* dessert," he said.

"Two birds, one stone. Sounds perfect," she said. "Is it strong?"

"It's got a little kick."

The cocktail tasted both sweet and smoky and featured a slice of caramelized banana on top. It tasted every bit as delicious as he'd promised, and after a few sips Layla felt as relaxed as she did when she was home alone in front of the fireplace in her robe and slippers.

But this was so much better.

She looked around the room at the other couples, some of them sitting so close you knew by looking at them that they were in love. Some looked like they were on a successful first date that they hoped would turn into a second and a third. Toward the end of her marriage, when she had all but checked out emotionally from Liam, going out to dinner was more about hunger and practicality than it was an opportunity to

319

connect or spend time with someone you actually wanted to be around.

"It's been a long time since I've had so much fun," she said. "I'd forgotten how much I *liked* having fun. Also, I think this cocktail is a little stronger than I'm used to because that was probably a weird thing to say."

"Will I need to carry you out of here?" he teased. "Because I can, Layla. I can throw you right over my shoulder in front of all these people."

A feeling of warmth spread over her and it had nothing to do with the bourbon. "You might," she said.

"But yeah, I get it. Fun is not the predominant emotion before, during, or after a breakup. But this is." He lifted his glass and clinked it against hers.

The waitress stopped by their table ten minutes later. "Would you like another?" she asked.

"Layla?" Josh asked.

She shook her head. Better to quit now before something weirder than the having-fun thing came out of her mouth. Like how much she liked him and how handsome he looked and how good he smelled and *goddammit,* she did not want to throw him back just because he'd been the first man after Liam.

Layla's seat was closer to the waitress, and when Josh leaned over to say, "We're good for now, thanks," he rested his hand on Layla's thigh for a moment.

She might not have wanted another cocktail, but that didn't mean she was ready to leave their nook. She was enjoying the way Josh kept looking at her. Fun was awesome, but flirting was even better, especially when you couldn't remember the last time you'd done it.

Their glasses were empty, but they lingered for another half hour. Their conversation was animated and there were a few more times when they touched each other — a hand on a leg or a shoulder to emphasize a point. She wondered if he felt it, too. There was nothing quite like that spark, that crackle of electricity when you realized the man you were sitting next to was someone you had chemistry with. *I could sit here for the next twenty years,* she thought. She smiled, because that was not the thought of a completely sober person and she never wanted to look that far ahead ever again. Better to stay in the present and appreciate how good things were right now. But it was also the thought of someone who was starting to believe not only that there was more on the horizon, but that she might be lucky enough to grab it with both hands.

"You ready to go?" he asked.

No. "Yes," she said.

Josh paid the tab and followed her as they walked through the restaurant, which was no longer as crowded as it had been when they'd arrived. Layla pushed open the door and took a deep breath of the cold winter air to clear her head. Before she even knew what was happening, Josh grabbed her hand and pulled her back toward him and gave her the kind of knock-your-socks-off kiss made a million times sweeter by the total absence of its anticipation.

Layla didn't have time to overthink it or even think about it at all before it was suddenly happening. There was none of that awkward fumbling that sometimes happened when you kissed a person for the first time. Later, when Layla looked back, it seemed to her that he simply couldn't wait until they were back in the car or on her doorstep. That the urge had been so strong he'd said to hell with it and kissed her right then and there because he just couldn't wait another minute.

She lost herself in the kiss. Their mouths seemed to fit together exactly, and Layla

322

didn't care who might be observing them or that they were kissing on a street corner like a couple of teenagers instead of two people in their thirties. It felt so good, like she'd been wandering in the desert dying of thirst and he'd put a glass of ice water to her lips. Except that his lips were warm and there was nothing cold about that kiss.

They were silent as they walked to his truck. Josh reached for her hand, and that was exactly what she needed at that moment. It was like he was saying, *That was not just a kiss. I like you and I'm holding your hand because this is the beginning of us.*

They made small talk on the way home, but Layla had so many thoughts running through her brain. *That felt so good, are we going to do it again, what are you thinking?*

Josh pulled into her driveway, parked, and turned off the engine. "I'll walk you to the door."

Her heart pounded in anticipation, but as soon as they reached her front door, he kissed her again and her nervousness faded away, replaced by how good it felt and how much she wanted this.

"Is this okay?" he asked.

She knew he wasn't only talking about the kiss. He was checking with her to see how she felt about the seismic shift their friendship had just taken. Friends with potential was now something real, something deeper, as they took the first steps toward being in a romantic relationship again. "Yes."

"You better go in. It's cold."

Was it? Layla barely noticed the temperature, but it was ridiculous to stand outside kissing when it was barely twenty degrees.

"Thanks for tonight. It was a lot of fun," she said.

He kissed her again, softly. "It was a lot of things. Talk to you tomorrow, Layla."

She watched him walk back to his truck and then she went inside and wished that tomorrow would hurry up and get here.

CHAPTER 39

JOSH

Josh and Jordan were playing a highly competitive game of pool in Jordan's basement. Their two other brothers were there, too, along with their kids. The wives were having a girls' night out, and it was complete pandemonium, because the brothers ran a much looser ship than their spouses did.

Kimmy used to love those nights out. Josh's brothers' wives had become her friends, and Josh hoped she didn't lose them in the name of family loyalty.

Sasha and her female cousins darted in and out of the room, screaming while being chased by their male cousins, who seemed hell-bent on terrorizing them. "Holy shit, they're loud," Jordan said.

Josh laughed. "Every time I leave one of these gatherings, I wonder if I've suffered permanent hearing damage."

"But it's a small price to pay for . . . this,"

325

Jordan said, gesturing toward his beer and his pool cue.

Something made a loud crashing noise upstairs. Josh shouted up the stairs. "Everything all right?"

His brother James shouted back, "Everything is under control."

"I doubt that," Josh said. "But also, not our problem." They'd already worked out the details ahead of time by rotating the responsibility of caring for seven children by dividing it up among the four brothers. Two stayed upstairs with the kids, which left two of them free to play pool in the basement. "Everybody wins," they'd decided.

"I'm not sure I do, considering Amber and I don't have any kids yet," Justin had said. The newlyweds were actively trying to get pregnant and planned to have their kids close together, since they'd gotten a bit of a later start than the other brothers.

"Think of it as a karma deposit," Josh had told him. "Besides, our kids will make excellent babysitters when they're a little older and then they can watch yours, so you're welcome."

"How's it going?" Jordan asked as he lined up his shot. "You gonna give the online-dating thing another try or what?"

"I'm definitely not."

"Then what's your plan, man?"

"I don't need a plan." Josh took a drink of his beer. "I met someone. We've been spending some time together. Quite a bit, actually."

"Who is she?"

"Her name's Layla. She's the music teacher at Sasha's school." He was about to call her his friend, which was true, but they were friends who'd traded kisses and were now in a transitional phase, it seemed. And he wanted more of those kisses.

Lots more.

"Oh, yeah," Jordan said, pumping his fist. "That's what I'm talking about. Little brother is back in the saddle."

"I wouldn't go that far. It's pretty new."

"Yeah, so? You can still be into it. It's okay to have a good time, you know. With her or anyone else."

"I know. I guess I just thought it would be easier." That wasn't completely true. What he'd thought was that it would be exhilarating to go out and sow some oats. Date a variety of women at the same time if he felt like it. Do all those things he'd missed out on because he'd married so young. But now that he could do them, he had no desire to. It didn't seem exhilarating at all. It mostly seemed exhausting.

"It's not like before if that's what you're worried about," Jordan said. "It wouldn't be cheating now. All I'm saying is that it's okay to play."

Josh took a long drink of his beer. "Yeah, I know."

Jordan's coworker had a sister who needed some electrical work done and he'd told the coworker all about Josh and given a glowing recommendation.

"Seriously, what have I told you about doing that?" Josh said when Jordan told him to expect a call. When friends and family referred him, it often ended up being a job he wouldn't have accepted otherwise. The work they needed done was rarely in line with his skill level and almost all of them balked at his hourly rate. He'd asked his family to stop doing it, but he also had a hard time saying no once a business card or his phone number had been handed over and he received the call. Too many times he would discover all that was needed was another outlet or a dimmer switch or someone to hook up a ceiling fan or two. In this case, he hadn't even talked to the potential client on the phone, because Jordan had acted as the go-between and all Josh had was an address and a request to stop by in the evening.

He was surprised when he pulled into the gravel driveway of a home twenty minutes outside of town. The fence was crumbling, the siding was peeling, and he double-checked to make sure he had the right address. The last thing he wanted to work on was a crumbling fixer-upper, and the house's condition probably meant the cost of his services wouldn't go over well, either.

A woman who looked to be a few years younger than Josh opened the door. She was wearing a T-shirt and jeans and she had a smear of dirt across her sweaty cheek. She had dark hair and eyes and she looked nothing like Kimmy. "Hi, I'm Nikki. You must be Josh."

"Yep. Nice to meet you," he said. They shook hands and she ushered him inside.

"Thank you for doing this. The last guy I hired flaked on me as soon as the kitchen was done. I guess he had a better opportunity, or something came up. I told my brother I wanted to find someone I could trust, and I was so glad when I found out about you. I don't feel comfortable hiring anyone now without a personal recommendation."

"Sure," he said. "No problem."

"I bought this house as an investment. I'm an interior designer and I thought it would be a fun challenge to buy something, gut it, and decorate it from the ground up. I must have temporarily lost my mind, because I'm in a little over my head. It needs a lot of work. But the price was right, so here we are."

"I'm guessing some of your problems are electrical," he said.

"I had an inspection done and I've got a list of things that range from mildly annoying to super unsafe."

"Can I see the inspection report?" he asked.

She fetched it from another room, and he scanned the items that needed to be addressed, ranging from critical to low-priority. "Is it hopeless?" she asked.

"No. It's not hopeless. But it could get expensive." Family referral or not, he'd worked hard to get where he was, and he wasn't going to start slashing his rates now. He didn't have to.

She didn't blink when he gave her his hourly rate and the number of hours it would probably take.

"I can do that," she said. "Budgeting for the worst and then doubling it was the only smart thing I did."

She was often there when he worked on the house, and over the next few days he learned that she'd recently moved back from the East Coast after a bad breakup. "My brother

330

thought I was crazy to buy this house, but I needed something to tear down and build back up. I guess that's what you do when your own life crashes and burns."

Once he'd gotten inside and discovered how much she'd already done, he realized that the house had a ton of potential. She told him that the roof and siding were being replaced next and she'd showed him the rest of the plans one day when he was taking a break for lunch. She'd spread everything out on the brand-new quartz countertop and pointed to various things on the blueprints. "I bought it at the right price — I have a suspicion the previous owner might have died upstairs — but it was exactly what I was looking for. I should still be able to sell it for a nice profit even with all the work I'm putting into it."

"I don't think you'll have any trouble selling it," he said.

"What about you?" she asked one day. "What's your story? How'd you get into this line of work?"

He told her that he didn't like to sit for too long and that he liked working with his hands. "I knew college wouldn't be for me, but I still wanted a career."

"Looks like it worked out for you."

He smiled. "I guess it did."

The project was growing to a close and he

told her he could probably finish up in the next day or two. "Oh," she said. "Okay." It was hard to miss the look of disappointment on her face, and Josh felt the first stirring of unease and something else.

Something that felt like yearning.

He'd be lying to himself if he said he didn't enjoy seeing Nikki's face light up every day when she opened the door. She often stopped to watch him work for a few minutes, and the conversations were enjoyable, easy. She was funny and she was smart, and she seemed like a woman who'd risen from a setback and would do fine on her own.

Later that day, when he was finishing up with the new subpanel he'd installed, she brought him a bottle of water. "Thought you might be thirsty," she said.

"Thanks. I am." He took off the cap and drank.

"Would you like to go out sometime?" she blurted.

He took a deep breath. "I would," he said. "If I wasn't married."

"Oh, my God. I'm so sorry. You're not wearing a ring. I just thought . . . it seemed like we . . . Oh, God."

"Most electricians don't wear them on the job. It's a safety hazard."

"I'm absolutely mortified."

"Seriously, it's okay. I never said anything . . . You didn't know. Please don't be embarrassed."

He'd driven home that night hoping to light a spark with the woman he was married to, but all he got for his effort was disappointment. He'd picked up dinner and taken Sasha to the park to give Kimmy some alone time, and later, when Sasha was asleep, he asked her to put down her phone and come to bed, which had always been their signal for "I need to connect with you."

She barely looked up from her phone and said she'd be there soon. But he knew she wouldn't. She would remain on her phone until long after Josh had given up and fallen asleep.

She was never without it. It was as if she had to be on high alert at all times in case there was some kind of political scandal that she needed to be aware of. But there were so many political scandals, he wondered how anyone could keep track of them anymore. Social media had changed the game and not in the positive way everyone had thought it might. Josh had little patience for social media himself. He had a Facebook profile that he set up mostly as an easy way to share pictures and information about Sasha with his family. But once he started using a smartphone, he could just as easily text that information to them — even his dad, who swore he'd never have time for any such thing and who now delighted in using that very same phone for a variety of helpful tools. Over the years, Josh's Facebook profile had slowly grown dormant, and he no longer remembered the password. But Kimberly spent every waking moment on her phone getting into political fights with people on Facebook and Twitter.

"Why do you even bother?" he asked her once, because he was fed up with the sight of her nose buried in that tiny screen and he was tired of competing with it for her time.

"Because I care," she said. "I don't know why you don't."

"I do care. I'm informed and I vote, but I don't have to go online and tell everybody how I feel about things to prove I care about them. You're all just shouting into the void. You're not going to change their minds and they're sure as hell not going to change yours. It is a waste of time."

"It's what's wrong with our political climate," she yelled.

"Not burying my face in my phone and getting into arguments with complete strangers is what's wrong with our political climate? This is what's wrong with our entire world," he shouted, pointing at her phone, every bit as angry as she was. "All anyone does anymore is fight. It has gotten us nowhere. We are a nation divided. Period."

We are a husband and wife divided, he thought, and not just when it came to their level of political participation. He scrambled to think of one thing that unified them by then other than Sasha, and he couldn't come up with one. They had no shared hobbies. Hell, they didn't even have a shared TV show. He would always remember the two of them on that old, lumpy hand-me-down couch watching *Lost* with a bowl of popcorn between them and a blanket over their laps. Kimmy would sometimes fall asleep after the show when the next program came on, and he would look down at her head in his lap and be filled with peace.

The ennui of a long-term relationship that had been on life support for a couple of years already didn't exactly provide the best environment for giving your spouse the attention they deserved, and it worked both ways. How many times had he tuned her out when she told him a story about the people she worked with, whom he couldn't care less about? They had reached an impasse where no one was happy, and they were edging closer to miserable every day. But they were a family, and so he'd lowered his voice and so did she.

Politics was the only thing outside of Sasha that Kimmy seemed to care about, all anyone in her professional circle seemed to care about. Not long ago, they'd gone out to dinner with some of her work friends, and one of Kimmy's male coworkers had made a snide remark when he asked Josh where he'd gone to college and Josh replied that he was an electrician and hadn't gone to college. The man had winced slightly, as if Josh's lack of a degree made him unfit to socialize with them. Josh had smiled and politely pointed out that it was nice not having any student-loan debt and that his first employer had paid for him to become an electrician. The man hadn't said anything more after that.

Josh had remained loyal to his first employer right up until the day the company was bought out by a bigger company. Some of the forthcoming changes didn't sound all that great to him, so he'd decided to go out on his own, and that had been one of the best decisions he'd ever made. He could have made even more money than he was currently making if he wanted to pursue some of the really lucrative opportunities he was qualified for. He didn't, because that might mean not being as available to take care of Sasha, but he could if he wanted to.

He'd vented to Kimmy about her coworker

on their way home. "Is that how you feel about my lack of a degree, Kimmy? Because my job, the one your coworker turned his nose up at, paid to put you through college so that you wouldn't have student loans, either."

"No," she said. "Of course I don't think that."

"I hope not," he said. But he could see that she was moving closer and closer to a world that wouldn't welcome him and that he had no interest in being a part of anyway.

"I can't believe you'd even think that I would," she said, and she started crying. "And the truth is you make more than him. Much more."

"I'm sorry," he said, although there wasn't anything to be sorry for other than that they were not the same people anymore and maybe the sorry was because he couldn't fix it, and neither could she.

"I'm sorry, too," she said.

By then they both knew the marriage was in serious trouble, but it was easier to focus on the day-to-day routine they'd fallen into — Kimmy with her phone and Josh with mindless television and household chores that didn't really need to be taken care of. Going to bed each night at different times so they could jam the wedge even further between them.

He made another attempt at closing the divide between them. He'd thought that maybe they could pick a travel destination that would bring them back year after year, just the two of them. They were both too busy living their lives and taking care of their daughter to remember what had gotten them this far in the first place — their undying love and their you-and-me-against-the-world philosophy.

"Let's go somewhere," he said to Kimmy one morning when it was just the two of them sitting in silence drinking coffee in the kitchen. "Let's go sit on a beach. Pack your bikinis. Pack all of them," he said.

"I was thinking of Florida," she said. "We could take Sasha to Disney World."

Frustrated, he opened his mouth to clarify that this was not a family trip, but what he didn't know was that Sasha had come into the room, and because his back was to her he only realized she'd overheard Kimmy when she started screaming in delight. "Yes! Disney World," she said. "I want to go."

And he would also never know if Kimmy had seen Sasha come into the room and if she had said it out loud on purpose.

He confided in Jordan and told him everything that was suffering in his marriage and admitted that he'd thought about starting something

338

with Nikki. "I'm sorry," Jordan said. "I thought everything was fine between you and Kimmy."

"It looks fine on the outside" was all Josh said.

"Well, you didn't act on it so it's not a big deal," Jordan said.

But it was a big deal, at least to him because it was indicative of just how broken the marriage was and he'd better figure out something to fix it as soon as possible.

Technically, he had remained faithful to Kimmy, but he'd cheated on her in his mind. He couldn't even look at those quartz countertops in Nikki's kitchen without imagining all the things he wanted to do to her on them.

Nikki wasn't around for the last couple of days he worked at her house. On the last day, he laid an invoice on the kitchen counter. The check landed in his post office box two days later and he never saw her again.

Jordan lined up another shot and missed. "Damn," he said. "So, is this new woman like a rebound or the real deal or what?"

"I have no idea," Josh said. So far, he liked what was happening between him and Layla. He liked it a lot. It felt easy and fun, but it did not feel like a fling, either, and he didn't quite know what to make of that. What if Layla *was* just a rebound? What if he was a rebound for her? He could see himself falling for Layla, hard, but he also didn't want to be the guy who couldn't be alone and fell too fast. His track record when it came to rushing into things wasn't great. "Taking it slow for now."

He'd expected to have a few casual relationships before he met someone like Layla. Except that casual had never really been his style. Plus, he had Sasha to think of and no desire to subject her to a revolving door of girlfriends. He'd already decided shortly after he moved out that he'd have to be pretty far into a relationship before he'd even consider introducing the woman to his daughter. But Sasha and Layla already knew each other, so that process might be easier for all of them. He and Layla were both somewhat emotionally unavailable, but that just gave them one more thing they could relate to in each other.

"You second-guessing the divorce?"

"No." But was that true? There had been times, especially lately, when he'd wondered if he and Kimmy had thrown in the towel too soon. They were getting along better now than they had for the whole last year of their marriage. Kimmy was never on her phone whenever they were in the same room together. She smiled at Josh and listened when they exchanged information about Sasha. She'd called him to let him know that she'd received an email about a sale on the work boots he liked, and they'd talked for forty-five minutes. Had they done everything possible to save the marriage? It was hard being here with his brothers knowing that Kimmy wasn't out with the sisters-in-law. He'd started to forget about some of the things that had led them down the path to their separation. And there was Sasha, of course.

"Maybe you just need to get laid," Jordan said.

"I need more than that. I need some kind of connection." It was the intimacy that he and Kimmy once shared that he missed so much. The inside jokes, cuddling on the couch, limbs intertwined, sex in the middle of the night because they'd been too tired at bedtime but couldn't make it until morning without coming together in the way they had been since they were eighteen years old.

"Maybe you're just one of those . . . what do they call them?"

"Idiots?"

"You're not an idiot." Jordan snapped his fingers. "Serial monogamists."

"Maybe I am," Josh said.

"All I'm saying is that you're free to be

with whoever you want. You're a single man with a good job and you're not hideous and you're pretty nice."

"Not quite single. Not legally, anyway."

"A final piece of paper isn't going to change anything. You don't have to feel guilty anymore. You're free."

"Yeah, I guess I am." This time, at least, there was nothing to feel guilty about.

CHAPTER 40

LAYLA

"So, how are *things*?" Tonya asked, giving Layla a friendly little nudge. The gray sky barely hinted at the spring weather that seemed years away from arriving even though it was early March. At least it wasn't too cold. Layla was still wearing her parka, but if the weather held, she'd be able to swap it for a lighter one in the not-too-distant future. Then again, this was Minnesota, so it was more likely she'd still be wearing her snow gear until May.

Layla laughed. "You mean, how is Josh?"

"Of course that's what I mean."

"I'm not holding out on you. I'm happy to give you all the juicy details. I saw him last night."

"And . . . ," Tonya said with anticipation.

"Oh, sorry. I don't have anything juicy to report yet. But things are good. Lots of texting and talking on the phone." The first

343

thing Layla did every morning when she woke up was check her phone. Josh always sent a text to say good morning, and they occasionally spent their first few moments after waking up in their respective beds texting each other. Neither of them wanted to overwhelm the other, so they didn't get together every night that Josh didn't have Sasha. But on the nights they were apart, they spent hours on the phone like a couple of teenagers.

"Wow. The two of you must really like each other if you're willing to talk on the phone. But you're right. That's the opposite of juicy."

"There's been a lot of kissing."

That was perhaps an understatement. They'd only seen each other a few times since their first kiss on her doorstep, but Layla estimated they spent about ten percent of that time talking and the rest joined at the mouth. She couldn't get enough of the kissing, and the novelty of one of them kissing the other whenever they felt like it had not worn off for either of them.

Not even close.

Tonya sighed. "Kissing is so underrated. I'm going to kiss Tim when I get home. Just lay a big old kiss right on his mouth."

"You should," Layla said.

Annie waved as she was walking her boys in and then joined Tonya and Layla briefly on her way back to the parking lot. "I've gotta run, but I have to tell you that my kids love your song as much as I do, Layla. Seriously, they know all the words and we sing it at the top of our lungs on the way to school every morning."

"Thanks," Layla said. "Tell the kids we appreciate their enthusiasm. We need all the fans we can get."

Josh came out of the building and headed toward his truck. As he passed them, he threw Layla a smile and said, "I'll see you around five."

Layla smiled back and gave him a quick nod. "See you then."

To Tonya, she said, "We're going to cook dinner together. That's something else that's underrated. I like cooking with Josh. We open a bottle of wine and we make a meal and then sit down together and eat it."

"And then there's kissing," Tonya said. "For dessert."

"Always," Layla said. She turned toward Tonya, and the expression on her face was serious. "It really does feel good knowing that the person standing beside you in the kitchen wants you. And I don't just mean in a romantic capacity. It's so nice knowing that he gives a shit, Tonya. He wants to be there. And I want him to be there. It's a good feeling."

As she and Josh had already discussed, fun was in short supply when a relationship was grinding to its fateful end, but romance was something even more likely to have tapped out long before that. That was certainly true in Layla's case. If the opposite of love was indifference, well, Layla knew a lot about what that emotion felt like. She and Liam had spent very little time together during the last year of their marriage, and when they were together, romance seemed to be far down on the list.

"I know," Tonya said, reaching out to give her shoulder a squeeze. "I'm really happy for you."

"Me too." Being around Josh was fun and romantic and peaceful and Layla couldn't ask for more than that.

As Layla was walking to her car at the end of that day, she was already thinking about Josh and how much she was looking forward to his arrival when a man walked up to her and said, "Are you Layla Hilding-Cook?" *I am Layla Hilding,* she thought, but she said, "Yes."

The man handed her a legal-sized envelope and said, "You've been served."

Her thoughts were racing so fast that she barely remembered unlocking her car door and sinking into the driver's seat as she attempted to rip open the envelope with her other hand. *No,* she thought. *It was a done deal.* Her attorney had assured her of that.

But Liam must not have agreed, because according to the papers in the envelope, he wanted to reopen their divorce. Layla's hands were shaking so violently that she dropped her phone twice. Tears blurred her vision and it took her two tries to find the right contact. The receptionist must have sensed the desperation in her voice, because a few minutes later, for once, her attorney came on the line, and the questions — so many questions — tumbled from Layla's mouth.

It seemed that Liam wanted to reopen their divorce based on fraud. Layla had disclosed every penny of the money she had received from her parents, because it was not in her nature to be dishonest or hide things. That was Liam's game and the last thing she ever wanted to be was like her ex-husband. But according to her attorney, based on the papers in the envelope that she read to him over the phone, it didn't matter that Layla had disclosed the money.

347

She had hidden it from Liam during their marriage and now someone had put a bug in his ear that maybe he should make sure she hadn't been hiding anything else. And now, for good measure, he'd decided that maybe he was entitled to some of the money in Layla's retirement account. And all the attorney fees for this round would be hers to pay, of course.

As she'd learned during the disclosure of their assets, Liam didn't have a lot in his retirement account because he'd liquidated some of it in the last ten years.

To keep them afloat, he'd said.

Them.

He'd been very vocal about that, almost as if he'd been expecting her to *thank* him. As if his mismanagement of their finances and the bailout the retirement money had provided should somehow be her problem to share even though she'd known nothing about it at the time.

"Is this something that could actually happen?" Layla asked her attorney. "In what world would this be even remotely fair?"

"Divorce is rarely about being fair," he said. "We can fight it and you'll probably win. You didn't have anything else, did you? Anything you didn't tell me about?"

"No," she said. And that was the truth.

She had her retirement and she had the yearly gift from her parents, and she could not believe this was happening.

"Don't do anything. Don't contact Liam. Don't talk to him about this. I'll get back to you tomorrow and I'll let you know what the next steps will be. Keep your chin up. At least he's not asking for alimony."

Layla made a mental note to fire her attorney when this was over. "Well, at least there's that," she said. Then she hung up the phone and made a call to Liam's assistant, fabricating an emergency that made it necessary for her to know exactly where she could find him.

Liam was waiting in the parking lot of the surgery center when she pulled in. Good. That meant his assistant had already tipped him off and he was worried about having a conversation with Layla within earshot of the client he was meeting with. When he spotted her, he hurried toward her car as if he thought she would let him get in. She got out and she slammed the door and it didn't matter that she hadn't made it inside the building because everyone could probably hear her from the parking lot.

"I asked for nothing," she screamed. "I walked away from everything we had, and if you fight me on this, I will do whatever it takes to ruin you financially. I will come after every single penny you ever manage to earn in the future. I will bankrupt myself doing it if I have to."

The depth of her anger and the conviction he must have seen on her face stunned him momentarily. Then he said, "I never thought you would say something so ridiculous. You're insane."

"You've never seen what I'm capable of, Liam." And there was something in her tone that was so evenly calm and yet so chilling she wondered if she was having some sort of psychological break. He must've heard it, too, because for once he kept his mouth shut, and she could see the worry that creased his forehead. The doubt that showed itself in his eyes. The look on his face told her that he might have finally realized he'd gone too far and there was a reason you didn't back wounded animals into a corner: They always came out swinging. Then he turned on his heel and walked back into the building.

She kept it together on the drive home, although she didn't remember any of it, and she barely made it into her driveway before screeching to a halt and slamming the car into park. She laid her head on the steering wheel. The tears came then, great heaving sobs that shook her body.

She'd heard a song when she was on her way to check into the Holiday Inn Express the night she left Liam. It was on a playlist she'd been listening to in the car on her way to work in the morning, and it was the Dixie Chicks' version of Fleetwood Mac's "Landslide," which had always been one of Layla's favorite songs.

Tears rolled down her face as she drove. *Can I sail through the changin' ocean tides? Can I handle the seasons of my life?* She didn't know the answer to those questions that night. She was, at that moment, smack-dab in the middle of the hardest season of her life, and she didn't know if she could handle it.

But she had, and she was not going back to that shitty time in her life.

Layla let out one final heaving sob but kept her forehead on the steering wheel, too spent to get out of the car. She liked to think that maybe she was on the brink of one of those good seasons, and if the hard one had taught her anything, it was that it had made her stronger.

She barely registered the car door opening and then she heard Josh's voice as he crouched down next to the driver's seat and said, "Hey," in a voice that was so soft and gentle the word felt like he'd wrapped her in a soft blanket.

She lifted her head from the steering wheel and laid it on his chest. "Hey." Norton pushed his face into the mix, and his cold nose nuzzled her wet face.

Josh didn't ask questions. He rubbed her back and finally she looked up and dragged her sleeve across her tear-swollen face. He kissed her forehead so tenderly that she started crying again. "Take Norton and go inside. I'll put your car in the garage," Josh said.

She nodded and he handed her Norton's leash and they traded places. Once inside, she washed her face and changed her clothes, and they did not cook together that night. Josh ordered takeout and urged Layla to eat. If Liam was baggage, Layla had just dragged the biggest suitcase she owned into the equation as she told Josh every shitty thing he'd done to her and how much this worried her and how hard she would fight. Maybe it was too early to say the things she said, but this was her reality and Josh could take it or leave it.

Besides, they'd started breaking every one of those new-relationship rules the night Layla told Josh they existed in the first place.

And now, she was fairly certain they were both too invested to care.

CHAPTER 41

LAYLA

The crowd clapped and shouted when
Brian and Layla took the stage on a Friday
night. Brian's friend had once again asked
Brian to cover his gig at the bar he and
Layla had played at on New Year's Eve. No
food poisoning this time; he just wanted the
weekend off, and Brian and Layla were
more than happy to take his place. And this
time Layla had invited Tonya and Annie and
their spouses.

And Josh, of course.

If Layla had enjoyed herself on New Year's
Eve, it was nothing compared to the way
she felt now, guitar in hand and Josh and
her friends sitting up front at the table she'd
reserved for them. She took it all in — the
applause and the energy she drew from the
crowd. Their smiling faces. They closed out
their second set with "Thankful," and everyone Layla and Brian had invited cheered

354

loudly. Annie got out of her seat and sang along, giving them her own personal standing ovation at the end. It was the first time they'd played the song for a live crowd, and when the applause finally died down, Brian let them know where they could purchase it if they were so inclined.

During the break, Josh was right there, his arm slung around her shoulders, mingling with Layla's friends like he'd known them for years. "Are you having a good time?" she asked him.

"I'm having a great time," he said, and he tipped her chin up and gave her a quick kiss that sent shivers up and down her arms.

Layla excused herself to go to the restroom, and Tonya went with her. "Good Lord, you should have seen the way Josh looked at you while you were up there doing your thing," Tonya said as they were washing their hands. "That man is smitten."

Layla was well aware of the way Josh had been looking at her. She had mixed feelings about it, because as much as she enjoyed being the recipient of his adoring gaze, it stirred up some memories of her early days with Liam. "That's how I lure them in, apparently."

"What do you mean?" Tonya asked.

Layla leaned toward the mirror and reapplied her lipstick. "It feels a little like I'm repeating a pattern. New gig, new guy. I've never admitted it out loud, but there were times I wondered if Liam had only been interested because I was the lead singer in a popular band."

Shiny, shiny Layla.

"And yes, I do know how ridiculous that sounds."

"If that was true, it was Liam's problem. Not yours. You are way more than just a girl in a band."

Deep down, Layla knew Tonya was right. But sometimes it was hard to accept it herself. "Tonight feels really good. I feel like I'm being true to my authentic self. The one that sort of disappeared into someone else's idea of what that should be."

"Then maybe it's not a pattern. Maybe it's a do-over," Tonya said.

"Do you know what else I'm going to do? I'm taking back my name. I've been meaning to do it, but I've been dragging my feet because I have to take the day off and go to the Social Security office and stand in line and that sounds about as appealing as going to the DMV. But after what happened the other day when Liam had me served in the school parking lot, I never want to hear my old name come out of anyone's mouth ever again. I just want to be Layla Hilding. I am going to walk out of there feeling like I'm me again, and I have never wanted to check an item off my to-do list as much as I want to check off this one."

"Atta girl," Tonya said. "That is something we will definitely need to celebrate. Ready to get back out there? It's about time for you to get up on that stage and entertain me."

"Do you know what Brian and I need to really round out our act? A backup dancer. Come on," Layla said, laughing. "It's your time to shine."

"Be careful what you wish for. One more glass of wine and I'll probably do it."

When the night was over and Josh drove them back to Layla's house, she was still flying high on the adrenaline of a successful performance. Josh killed the engine and followed Layla to the front door. He'd brought Norton with him, so the first thing they did was rouse the sleeping dog and let him out in the backyard to do his business. Then either Josh would kiss her good night and head home with Norton or they'd both stay. Norton ambled back through the sliding glass door and flopped down in his bed again, and Josh answered Layla's unspoken musing with his mouth when he pressed it against hers. They stood in the kitchen making out in the dark, and then Josh nudged her toward the hallway, where she slipped her hand into his palm and led him to her bedroom. They fell onto the bed, and Josh twisted his fingers in her hair and pulled her head back to reveal the length of her neck, which he nibbled and sucked, eliciting a loud moan from Layla.

He tugged her shirt from the waistband of her jeans, and they quickly helped each other out of their clothes. Josh explored every inch of her with his hands and his mouth, like someone who'd been waiting a long time to unleash the pent-up passion he let rain down on Layla. It had felt like forever since she'd been intimate with anyone, and the last few times she and Liam had been together had seemed more like an obligation on both their parts. Now Layla touched Josh's body with a similar urgency, running her hands down his chest and lower, skimming across his stomach, enjoying the way his breathing grew ragged and how it seemed like he was barely maintaining control. It was a big step for them, but Layla told herself that it didn't have to mean anything; it could simply be something she wanted to do because she felt safe and it felt good and it had been a while.

When it was over, their movements slowed, became less frantic, gentler, and she felt the first wave of pure relaxation wash over her. Josh got up to take Norton out and when he slid back underneath the covers, he wrapped his arms around her and she could not think of a single place she'd rather be than right where she was.

CHAPTER 42

LAYLA

The next morning, Layla brought Josh a cup of coffee in bed. He sat up and she handed it to him and snuggled back under the covers with her own cup. It was snowing hard, which didn't bother her at all, because it was cozy and warm inside and neither of them had anyplace they needed to be.

They were still in bed and were on their second cups of coffee when Layla's phone rang, and GUITAR SHOP BRIAN flashed on the screen.

"Hey," Layla said. Maybe they'd left something behind last night or someone had reached out to book them for another show.

"Brace yourself," he said.

She sat up so fast she splashed a bit of coffee on her white comforter. "Damn," she said, blotting at the stain with the hem of the long T-shirt she'd thrown on to make

360

coffee. "What? What's wrong?"

"Oh, it's good news, Layla. It's *phenomenal* news."

She could handle a coffee stain for phenomenal news. "What?" she yelled. "Tell me."

"Our little song has had a very big development." Their daily average for downloads was now around three thousand, which sounded like a lot but really wasn't. Not in such a crowded marketplace full of infinite choices.

Tiny fish, big huge pond.

"Because we played it last night?" she asked. "Don't get me wrong, it was a good-sized crowd, but I didn't think it would be enough to make a difference."

"No, not because of last night. We showed up on a playlist, Layla."

"No way," she said. She knew immediately that Brian wasn't talking about a user-created playlist. What he meant was that they'd landed on one of the algorithm-driven playlists that matched song and listener data. It was a serendipitous event completely out of their control, and it was the holy grail of good luck for independent artists hoping to stand out.

"Yep. I can't believe it, either."

"How many downloads?" she asked.

"Fifty thousand."

"Holy shit."

"We might actually make some money, which I desperately need because the guitar shop is barely operating in the black."

Layla hadn't thought much about their income potential; she thought it was cool that they'd made back their operating costs and that a little money had started trickling in.

"I'll track everything. Prepare for hourly updates."

Brian was much more interested in the analytics than Layla was. He kept a spreadsheet and he tracked their downloads, and the data geek inside him would be busy in the coming weeks.

"Keep me posted," Layla said.

"Sounds like Brian had some very good news to share this morning," Josh said.

"The best kind." Layla brought Josh up to speed and answered his follow-up questions.

"Maybe you're getting a second chance to do the thing you weren't quite ready to stop doing," he said.

"Yeah," she said, laying her head on Josh's chest when he put his arms around her and pulled her in close. "Maybe I am."

They might have stayed in bed a little

longer, but Josh's stomach growled, so they got up and made a huge breakfast of bacon and eggs and toast, and it felt like they'd been making breakfast side by side for years. There was something about it that just felt so easy to Layla, and she practically danced around the kitchen, still flying high from the news Brian had delivered and a morning made even sweeter by what she and Josh had done the night before and once more around 3:00 A.M.

She could do these things now if she wanted. She could have a second chance at a music career, and she could have a man in her bed and that same man in her kitchen the next morning, and she did not have to answer to anyone. She looked at Josh standing at the stove pushing the eggs around in the skillet as she turned the bacon and she thought that maybe she would enjoy doing this on regular basis.

After breakfast, Josh headed home. He was helping one of his brothers with some sort of home-improvement project, and he told Layla he'd call her later. She poured another cup of coffee and sat down on the couch. She didn't turn on the TV or reach for a magazine or book. She watched the snow falling outside the living room window and savored the absolute joy and peace she felt within the four walls of the small house that Liam would have absolutely hated.

Layla thought they were on their way to have a late lunch the day Liam dragged her to the open house in a newly constructed, gated neighborhood that was all the rage. They were still living in their loft, and the suburbs had been beckoning for some time, especially for Liam. She'd be lying if she said she didn't long for a yard and to not share walls with other homeowners, but they could afford the loft, and buying a house would bring all kinds of additional costs along with a higher monthly payment. They'd have to buy lawn-care equipment and a snowblower and Liam would undoubtedly want to landscape the yard and finish the basement. They had watched their friends do these things and they'd listened to them brag about how it was all so horribly expensive but totally worth it in the end.

Layla might not have argued about going to the open house, but she was only going through the motions. She declined the fact sheet the Realtor offered her, and she followed Liam silently from room to room, showing little enthusiasm.

"Look at these cabinets," Liam said in the expansive gourmet kitchen, opening and closing them like he was a game-show host enticing the contestants about what was up for grabs.

"They look pretty solid," she said.

"This island is massive," he said. "I bet you could get seven stools around it."

"Probably."

"Layla, you've got to see this," Liam yelled. She had fallen behind as the Realtor described the features of the home for a rapt Liam. She caught up with them in the sprawling living room in the back of the house, with soaring twenty-foot ceilings and a whole wall of windows looking out onto a golf course.

Liam loved to golf.

Liam made all kinds of deals on the golf course.

Ten bucks said he was going to claim that this house would practically pay for itself.

"Isn't it gorgeous?" the Realtor asked.

"How often do golf balls hit the windows?" Layla asked, and it must have been the wrong answer to the question, because Liam looked disappointed.

"Not very often," the Realtor said.

She and Liam finally made it to lunch. He studied the fact sheet as the waitress took their orders. "The basement is plumbed for a wet bar," he said. "We could also put another bedroom down there."

"I don't even want to know what the payment would be on a house like that," Layla said.

"You didn't like it?" he asked, and he looked at Layla like the possibility of that flabbergasted him.

"I didn't say that. It's a beautiful house, but I can't imagine we could afford it."

"We can. I've already run the numbers."

"You've already run the numbers?"

"That's what I just said."

"I would need to see those numbers," she said.

The waitress appeared and set down their meals. Liam picked up his fork and stabbed at his pasta. "It feels like you're trying to tell me what I can and can't spend my money on," he said, his voice growing more frustrated with each word.

"I work too, Liam."

"I never said you didn't." She saw the look on his face — fleeting — but she saw it. It was the look that said, *Yes, you work, but we both know I'm the real breadwinner.*

You could leave him, she thought. *You really could.*

Things had been calm for a good long stretch by then, and Layla didn't have the energy to rock the boat. She told herself that all marriages had land mines — the topics you avoided because you didn't want to spoil what was otherwise a drama-free afternoon: the borderline alcoholic who was loving and gregarious as long as you kept the bar tab open but didn't let them get too wasted, or the obsessive flirt who rode the line between acceptable and nonacceptable a smidge too hard at the neighborhood block party.

"We've got a ton of equity in the loft. I'll get the financing in place. I'll show you exactly how we can afford it."

Instead of arguing, she took a bite of her sandwich, because Liam was going to do exactly what he wanted, anyway.

In the weeks that followed, somewhere off in the periphery, she knew that Liam had talked to a mortgage broker and that he'd asked the Realtor to write up an offer. She had run the numbers herself and, technically, they could afford the payment. But it would strain their budget, and the payment was not something Layla could carry on her own if it ever came to that. Soon, paperwork would be forthcoming, and just the thought of the battle that would likely ensue if she were to draw her line in the sand made Layla's temples throb.

Liam came to the dinner table a few nights later looking like someone had taken the wind out of his sails. "What's wrong?" Layla asked.

"Nothing," he said. They ate in silence for a few minutes and then he said, "The mortgage company wants us to put more money down. Twenty grand more."

Layla knew exactly how much they had in their savings account, and forty-two hundred wasn't going to cut it. "I'm sorry," she said, although it certainly wasn't her fault.

He looked so utterly forlorn that Layla could feel his pain. "Now would be a good time to tell me about that winning lottery ticket you were waiting to surprise me with." He mustered a sad smile despite the crushing defeat he wasn't at all accustomed to.

She thought of the yearly monetary gifts she received from her parents and how hard they'd worked their entire lives as she looked down at her plate instead of at Liam. "No lottery ticket," she said, and the issue of whether they could afford the house suddenly evaporated, leaving Layla feeling as light as Liam was heavy.

And then a week later the universe rubbed salt in his wound and Liam lost his job.

A company merged with the one Liam worked for, and in the space of twenty-four hours he found himself out on his ass along with ten other sales reps. Liam had become a pro at job-hopping for a better opportunity, but this was the first time he'd been on the other side of it, and he ranted endlessly about the horrible company that had had the audacity to let him go.

Layla took the news in stride. This was why she never stopped giving those music lessons. This was why she would never leave her job. This was exactly why she didn't want to buy that big beautiful house.

Liam spent the first few days of his unemployment moping around the house in his bathrobe with his coffee cup in the morning and a glass of whiskey in the evening. He locked himself in the spare bedroom that they used for his home office, and Layla could hear him on the phone talking to headhunters. Commiserating with his former coworkers.

Some couples had another baby. Some made a career change that buoyed the mood of the household and thus, the whole family. Some bought a vacation property where they could relax and tell themselves how good it would be for the relationship. "This was all we needed," they'd tell themselves when they were back on solid ground again.

Liam always found a new job, one that came with enough money to get them out of whatever financial mess he'd apparently gotten them into. Layla would feel relieved because the problem she had no idea how to keep solving would be solved by Liam instead, which only seemed fair since he was the one who'd gotten them into the mess in the first place.

In this case, after three weeks of grueling interviews, Liam landed his highest-paying job yet, leveling up to the role of regional sales manager. It was a much better job than the one he'd had — with a much higher salary — and would you believe it, it came with a sign-on bonus, too. One that was more than enough to appease the mortgage company for the down payment on the new house.

"We're going to be so happy in that house, Layla," he said that night when they went out to dinner to celebrate. He'd ditched the bathrobe and he strutted into that restaurant dressed to the nines and holding Layla's hand like a man who was on top of the world.

There was nothing else they could buy.

Maybe, now, Liam would finally be happy.

"Once we get moved in and settled, maybe you can go off the pill. You said you were going to, but I saw them in the bathroom the other day."

That was true. She had told him she would stop taking them soon, but she'd kept on filling the prescription anyway. She was almost thirty-five and the babies would have to be closer together than the three years she'd originally envisioned between them, and that was only if she could replace some of her current indifference with the love she had once felt for Liam.

"I really want to have a family," he said. So, maybe there was still something Liam wanted after all.

Layla wanted one, too, but she would not bring a baby into a home that wasn't happy.

They could go to counseling.

They could have a date night every Saturday, no excuses.

She could take up golf.

Maybe if things improved, Layla would feel secure enough to start the family Liam so desperately wanted.

Things will get better, she thought. *Stay positive,* she told herself. But red flags had a way of looking pink when you viewed them through rose-colored glasses.

CHAPTER 43

JOSH

Josh and Layla went out to dinner and then took Norton for a long walk. Dirty melting snow covered the sidewalk and speckled the dog's white fur as he splashed through the puddles, necessitating a bath when they returned to Josh's place. Layla helped wrestle him into a bathtub filled with warm water as Norton flailed about, shaking and dodging their hands as the water turned gray.

"I'm taking Friday off," Layla said. Norton shook for a good ten seconds after the final rinsing, drenching them both. "I'm going to the Social Security office to fill out the paperwork to take back my name."

"Sounds like Friday's a big day for you." Josh envied how much further along Layla was in tying up the loose ends of her divorce. Sometimes he felt he was still stuck in the starting blocks and sometimes it shocked him that he and Kimmy each had their own place, their own routine. Would Kimmy change her name, or would she keep it because of Sasha? It didn't matter at this point, because until they signed the damn papers, neither of them would be moving forward on anything. Josh threw a towel over Norton and rubbed him vigorously, and when he escaped, the dog all but mowed Layla down in his haste to get out of the bathroom and away from them. Josh helped her up and now they were both as wet as the dog. "Want to meet for lunch after you're done at the Social Security office? I'm finishing up a job in the morning and I haven't scheduled anything for the afternoon."

"Definitely," she said.

He reached over and peeled her out of her shirt. Her lacy bra was wet, too, so that clearly needed to go. "Guess where I'm taking you right now?" Josh asked, taking off his own soaked T-shirt.

She looked sexy as hell when she said, "Straight into a warm shower and then your equally warm bed, I would hope."

In response, he reached over and turned on the shower and as they waited for the water to heat up, he took off the rest of her clothes. She reached for the button on his jeans and popped it open. She lowered his zipper with so much enthusiasm that — if Josh had been a younger man — it might have caused him to finish a bit prematurely because the feeling of being desired was like a drug he would never get tired of. He wanted to be with a woman who wasn't going through the motions like it was a chore she had to complete before she was able to do what she really wanted. Josh had once said to Kimmy, "I'd rather you just shoot me down before anything gets started. That way I won't be under the illusion that it's something you wanted to do. I can tell when your heart's not in it."

Stop thinking about Kimmy.

Once he and Layla stepped under the spray and he'd run his soapy hands over every inch of her, he wasn't doing much thinking at all. After the shower and the sex, as Josh and Layla cuddled in his bed, their limbs intertwined and her head on his chest, he twirled his fingers in her hair and pulled her closer. She let out a soft murmur and pressed her lips to his skin.

"Why did you stay with him for so long?" Josh asked. There wasn't much he didn't know about Layla's past by then, and she'd told him what Liam had done to finally send her out the door for good. But even before

374

that, she'd put up with a lot, and there hadn't been any children to consider.

"I struggled with the answer to that question for years," she said. "Stubborn pride? A reluctance to admit that maybe I shouldn't have married him in the first place? Our relationship wasn't perfect, but I thought perfection in any relationship was an unattainable and unrealistic goal. It's easier to leave a train wreck than it is to leave a relationship that's not really working but still has enough of the good things to sustain it. I thought he would change. If I'm being honest, I had a lot of time invested by then and I thought I could be the one to change him. Turns out I was wrong about that."

"When I got married at eighteen, I didn't ever want things to change. I couldn't fathom that they might, or that I would want them to. Or that she would. I thought all marriages had rough patches and I was determined to stick them out. And yet you and I both reached the same outcome, so who really knows anymore about anything."

"Those are some wise words," Layla said. "Who really knows anything?"

Disney World was not at all what he'd envisioned when he'd told Kimmy he wanted them to get away, but for a family vacation it was a great call. Sasha was the perfect age to enjoy the parks, and they suspected she liked the resort's swimming pool even more than she did the rides.

Josh splurged on a suite when he booked the trip so that he and Kimmy could at least try and have some privacy. They even had their own secluded balcony. It might not have been the romantic reset he'd envisioned, but they could make it work. They were on vacation, after all, and it had been a while since they'd taken a break from their jobs to enjoy their daughter.

On their second night, Josh called room service while Kimmy supervised Sasha's bath. He ordered a couple of fancy mocktails. Added an appetizer sampler and a piece of cheesecake.

"I ordered a few things from room service. I thought we could sit out on the balcony for a while, just the two of us."

"Sure. I'll read Sasha her books and put her to bed."

"I can do it. You did the bath."

"It's okay. I don't mind."

Josh kept his expression blank. Maybe she'd prove him wrong. They were on vacation, after all. "Okay."

But he wasn't wrong.

Because after the room-service waiter arrived with their drinks and the food and Josh waited patiently on the balcony for Kimmy to join him, he already knew what he'd see when he went inside and poked his head into Sasha's room. It was just as he'd suspected: Both of his girls were fast asleep. One because she was exhausted and the other because she'd rather do anything than spend time with her husband alone.

He returned to the balcony and took a big gulp from one of the mocktails, wishing he'd ordered a beer instead. The appetizers and dessert no longer held any allure. He spent a lot of time on the balcony that night, lost in his own thoughts, before finally going to bed alone.

He'd promised himself that he wouldn't say anything in the morning, but he did. With a flick of her eyes, Kimmy noticed the room-service tray with its congealing food and didn't acknowledge it, which hurt more than her failure to appear the night before.

"I thought you were going to join me," he said.

"We walked a lot and I was tired. Weren't you?"

"I'll never be too tired to spend time with you."

"I thought this was a family vacation."

"It is. I'm on vacation with my daughter and my wife. Or maybe 'roommate' is a better word."

"What's that supposed to mean?"

"It means exactly what it sounds like. If there's another word that describes literally turning your back on your spouse every night and wrapping yourself in seven layers of blankets because God forbid, he tries to touch you, then it means whatever that word is."

"I don't turn my back on you every night."

"Okay, Kimmy."

"Is this really what you want to do right now?"

"Discuss our lack of intimacy with my wife? Yeah, maybe. Because who knows if you'll ever hear what I'm saying?"

"Stop fighting," Sasha cried from the doorway. She was wearing her swimsuit and her Mickey ears. At that moment, Disney World was not the happiest place on earth for any of them.

They stopped immediately, ashamed because they were usually so much better at hiding their marital discord.

Or so they thought.

CHAPTER 44

LAYLA

Layla slept in the morning of her day off.
The sun had already risen, but that was a
bit of a misnomer, because when she pad-
ded out to the kitchen in her robe and slippers, there was no sunlight to be seen. The
day was starting out dark and dreary, but
she didn't really mind. She brewed a pot of
coffee and settled on the couch with a
steaming mug and her journal.

She'd started adding things she was grateful for when she wrote in her journal. That
morning, she wrote down that she was
grateful for a rare day off during the week.
She was grateful for Tonya, who had helped
her get through the last year. She was grateful for the downloads of "Thankful" which
had passed two hundred thousand, a number that blew her mind and was generating
a measurable income. She was grateful that
she and Josh had found each other and for

the common ground they shared.

And last, but certainly not least, she was grateful to her parents for giving her those yearly gifts and the ability to land on her feet after walking out the door the night she left Liam.

A month after Layla and Liam moved into their new house, a flyer appeared in their mailbox inviting them to a mixer for new residents interested in learning more about the development's members-only country club.

"Where did that flyer go?" Liam asked a few days later.

"I threw it out," Layla said. "You already have golfing privileges. Why would we join the club?"

"Because a social membership would give us more amenities. There's a pool and a restaurant. It's a great way to get to know people."

"I thought you always said you weren't interested in joining a country club. You didn't want to be tied down."

"I mean, we're pretty tied down already. We live on a golf course now."

"I know," Layla said. "A ball hit the living room window the other day and scared the crap out of me." It had only happened once since they'd moved in, but she was shocked that the ball hadn't broken the glass. "You should have seen me jump. No wonder the Realtor didn't answer my question about that."

"I think it might be something we'll just have to get used to. So, what do you think? Should we go to the mixer? Just pop in for a few minutes and if we hate it, we can bail?"

Layla had no desire to join the country club. The swimming pool wasn't a huge draw, because her skin burned so easily, and she always found herself alone in the shade wearing a huge hat while everyone else splashed in the water or sprawled out on their chaise longues. But even if she did want to join, the social membership and its high monthly fee were simply out of their reach.

"We can't afford it," she said. As she'd predicted, the new house had strained their budget. There were times their checking account balance had dropped below a comfortable threshold, but the house payment — and their other bills — never went unpaid. Every few months, Liam would swoop in with a big commission and build their bank balances back up again. But there was always something new that he wanted, and what if there was a day in their future when he couldn't swoop in? Layla couldn't sleep sometimes when she thought about how they were one medical disaster or long stretch of unemployment away from total financial ruin. None of this bothered Liam. His philosophy was that you had to have the biggest, the best, of everything. He wanted to enjoy life in the present with little regard for what might be coming down the line. They were living the dream. Beautiful home, nice cars, and a country club membership if Layla would just get on board.

"I know we can't," he conceded. "Not right now, anyway. But the mixer is totally free, and you might hit it off with someone who lives in the neighborhood. Maybe they have a book club you can join."

A book club might be nice. Maybe they'd meet some new couples she and Liam could get together with for a barbecue in the warm months or a game of cards during the endless Minnesota winters. Honestly, they could use some more friends. Make a fresh start, socially speaking.

"I guess it wouldn't hurt to pop in," Layla said. "I think the flyer said it started at six thirty."

The term "mixer" was a bit misleading; to Layla, it looked like a full-blown event. There were waiters passing trays of hors d'oeuvres and signature cocktails. There would obviously be a band, because there were a drum kit and a couple of guitars on a stage, lacking only the musicians who would be playing them at some point. Looking at the stage and the instruments filled Layla with the kind of wistful longing she had learned to tamp down.

The men were all wearing jackets, and the women were in dresses or tight, formfitting pants and tops with plunging necklines. Layla was happy she'd worn a pair of heels with her skinny jeans, camisole, and blazer, and had taken the time to give herself a blowout in lieu of her usual ponytail. She was even wearing lipstick, and Liam had commented on how nice she looked when she walked into the kitchen.

She had just accepted one of the signature cocktails — something purple that smelled delicious — when she turned back around and came face-to-face with Suzanne.

"Layla! Hi," Suzanne shouted as she threw her arms around Layla. "I was hoping I'd see you here."

Confused, Layla hugged Suzanne back and shook her husband's hand when the introduction was made. Liam didn't seem surprised to run into Suzanne, if the relaxed expression on his face was any indication.

"Do you live in this neighborhood?" Layla said.

"Yes. I assumed you would know that. I post about it all the time."

For several years after their wedding, neither Liam nor Layla had seen much of Suzanne around town, and Layla thought maybe she'd moved away. She popped back up again when everyone Layla had ever known decided to get on Facebook, including her and Liam. Liam had accepted Suzanne's friend request; Layla had not.

"Why did you accept her friend request?" Layla asked when Liam mentioned it.

"I didn't see any reason not to. It's not a big deal," he said.

Suzanne kept sending Layla friend requests and badgering Liam about it until Layla finally accepted and then promptly scrolled past the endless photos of her children and husband as Suzanne shared every carefully curated second of their lives.

The matching, color-coordinated outfits.

The holiday photo shoots that took place in the library of Suzanne's home, all of them decked out in orange and black for Halloween and an explosion of tartan plaid and white snowflakes for the winter holidays.

The red of Valentine's Day and the head-to-toe green for St. Patrick's Day rolled right into the pastels of Easter.

Layla hid Suzanne so she didn't have to see the posts at all. But sometimes an interaction between Suzanne and Liam — a comment, a shared funny meme — would make its way onto Layla's timeline and her intuition would give her a little nudge. A little warning. *Maybe you should pay attention to this,* it said.

And now Liam had moved them right into Suzanne's neighborhood. Layla might not have known she lived there, but Liam sure did. It was a large residential development, so unless Suzanne lived on their street — and Layla didn't think she did, because she and Liam had met most of their closest neighbors, at least in passing — the chances were good that Layla wouldn't run into Suzanne unless she wanted to. If she confronted Liam about it, he could argue that he wasn't hiding anything about who lived in the neighborhood from Layla. It was all right there in Suzanne's Facebook posts.

Layla received her second shock of the evening when she ran into Rick, Storm Warning's former bass guitarist, on her way back from the bathroom. "Layla!" he shouted, throwing his arms around her and giving her a big hug.

"Oh, my God. Are you playing tonight?"

"Yep. Formed a new band a couple years ago. We're building a pretty steady following on the country-club and private-event circuit."

"Wow. I must really be out of the loop. I didn't know."

"You should sit in with us tonight."

"Thanks, but I'm here with my husband. We moved into the neighborhood a few months ago and just popped by to check it out."

"Feel free to join us onstage if you change your mind. I better go. We're going on soon. Man, it's great to see you again, Layla. Reminds me of old times," he said.

"You too."

Once the band started playing, Layla took it all in. She had told Liam about running into Rick as soon as she returned from the bathroom. "Cool. I hope they play some of my favorites," he said.

They did.

The set list wasn't exactly the same and they'd added a lot of current songs, but when they played the songs they used to play at Connie's, Layla closed her eyes, transported, remembering how she felt back then and longing to experience it once again.

She didn't say much on the way home. Liam had had too much to drink, so he slumped against the passenger-side window as she drove along the darkened streets of their new neighborhood. "The country club membership would practically pay for itself," Liam said. "Do you know how many sales are made over drinks in the dining room?"

"We can't afford it," she said, and her tone

was firm. No matter how much fun she'd had, the numbers didn't lie, and if she didn't shut this down right now, his desire to join would only grow. The country club would become the new shiny toy Liam would want.

"I think we can," Liam said, and the steel in his tone matched hers.

Neither of them said anything during the rest of the short drive. But Liam brought it up again when they were getting ready for bed. "You can't tell me you didn't have a great time tonight," he said. His tone was much sweeter now.

"I did have a great time," she said as she stepped into her pajama pants and pulled a T-shirt over her head. "And now I'm tired and I want to go to bed." She didn't have the energy to argue with a man who made his living talking people into buying whatever he was selling.

"I think we should consider it."

"No, we absolutely shouldn't."

"I know what this is about. This is because of Suzanne," he said.

"I don't give a shit about Suzanne. In fact, I give so few shits about Suzanne, she's not even a factor in this equation. We can't afford it. It's too much money and I'm not going to lose sleep worrying about how we're going to pay for it. I can't handle it anymore."

"This is not about what you can handle, Layla. I don't know why you always have to make it about you."

"I'm not trying to make this about me." She had bypassed staying calm and had gone straight to yelling, and the top of her head felt like it was about to explode. "You say that every time we hit a rough patch or a really rough patch or a patch where I didn't fucking know how we were going to pay our bills. Every single time I've gotten upset, you say, 'Layla, this is not about you.' But if someone's actions affect you and those actions send you into a panicked state of mind, then yes, it is about me. I am so goddamn sick and tired of keeping this boat steady. This boat," she said, waving her arms around to include him and her and the room they were standing in of the house they couldn't really afford. "I go to work all day and then I teach kids at night because somebody has to keep this boat afloat. And once I get it there, I don't need you coming along and rocking it. You drag me along behind you and all I'm trying to do is find some sort of footing. You love chasing the next big commission. You get higher than a kite from it. But you know what, I used to get high chasing what I loved, too. But I had to give that up."

"Yes, I know, because you haven't ever

stopped talking about that. Poor Layla," he said. "She wanted to be a rock star and Liam took it away from her. But did you really think you were going to be a rock star, Layla?" The look on his face said that he sure hadn't and that she'd been a fool to think she could.

It was odd how much time you spent getting to know someone at the beginning of a relationship. The corny conversations when you desperately wanted to know their favorite color, favorite meal, middle name. But you learned a lot more about a person at a relationship's demise than you ever knew about them at its inception, including how badly they could wound you with their words.

"It was never about being a rock star, you asshole. It was always about doing something I loved that I wasn't ready to stop doing yet."

Liam slept on the couch that night, and the next morning, when Layla woke up in their bed all by herself, she started to think about what she wanted out of life. What she might do. The thoughts seeped in like smoke under the door. *What if I left? What if I just said, "I'm done"?*

Would it blindside Liam? What about her friends and family? Would they be shocked? Did she even care?

A few months back, Layla had taken out a

piece of paper and written all of Liam's good qualities on one side and his bad qualities on the other. Liam had lots of good qualities that she couldn't ignore. He was kind, generous, affectionate, and a good listener. He was committed. But he was also horrible with their finances and he was never happy with what he had. And being a good listener didn't really matter when he heard what Layla said but then did whatever he wanted anyway.

Layla did not relish the thought of blowing up her life. But she told herself it would probably feel like those moments right before you threw up or ripped off a Band-Aid that had really adhered itself to your skin: not pleasant, but once it was over, you felt so much better that you wondered why you waited so long for the relief.

It was a full day after Liam spent the night on the couch before they started talking to each other again. "I heated up some of that leftover pasta for lunch and made you a plate," he said.

"Thanks." And then, a little later that afternoon, Layla said, "I picked up the dry cleaning. Your suits are in the closet."

Liam smiled at her. "Thanks."

She had known for a long time that she and Liam needed marriage counseling. Maybe she could ask around and get a recommendation. They could talk it out with an impartial third party so that Layla wouldn't have to feel like the bad guy. Maybe Liam would listen. She would listen, too.

They might have temporarily mended fences, but Layla did not trust that Liam hadn't used their credit card to put down a deposit on that country club membership anyway, and she'd been checking the account daily. If her laptop battery hadn't died and she hadn't grabbed Liam's iPad instead, Layla would never have seen the Facebook chat window he forgot to close. The one that went back almost eighteen months and was filled with his and Suzanne's frequent declarations of undying love.

When Liam came home from work that night, she handed it to him.

He didn't deny anything.

He didn't fight for her.

He almost seemed relieved.

Layla went into the bedroom and when she came out, she was rolling a suitcase behind her. "I'm done, and I'm leaving you."

Layla's marriage to Liam reminded her a lot of that frog analogy, the one where the frog is sitting in a pot of water, but the temperature increases so slowly it doesn't realize it's being boiled alive. By the time Layla pulled her head out of her ass, the water she'd been sitting in for years was boiling but good.

She stood up and put her coffee cup in the sink. The last thing she wanted to do on such a cold and miserable day was venture out and then stand in line at the Social Security office. But after today's errand, Layla Hilding-Cook would once again be known simply as Layla Hilding. She was already anticipating the satisfaction she would feel when she returned home and drew a heavy black line through the item on her to-do list. It would be like a rebirth of sorts, the next season of her life.

A better season.

Layla held her umbrella tight as she walked along the sidewalk to the front door of the Social Security office, the rain looking more like sleet as it hit the ground with a plop. The line was every bit as long as she'd assumed it would be, but as she stood waiting her turn, she smiled and thought about how one short year could make such a difference. Maybe she was meant to savor the recollection of the past and of how far she'd come because it made what was about to unfold so much sweeter.

When it was finally her turn, she handed over the necessary documents and walked back out the door ten minutes later. Her phone pinged with a text from Josh: Ready for lunch?

Yes, starving!
See you soon. Xo

Ready for lunch, yes, but also the rest of her life.

CHAPTER 45

LAYLA

Layla pulled the collar of her coat tighter around her neck. She and Tonya stomped their feet to keep the blood flowing, their breath coming out in icy puffs as they watched the cars in the drop-off line inch forward. "Spring must be canceled this year," Layla said. "I think we're stuck in second winter."

"And we still have third winter to look forward to," Tonya said. "In April."

"Brian and I have plenty to keep us busy inside." It was hard to miss the enthusiasm in Layla's voice as she gave Tonya the latest rundown on the marketing efforts they had set in motion in order to capitalize on their newfound popularity. Facebook, Instagram, and YouTube, live videos, tweets! Everything was happening so fast, and sometimes it felt like all she and Brian could do was hang on and enjoy the ride. The texts between them were fast and furious as they exchanged information and ideas.

Josh and Sasha arrived, and Josh's eyes lingered on Layla as they exchanged a knowing smile. Their lunch on Friday had turned into spending the weekend together, which turned into Josh not going back to his own house until late Sunday evening. Layla smiled when she thought about the time they'd spent together and the things they'd done.

Maybe she wasn't so cold anymore.

She thought about Thursday, when Sasha would go back to Kimberly's and she and Josh could be together again. The anticipation of it felt almost as intoxicating as the reality, and if she could bottle that feeling and sell it to others, she'd be a millionaire.

"Looks like things are humming along with Josh," Tonya said after Josh and Sasha had made their way into the building. "That look he gave you was *smoldering.*"

"You know that feeling when things are still pretty new, but you can tell you're on the brink of taking it to the next level?"

"I do," Tonya said.

"That's how it feels with Josh right now." Layla floated through her days and nights, high on the thought of Josh and the budding realization that she was falling in love with him and that it seemed like he might feel the same way. It was the polar opposite of how stressed-out and unhappy she'd been at the end of her relationship with Liam, when her life had felt like a long hard slog through quicksand. This was so much better in a million different ways. A year ago, if someone had told Layla that in twelve short months she would be this happy, she wouldn't have believed them.

Layla squinted at the parking lot. The woman hurrying toward them looked a lot like Kimberly. As she drew closer, Layla could see that it was definitely Josh's soon-to-be-ex-wife. The strap of a child's tote bag hung from her arm, and she carried a plastic container of some sort in her hands.

"Hi," Kimberly said when she reached them. "Did Sasha already go in? She wanted to bring her American Girl doll to school for show-and-tell and thought she had it at her dad's. I just missed them at the house."

"They've already gone in, but I'll make sure she gets it," Layla said.

Kimberly handed her the tote, but when Layla kept her hand out for the container, Kimberly held on to it. "Oh, that's not for Sasha." She was looking over Layla's shoulder toward the entrance of the school building, and she must have spotted Josh on his way out, because she raised her hand and gave a little wave.

"Hey," Layla heard him say as he came up behind them. "Did Sasha forget something?"

"She called me from your phone when you were in the shower because she wanted to bring her American Girl doll to school. She thought it was at your house."

"I'm sorry, I didn't know she called you. She didn't say anything to me. I would have waited, or we could have swung by and picked it up."

"It was no trouble," Kimberly said. She paused, looking at Josh. "Did you do something different to your hair?"

"Nope."

"Oh, it looks different. Not different bad," she said quickly. "It looks nice." She handed the plastic container to Josh. "Here. I made those blondies you like. The recipe makes so many, and I thought you might want to have some at your house."

"Oh," he said, sounding surprised but also like he was touched by the gesture. Layla remembered that Josh said Kimberly had taken up baking.

"They're the ones with the white chocolate and the peanut butter chips," she said.

"With the sea salt on top?"

"Yep. I used extra salt like I did that one time when you said they were really good."

"Well, thanks."

"It was nothing."

Josh turned to Layla and Tonya. "Have a nice day."

"You too," they said, and Josh headed toward the parking lot, Kimberly falling in beside him. Layla watched as they walked side by side, chatting the whole way.

"Well," Layla said under her breath.

"Yeah," Tonya said.

At lunchtime, when Layla was heating her leftovers up in the microwave, Tonya waited with her, spooning yogurt out of the container as she leaned up against the counter. "I don't know how much you should read into that," Tonya said.

"I'm trying not to." But her thoughts had returned to it no matter how hard she'd tried to put it out of her mind.

"Who wanted the divorce, do you know?"

"He said he was waiting on her to file the paperwork, so I'd always assumed she was the one who asked for the divorce. They got married right out of high school. Josh said they'd grown in different directions and weren't the same people anymore."

Layla thought she knew about Josh's split

from Kimberly. Except that when she really thought about it, the way she had been all morning, she realized that it was a completely different scenario from her separation from Liam, which had been frustrating, heated, and no-doubt-about-it final.

Much different.

Josh and Kimberly had spent half of their lives together, and their separation seemed amicable, friendly. The type of split that still fostered feelings of kindness and not the urge to throw something heavy at your spouse's head during the heat of an argument that had gone completely off the rails. And they had a child, so they would always be in each other's lives.

"Maybe she's changed her mind," Layla said. "Maybe he was the one who fought for them to stay together, and her coming around now with her blondies and compliments about his hair opens the door to reconciliation. A while back, Sasha announced in class that her parents were getting back together. I didn't put too much stock in it, but I asked Josh about it and he told me there wasn't any truth in it." When Josh was with Layla, he certainly didn't act like a guy who wanted to patch things up with his ex-wife.

"He's not legally divorced, which was

something I hadn't worried about until now," Layla said as the microwave dinged. "Now I'm getting a front-row seat to what his life must have looked like with her when it was good."

"What are you going to do?"

"I'm going to talk to him like a mature adult and admit that maybe I've gotten a little ahead of myself. Cool things down at least until the divorce is final. My gut says he's a good guy, but I've been wrong before and there's no reason to hurry. If it's right, it will still be there." Layla wanted it to work out, but if she'd learned one thing from her relationship with Liam, it was that people didn't always tell you what they were thinking.

And Kimberly hadn't looked like someone who was building a custody case against her soon-to-be-ex-husband; she looked like someone who wished she had him back.

CHAPTER 46

LAYLA

Layla sat on her thoughts for a couple of days, wishing she could convince herself that what she'd seen had been no big deal and didn't warrant a discussion with Josh. However, her gut would have no part of that, and when he arrived with Norton on Thursday night, right after he kissed her, the first thing she said was "Can I talk to you about something?"

"Sure. What is it?"

She hesitated, and the smile faded from his face. Now he looked a little worried. "I'm falling for you," she said. "Hard."

His smile returned. "I feel the same way."

"But I think we need to step back for a bit. You're not legally divorced yet and Liam is trying to make things difficult for me. When I saw you with Kimberly at school the other day, it really hit home that we've

401

got some loose ends that need to be tied up."

He didn't say anything right away, but then he looked into her eyes. "Is that what you want?"

No. "I can't call you mine if you still belong to someone else," she said.

"I don't belong to her," he said. "But I understand and I'm okay with waiting until the papers are signed, especially if Kimmy tried to use my relationship with you as a reason to build a custody case. Not that she knows about us."

"But that's part of it. You shouldn't have to worry about that, and you wouldn't have to if you were divorced. I feel like we're hiding something from her, and I don't like that feeling."

"I don't like it, either."

"I'm not going anywhere," she said. She would be right there waiting, and if he didn't return to her, she would always remember him fondly. Maybe he *was* meant to be her rebound, her buffer between Liam and whoever came next. And maybe she was meant to be his.

Or maybe they would find their way back to each other because there was no one else they'd rather be with.

"How about one more night?" Josh said.

"We'll do everything we planned and then tomorrow we'll go our separate ways until the dust settles."

She smiled. "Absolutely." Josh wasn't a drug she couldn't give up. She was thirty-five years old, and the practical, cautious side of her had made the decision to put their relationship on the back burner for a while, and it was the right decision. But it soothed some of the pain when she realized he wouldn't be walking out the door quite yet.

"I've already taken you-know-who on a W-A-L-K, but how about going for one with me?"

"Sure," she said.

Outside, he reached for her hand. She wished she could throw caution to the wind and forget about everything but how good it felt to walk with her hand held tightly in his, but she couldn't.

He didn't try to talk her out of it, not that she'd expected him to, and in the silence, she could almost hear the wheels turning in both their heads.

"It's weird," she said. "Life."

"It is."

"I've been thinking a lot about where I was ten years ago and how I'm in a totally different place than what I'd imagined."

He let out a short laugh. "I can relate but double that to twenty."

"Maybe what's coming is better than we imagined," she said.

"I hope so."

They walked for a long time, and when they got back to Layla's he took her hand again and led her to the bedroom. She was glad they'd decided on one last night together. And the next morning, when he slipped from her bed after placing a kiss on her temple, only time would reveal if there would be more.

CHAPTER 47

JOSH

To an outsider, the morning drop-off looked the same: He and Sasha would walk from the parking lot to the sidewalk and then to where Layla and Tonya stood next to the curb. They still exchanged good-mornings, and then they'd walk into the building. Sometimes, Sasha would have news to share with Layla or Tonya, and Josh would wait patiently. He still smiled at Layla and she smiled back, but the interaction only served to highlight how much he missed seeing her, talking to her, every day. On his way out, he told Layla and Tonya to have a nice day and then he walked to his truck.

They were two weeks into their cooling-off period by then, and while Josh knew that Layla had been right to ask him to wait, it didn't make their time apart any easier. He wasn't pining for her like some lovesick teenager, but he felt her absence in the lack of communication. He felt it when he reached for his phone to call and say good night after Sasha was in bed and it was just him and Norton sitting on the couch. Josh felt like he was in a state of arrested development. He knew how to be an impulsive eighteen-year-old who married the first woman he fell in love with and then a young adult who had to get his shit together and become a good husband. Now he was a single dad in his late thirties who was starting over, and he felt like a tourist in a strange land trying to figure out how all the pieces fit together.

Sometimes he thought the break was unnecessary because he had feelings for Layla, strong feelings, and he wasn't interested in anyone but her. But he knew he had things he still needed to do. Kimmy had finally received the divorce paperwork and she'd asked Josh to come over and sign everything, so now he'd be one step closer to putting this chapter of his life to rest. He hadn't realized until Layla asked if they could take a step back how much he needed the closure himself.

Josh rang the buzzer to Kimmy's condo around ten thirty. She'd told Josh she had taken the day off, but when she opened the

406

door, she looked far more put-together than someone who planned on relaxing for the day. She'd done her hair and makeup, and instead of sweats she was dressed in jeans and boots and a low-cut sweater. He caught a whiff of the perfume she'd been wearing for the last ten years, which he could identify on anyone who came close enough for him to smell it.

"Hey," he said as he shook the rain from his hair.

"Come in," she said. "I made coffee. Would you like a cup?"

"Sure. Thanks."

She brought him the coffee and a slice of banana bread that still had steam wafting from it. "I felt like baking. This weather is so dreary," she said.

"Smells good." He took a big bite. "Tastes good too."

Kimberly sat down across from him with her own coffee and banana bread, and they ate in silence. When Josh was finished, he said, "Do you have the papers? I can sign them and get out of your hair. I'm sure you've got something more fun planned for your day off."

She stood up and took their plates to the sink, and that was when Josh's anxiety over their custody arrangement creeped back in.

"Kimmy?" he said.

She turned around, and Josh could see that her eyes were filled with tears. "I don't have them because I haven't filed yet."

"Why not? I won't give up a single minute of my time with Sasha. I want you to know that." He said it calmly, but inside his heart was pounding.

"It's not about Sasha," she cried as the tears ran down her face.

He didn't have to ask her what it was about, because suddenly he knew.

He'd spent half his life with her. He knew everything there was to know about her, and the only thing he didn't know was why it had taken him so long to clue into what was causing the delay. His anxiety and fear over losing time with his daughter had overshadowed any other concerns.

Kimmy was crying louder now. Because she was upset, his first instinct was to comfort her the way he'd been comforting her since they were eighteen, but then two thoughts popped into his head. The first was that comforting Kimmy was no longer his responsibility, and the second was that it was hard to comfort the person who'd informed him on an otherwise normal Tuesday evening that their marriage was over and that she wanted a divorce.

He'd come home from work and found Kimmy in the living room staring off into space. The TV wasn't on. There was no music playing. Her face wasn't buried in her phone, and that should have been the first indication that something was up.

"Where's Sasha?" he asked.

"She's at your mom's baking cookies with the cousins."

"Nice," he said, because that was something his mom did often — invite all the grand-children over to make a giant mess of her kitchen and then return them jacked up on sugar but bearing a plate of sweet treats that Josh would help himself to.

Kimmy had a pained look on her face, and she got up from the couch and paced the length of the room, turning on her heel, back and forth.

"What's up with you?" he asked.

"Don't you want things?"

What in the hell kind of question was that? "Like what?" he asked.

"I don't know. Different experiences. More life choices."

"You're going to have to be more specific," he said. "You had plenty of choices. We both did. You made yours and I made mine and there were plenty that we made together."

"I mean like seeing what's out there. When I

went to college it made me wonder about other things I might have missed."

"What exactly are you looking for out there?" She was starting to piss him off, because it almost sounded like she blamed Josh and their marriage for limiting those choices.

"I don't know," she cried. Now, in addition to the pacing, there was hand wringing.

"Are you cheating on me?" That would certainly explain why they never had sex anymore.

"No!"

"Then what is this really about?"

"I don't know if I want to be tied down anymore."

"Tied down as in married to me?" he asked. She didn't answer and she wouldn't look at him. "Wow, Kimmy. I'm sorry this marriage is such a hardship for you." Hearing the anger in his voice made her cry, which made him even angrier.

"It's not a hardship," she said.

"Sure sounds like it is."

"We were so young," she said.

"Yep," he agreed.

"I've changed. You've changed."

"Yep," he said again. "But what about our daughter? Has she changed? Because she will. This will change her forever." It broke his heart to think of the ways in which Sasha's heart would shatter, and at that moment he understood why couples stayed together for the kids.

She recoiled visibly, because he'd stabbed her right in her heart by mentioning Sasha, and the pain he inflicted felt good, felt justified. She didn't answer him, because what could she say? And what were they supposed to do now? Was he supposed to move out? Was she?

They decided to go to marriage counseling, but after three sessions, Kimmy said she didn't want to go to counseling anymore.

She just wanted to go.

Once again, Kimmy could barely look at Josh. "I want our family back. I want you back. I hate what we've done to Sasha."

"So, now that you regret your decision, we should just give it another go because look what it's doing to our daughter? To you? Have you conveniently forgotten the complete shit show this marriage devolved into over the last couple of years — which our daughter definitely noticed, by the way. Do you think breaking up our family was easy on either of us, because it wasn't easy on you and it wasn't easy on me and it sure as hell wasn't easy on Sasha. Is this what you want her to grow up seeing? Us fighting

411

and then getting our act together and going through periods where we both have to try harder than we've ever tried before to do something that should be, if not effortless because marriage is a lot of fucking work, but at least enjoyable? Because that's the last thing I want."

"It was my fault," Kimmy said. "I was wrong. There was nothing I wanted that I didn't already have at home with you and Sasha."

"You wanted to sow those oats. You wanted to see what was out there. What happened to that?"

She remained silent, because the grass hadn't been greener and they both knew it.

"You'd been holding me at arm's length for a long time and I wasn't happy, either," Josh said. "I hadn't been truly happy in years."

She looked like he'd slapped her across the face. "Why didn't you say anything?"

"I tried to. I tried to talk to you and connect with you and show you I was unhappy and when it didn't work, I gave up for the same reason you are now sitting across from me thinking we could give it another go: I didn't want to break up our family. I love you, Kimmy. I will always love you. We have been together way too long for me not to feel something toward you for the rest of my life. To want what's best for you the way I always have. But now that some time has passed, I realize that I want what's best for me, too. We're young and there's a lot of living left to be done, and it should be done in the happiest, most satisfying way we know how. Sadly, this is something Sasha will carry with her for the rest of her life. But we can't help her adjust and heal if we keep giving her false hope. That's what a reconciliation would be, and it's a reconciliation I don't want. I think you're scared to go it alone, but you shouldn't be. You'll be fine and we will always be linked because of our daughter. We don't have to burn the house down just because we don't all live in it together anymore."

"I'm sorry I wasn't a better wife to you at the end."

"You just outgrew me. And I outgrew you." Kimmy got up and came back to the table with a box of Kleenex. Eventually, her tears subsided, and she took a deep breath.

"I'm going to file the paperwork myself," he said. "I'll make the call today."

"Have you started seeing someone?" she whispered.

"That's not what this is about," he said.

"I know, Josh. I'm asking because you

deserve to have someone who makes you happy."

"I'm not seeing anyone at the moment." The desire never to hurt Kimmy was so deeply ingrained that he would not mention Layla or how far they had already taken things before deciding to spend some time apart. "You're a good mom, Kimmy. I'm proud of everything you've accomplished."

He stood up and hugged her and she squeezed him back. "I need to get going," he said. "You were right. There *is* more out there. Go out and find it."

CHAPTER 48

LAYLA

"How does this work again?" Layla asked. She and Brian were sitting on their make-shift stage in a corner of the guitar shop at a quarter 'til nine on Thursday evening. They had fully immersed themselves in the social media side of things, and Brian had added the links for Facebook and Instagram and Twitter to their shiny new website. They'd scheduled an event, and at nine they would go live and sing "Thankful" for their new fans. Brian had been hyping it online for over a week. Facing them were two laptops on a stack of boxes that Brian adjusted for height.

"I'm setting up Facebook and Instagram to broadcast us simultaneously. We'll sing the song and then we can take questions from our listeners."

"I'm glad you have the technical side figured out, because I'm just a girl with her guitar who's ready to play."

"I just hope people show up," Brian said.

"But we won't be able to see them, right?" Layla said.

"No. We won't be able to see anyone. Is your guy watching? Pretend like you're playing for him."

"Oh. We're not really seeing each other right now."

"Shit. I'm sorry."

"No, it's okay. We didn't break up." But sometimes that was exactly how it felt. Layla would think of something she wanted to tell Josh and would reach for her phone before remembering they weren't doing that anymore, and that it had been her idea. "He wasn't legally divorced yet and I felt like things were getting pretty serious. We're taking a step back."

Brian nodded. "Understandable."

"And he's the first person I've dated since my divorce, and I'm his. And you know that *never* works out. The first person you get together with after a breakup is like a practice relationship, like a job interview for a job you don't really want so you can work out all the kinks before the next one."

"Hmmm," Brian said.

"And also, his wife — because technically they're still married — showed up with

416

some blondies and complimented his hair because I guess their split was amicable and not the disaster mine was. It looked like he's got some loose ends he still needs to tie up, you know?"

"I have no idea what a blondie is, but he seemed really cool."

"It's a brownie but with white chocolate. And he's a great guy. That's not the issue."

"Nothing wrong with making sure he's moved on and ready for something new."

"Exactly."

"But then again, overthinking can really mess up a good thing. Wouldn't you say?"

"I'm sensing that you have an opinion on this. You can give it to me straight," Layla said.

"I agree that he should definitely be divorced but throw out all that other bullshit about practice relationships. This is about faith and what your gut is telling you."

"My gut told me to wait and I listened to it."

"That was actually your fear that did that."

"No, it wasn't."

"It was. And it's understandable. Breakups suck and the last thing you want to do is fall in love and get your heart trampled on again. It's self-preservation. I know all about that. I even wrote a *song* about it."

"You've never been divorced," she said. "It's different."

"True. There are legal issues involved, which is why I agreed that he should be divorced. But let me ask you this? If the ink had dried on that divorce decree six months ago and there was nothing standing in your way, would you still be hesitating? Tell the truth."

"No. I was pretty much all in until she brought him blondies and complimented his hair."

"Forget about the blondies and the comment about his hair. A random woman standing in line next to me at a gas station once told me she liked the way I was dressed, and I still think about it. That was six years ago."

"Wow," Layla said.

"Men are not that complicated. We seldom turn down baked goods and we like it when a woman says something nice to us, especially if that woman is someone we used to care about. It makes us feel less like idiots or that there was something wrong with us. He'll tie up those loose ends and he'll be back."

Layla fiddled with her guitar as Brian gave the laptops a final adjustment. "Okay, we are good to go," he said.

"Brian?"

He sat down next to her and picked up his guitar. "Yeah?"

"I almost asked you out once. It was that night I stopped in right before you closed, and we played together. I thought you were nice and smart and handsome, and we had a lot in common. And then you mentioned your fiancée, so I didn't say anything."

He smiled from ear to ear. "I think we both know I'll be coasting on this until sometime in 2032."

Layla laughed. "As well you should."

At nine, they went live, and Brian addressed the attendees who were typing "hi" and "here" and "can't wait," and he shouted out greetings to them by name.

"Hey, nice to see you tonight, Matthew," he said. "Thanks for coming, Lauren, Darian, Cordelia. We'll give people a few more minutes to join and then Layla and I are going to sing the song that you guys have made more popular than we ever dreamed. We can't thank you enough for your support. You're awesome."

"Hey, Lisa," Layla said. "Hey, Brooke, Julie. Nice to see you, Scott."

"Hey, Grace," Brian said. "Hey, Stacy, Stefani, Amy. So happy you could join us

419

tonight. Leave a comment with your location so we know where you're tuning in from."

Brian was better at this than Layla was, but after she greeted a few more people by name and felt the genuine smile on her face, she relaxed, and it felt more natural. Fun, even. It filled her with warmth to see the support, and it was cool noticing how many people were showing up to watch them sing.

Brian played the opening notes of "Thankful," and she joined in. They played the intro a couple of times, slowly, gearing up. "What do you say, Layla?" Brian asked. "Ready to sing this song?"

"I sure am, Brian," she said, and they launched into it.

They sounded great, and the arrangement they'd decided on lent the song a slightly more intimate feel, which was what Brian said they should shoot for. "It's all about connecting to your audience," he told her. "The barrier between artist and listener is thinner than it's ever been. We can connect in real time. Form actual relationships with our fans."

It was such a strange sensation to speak and play and sing for an invisible audience. Layla knew they were there, watching through their phones, tablets, and computers, because she could see the little hearts and thumbs-up icons that flew across the screens of Brian's laptops. There were more comments now, too.

I love the song
What's next
You guys seem kind of old
Love you guys
Fuck, yeah

"So, we've got a surprise for you tonight," Brian said when the song ended. They'd been sitting on the news for over a week and were bursting to share it. "We've got something new to perform for you now. It's our next single and it'll be available at midnight tonight. Make sure you're following us and add it to your playlists."

They played the new song, Layla once again singing lead. It was called "Come with Me," and it was just as catchy as "Thankful" but slightly different in tone. Brian had looked through all the songs he'd written over the years, and they'd selected it because it was similar to "Thankful" but different enough so that it wouldn't seem like they were copying themselves. Layla thought it was superior to "Thankful" from a song-writing and technical perspective, but Brian would track and analyze the sales data to see if those qualities translated into downloads.

When they finished singing the new song, hearts flew up the screen again and the comments indicated that the song had landed, and they wanted more. Brian ended the livestreams, set his guitar down, and started laughing. "Jesus. We're not that old."

No, but for musicians trying to break in, they were pushing it. Brian was forty-four but had a more youthful appearance. Layla would soon be thirty-six, and she didn't look her age, either. Nor did she care.

"That's what happens when you put yourself out there," Layla said, laughing, too. "The internet will always have an opinion and they will happily share it."

"We sounded good and we can be proud of that. Might pick up a few more listeners if word of mouth continues to shine its light on us."

"Thankful" had popped up on a few more playlists and was gaining even more steam. And now they'd have their first follow-up. See if they could make it rain twice.

"Word of mouth is the best kind of marketing power in existence," she said. Someone telling a friend about a song they loved and convincing them to download it was the kind of organic support you couldn't materialize on your own, but when it happened you'd better harness it for all it was worth, and they intended to.

"So, 'Come with Me' will be available at midnight and I've set up all the links to be published on social media simultaneously."

"Thanks for taking care of all that." Layla was glad that Brian enjoyed the technical side of things, because she had little interest in it. She just wanted to make music.

"No problem."

Lost in her thoughts, she didn't hear what Brian said next. "Layla?"

"Sorry. What did you say?"

"You must have been daydreaming about our potential downloads," he teased.

"Busted," she said.

"I said I'll let you know how we do in the first twenty-four hours."

"Awesome." But she hadn't been thinking about the downloads. What she'd been thinking about was whether Josh had been watching the live video and how he was doing and if he missed her as much as she missed him and if he'd really be back like Brian said he would.

CHAPTER 49

LAYLA

"Will you just *look* at that," Layla said.

"Oh, I am," Tonya said. "It's a beautiful sight."

The cars in the drop-off line were moving forward with precision. Like a well-oiled machine, students stepped out of the vehicles, backpacks in hand, and waved to their parents, who pulled away from the curb, leaving room for the next car. Layla didn't even care that it was the last day of school, which meant they'd be right back to square one in the fall. It was nice seeing it finally come together.

Josh and Sasha arrived, and that was one more thing that had found its groove. It was almost as if they'd never had a relationship outside the one they had in the context of the school setting.

Almost.

Josh and Layla still greeted each other

with a smile, exchanged pleasantries, mentioned the weather. But underneath it all, Layla wanted to know how he was doing. She missed talking to him, walking Norton, cooking side by side. She wanted to ask how things were going with the divorce. How long it might be until he'd tied up those loose ends. But maybe he had. Maybe the cooling-off period had shown him that they'd moved too fast and he was having second thoughts. Had he decided she was his rebound the way Layla wondered if he would be hers?

Two weeks ago, Layla turned thirty-six. She and Tonya and Annie had gone out for happy hour, and the urge to text Josh after one margarita to ask him these things was so strong, she declined a second and went home early.

She and Brian were fully immersed in their budding career, and now that school was ending, Layla would have even more time to devote to it. They were doing live videos at least once a week, and they'd released their third song, a summer anthem called "Stick Shifting," that Brian sang lead on. It was about road-tripping to Colorado in a Jeep with your girl by your side, and it was doing well, but neither follow-up had made it onto a notable playlist or seen download numbers anywhere near as high as "Thankful."

"It's okay," Brian had said. "We're building our audience and it takes time."

They had to constantly grind, keep up with social media, and feed the machine daily. The tweets, the posts. Snapchat, Soundcloud, YouTube, Bandcamp. They'd hired a publicist with some of their royalty money. Her name was Barbie Petersen, and she had all kinds of great ideas for growing their audience, but she had also asked Layla to do some things she wasn't comfortable with, and Layla had pushed back. No, she was not going to pose in her bed wearing a white tank top and holding her guitar with artfully tousled hair. No, she was not going to film a video with Brian in which they would look at each other longingly and pretend how thankful they were to have found each other. Brian had put his foot down on that as well.

Layla was growing weary of looking at the screens of Brian's laptops. She wanted to perform in front of a crowd, hear their shouts, watch them sing along while they listened to the music. She would have thought that two up-and-coming musicians with a growing online fan base would find it easier to book local gigs, but they were finding it every bit as difficult as it had always been. There were so many bands and artists vying for the same opportunities, and they really needed to hire a manager to take some of the booking responsibilities off their shoulders. But neither of them really wanted to hire another person after already hiring Barbie. They were earning a nice supplemental income by then but had agreed to keep their operation as small as possible. Brian and Layla could reach a large audience online, but connecting with fans locally was the same crapshoot it had always been.

In June, one of Brian's local contacts told him about a new, upscale bar looking for musicians. Brian made a call, and thanks to their social media following and the digital calling card they could now present, they were hired on a trial basis. Maybe it would turn into something more, but for now, Layla was happy to throw a guitar strap over her shoulder and look at real human faces. When she wasn't with Brian, rehearsing or playing, she was sitting alone on her deck, guitar and journal by her side. She'd come full circle from where she'd been at this time last year, but she wasn't the same person and she took solace in that. And Josh, well, she'd pressed pause on that relationship, and he hadn't returned. She'd made her peace with the decision and she would be just fine.

Tonight would be the first time she and Brian had played live since they'd filled in for his friend back in March. That was the night Layla and Josh had slept together for the first time, and the memory filled her with such longing that she closed her eyes and indulged in filtering through the scenes of that night like a slide show in her mind: playing for the crowd, Josh talking to her friends, kissing Josh, waking up next to him in the morning.

Now there was no Josh and not enough live performing to feed her soul. Layla's days were filled with writing social media posts and pithy tweets and recording thirty-second Instagram stories and not only did those things not fulfill her, she was starting to struggle with completing them at all. And then she would tell herself how lucky they were, remind herself that she should be *thankful.* Wasn't this all she ever wanted?

At the bar, as they were tuning their instruments and warming up, Brian said, "Did you drink a coffee on the way over? You're bouncing. I don't think I've seen you this energetic in a long time."

It was true. It was almost like she had little springs in her shoes. She vibrated with energy and pent up creativity that she could hardly wait to unleash. "That's pure adrenaline, my friend. No caffeine needed."

"Josh coming tonight?" he asked.

"Haven't heard from him."

Brian opened his mouth, and she braced herself for the inevitable *I'm sorry. I guess I was wrong about him coming back.* But all he said was "You ready?"

"You know I am," she said.

"Then let's do this," he said, and he smiled at Layla and they high-fived and she felt like she was standing on top of a mountain waiting to jump, hoping the crowd would still be there to catch her.

They launched into their opening song, a cover of Carly Simon's "You're So Vain," followed by Fleetwood Mac's "Go Your Own Way." A respectable applause greeted them at the close of every song in their first set, and by the time they were midway through their second, the crowd had spilled onto the dance floor and the palpable energy reached all four corners of the room.

They closed out the second set with "Stick Shifting," which had become one of Layla's favorites even though she sang backup instead of lead. She remembered something she'd said to Josh when she tried to explain how performing made her feel. *Have you ever been driving in your car alone and it's a beautiful day and you're in a really good mood and the sun is shining and you've got the sunroof open and you're on your way to do something that you've been looking forward to? And then a song comes on the radio and it's one of your favorites and you sing along and you don't care how loud you're singing or if the car next to you notices your little concert for one?*

Layla might not have been in a Jeep with the top off, but she felt exactly the way she told Josh that performing made her feel. She couldn't stop smiling and she could have played for days, because every note she played and sang felt like a deposit in her happiness tank.

She downed a bottle of water during their break, itching for it to be over so they could play another set. Tonya and her husband came to say good-bye. "You are on fire," Tonya said. "I wish we could stay, but we told the babysitter we'd be home by ten. Early flight tomorrow morning."

Layla hugged her. "Sorry. I'm a little sweaty. Have a great time on vacation. Call me the minute you're back."

Layla dashed to the bathroom and made

her way back onstage, raring to go. Brian joined her and they ramped things up with "Rolling in the Deep" and "Take It Easy." The songs got faster and louder until they peaked with "Magic Man," and then they slowly brought the vibe back down.

"This is our last song," Brian said. "It's an original song called 'Thankful' and we want you all to know that we're thrilled to see you here tonight. We hope you'll come back and see us again."

Layla smiled at Brian. He gave her a thumbs-up and she flashed the peace sign back at him. She strummed the opening notes, and as she sang the words written by the man who stood beside her, it was as if she were hearing them for the first time. She'd been singing them for months, but she was finally *listening* to them.

I thought we'd have forever
Not an expiration date
The time I'd invested
Now straight down the drain
I wallowed and raged needing someone
 to blame
Hurt and broken I lashed out
Couldn't even say his name
It's hard to let go when you've done all
 the work

431

So much time and effort and none of the
  perks
It's old news
Bad news
Nothing meant to last
Get back in the game
Bring the lessons you learned from the
  pain
They said don't long for what broke you
It's in the rear view
Let go of the old
Make room for the new
I only half listened to their stupid advice
Because everyone knows lightning never
  strikes twice.
Be thankful it ended
It's not what fate intended
Let it crumble
Let it shatter
Years from now it won't matter
Make your peace
Draw your line
Hold firm for next time
He's out there waiting
Go and find him
So I guess the advice they gave me was
  true
Felt that spark again the night I met you
Picked myself up
Started living

And it happened by chance
It's true life's a journey
It's true life's a dance
Onward into the night
The love I found with you is the love that
    was right

As she sang, she heard Liam's voice so clearly in her head it was like he was standing next to her, whispering in her ear. *Did you really think you were going to be a rock star, Layla?*

Yeah, maybe she had.

And maybe she still could. There was nothing standing in her way, nothing to prevent her from pursuing a sky's-the-limit musical career.

But nothing would ever make her feel as good as the way she felt right then, singing for the crowd. And no one ever said she had to be a rock star to keep doing it.

The question wasn't "Who do you love?" It was "*What* do you love?" *What do you really want, Layla?*

She'd been chasing the answer her entire adult life, and there it was right there in front of her, blinking neon, shining even brighter than the lights beaming down on her.

This is what I love.

This is what I want.
This is what makes me happy.

If she'd really wanted to be a rock star, she would have become one. She'd have taken that rep up on his offer and she would have let them mold her in any way they wanted. She would have felt bad about leaving the band behind, but she would have done it anyway. And then, someday, she would have taken what the music executives had created and she'd have torn it down and built it back up into whatever she wanted, because other artists had done that exact same thing and she could have, too. But she hadn't done any of that. She'd blamed Liam because it was easier than admitting to herself that the dream had died, and she'd only been clinging to it because she wasn't honest with herself about what she really wanted. Maybe she truly didn't know.

Sometimes it took a while to figure someone out even if that person was yourself.

When the last note faded away, Layla set down her guitar, turned to Brian, and said, "I don't want to do this anymore."

CHAPTER 50

LAYLA

Brian looked shocked. "You don't want to sing with me anymore? Are you okay? Did I do something?"

"No, sorry. That came out wrong. I feel great and I want to perform with you anytime we have the chance. But I don't want to play for a computer screen. I don't want to do all the other stuff. I don't want to pose for pictures in my bed and I don't want to come up with clever things to say online. I don't want to keep hoping that we get picked up by a label. I don't want any of that. You're good at it and you seem to enjoy it more than I do. But I don't."

Never again would she go along with something that didn't feel right. Not with a man, not with a friend, not with her musical partner.

Not in any aspect of her life.

She started to say she was sorry, but that

435

was something she wouldn't say anymore, either. Not where her own happiness was concerned.

"All I need is to play in front of a crowd. It's like oxygen to me. I want you to take everything else and run with it. This will open doors for your songwriting. It already has. I will sing whatever you write. But I don't care what happens with it. That's it. That's all I can give you."

She wasn't leaving him in a bind by letting him go solo. He'd already confided that the money they were earning had allowed him to sock enough away that he could keep the doors of the guitar shop open indefinitely. And he'd received some promising feedback on a few of the songs he'd been trying to sell. He'd make it as a songwriter; Layla would not hesitate to put money down on that bet.

Brian looked at her with an expression of genuine warmth and understanding. "That's plenty, Layla. It's more than enough."

"Okay," she said.

"You want a beer? I'm going to grab one."

"A beer would be great."

Brian walked off toward the bar, and Layla set her guitar back in its stand.

I just wanted to keep playing.

She took a deep breath, and a peaceful

feeling settled over her. Then she scanned the crowd, and her heart leapt, because it turned out that Brian hadn't been wrong after all.

CHAPTER 51

JOSH

Josh had arrived mid-set, and he'd been standing near the back of the room, because there were no open tables. He'd waited patiently for her to finish playing, finish talking to Brian. Then he weaved his way through the crowd and walked up to Layla.

He didn't say anything; instead, he took her face in his hands and kissed her, because he'd been waiting a long time to do that again. He was no longer an impulsive eighteen-year-old, but that didn't mean he couldn't lose control every now and then. Layla wrapped her arms around his neck and kissed him back like they were the only two people in the room.

His divorce had been final for a few weeks, but he'd tied up a few more loose ends before going to the bar that night. His brother had set him up with the friend of a coworker, and though Josh's first instinct had been to say he wasn't interested, he went ahead and met the woman for a drink. She was smart and attractive, and it turned out that she kickboxed at the same gym he went to, although she went early in the morning and he went after work. She was funny and the conversation never lagged and there was not a damn thing wrong with her except that she wasn't Layla.

He'd also done a lot of thinking during their time apart, and he'd gotten comfortable with being alone. Not too comfortable, but he'd done all the things he was supposed to do, and it turned out those women's magazines knew what they were talking about. He'd spent plenty of one-on-one time with Sasha. He'd had plenty of alone time and he had his dog. Getting to know himself had taken a bit longer, but it turned out that he wasn't an idiot and there was nothing wrong with being a serial monogamist.

Josh had been notified of Brian and Layla's performance because he'd signed up for their newsletter one night when he'd been unable to get the memory out of his head of Layla singing in her basement. He'd never watched their live videos because he didn't have any social media accounts, but the weekly newsletter kept him informed of their accomplishments and he couldn't be happier for them.

"You hungry?" Josh asked.

"Starving."

"Want to get something to eat?"

She smiled. "Yes."

He helped her gather her things and they said good-bye to Brian. Over a late dinner, he told her about Kimmy's attempt to reconcile and how he'd missed the signs. He told her that the divorce was final. "It does feel better having those loose ends tied up, but I sure did miss you."

"I missed you, too," she said. "And I'm so happy that you're back."

CHAPTER 52

JOSH

Minnesota flourished in the warmth of the summer sun. Layla did, too, and she glowed with the kind of happiness that came from knowing exactly who you are and what you want. She and Josh had also found their rhythm, and while they hadn't picked up exactly where they'd left off, they'd discovered that what they had now was better because there was nothing standing in their way.

Liam had dropped his attempt to take Layla back to court, and her attorney said she could be reasonably certain she wouldn't hear from him again. "I hope you're right," she said, and then she told Josh she fired him.

A friend of Kimmy's had set her up with someone and they'd hit it off. Josh was happy for her, and Sasha seemed to like him. Sometimes it was hard for him to wrap his brain around his daughter spending time with a man who was not her father and who was not Josh. Maybe in time it wouldn't be so hard.

He'd decided to wait a bit longer before telling Sasha that he was dating her music teacher. He wanted to, but he liked to think he had learned a thing or two about jumping in too soon. When he'd talked to Layla about it, she said that she understood and wasn't quite ready for that, anyway. "I like the way things are right now."

"So do I," he said.

By then, there were no secrets between them. Josh knew everything that had gone wrong in Layla's marriage to Liam, the part she had played in its demise, and her regrets.

Layla knew everything about Josh's relationship with Kimmy, and some of the things he told her didn't paint him in the best light, either.

But that was real life and real life was messy.

Layla told Josh that she'd done a lot of thinking during their time apart and what she'd decided was that she didn't need to be his wife or have his child or live with him or any of the other things she'd done the first time around. "I'm not getting any younger, but I don't want to make those

442

decisions right now because I don't know for sure," she said. But she'd told him she wanted the option and the freedom to explore those things in the future if she so desired, and so, Josh had explained, did he.

"You know that 'if you choose not to decide you still have made a choice,' " he said.

She placed her hand on her heart. "Did you just quote Rush lyrics to me? Because you're speaking my love language."

Those lines were from a song called "Freewill," and they had always stuck with Josh because they were so simplistically yet profoundly true. "I did, and we have my brother James to thank for the fact that I know every word to every song on that album. He played it on a continuous loop for six months until my mom begged him to play something else. Backfired because we all had to listen to *Appetite for Destruction* by Guns N' Roses for a solid year."

"Man, that's a good album," Layla said.

Norton died peacefully in his sleep one night near the end of June. Sasha had been devastated, as he'd known she would be, and when she'd asked if they could get another dog, he'd found it impossible to say no. They went to the shelter and Sasha picked out a rambunctious two-year-old goldendoodle named Kevin who started stealing their shoes two seconds after they brought him into the house.

When Sasha wasn't with him, Josh spent almost all those summer evenings with Layla. They sat on her deck, Kevin on the floorboards by their feet. Layla always had her journal and her guitar and iced tea or wine, depending on what she was in the mood for.

One night, as Layla strummed her guitar, Josh said, "What is that song?" It was the same song she'd been strumming for a couple of weeks.

They'd swapped out the individual chairs on her deck for a loveseat, and Layla's hip was pressed against his as much as it could be while she was playing. She strummed a few notes and then reached for her journal and scribbled something inside. Then she reached for the guitar again. Maybe she hadn't heard him, because now she was staring out at the backyard as if she was lost in thought.

"Layla? The song. I can't place it."

She turned to him. "That's because no one's ever heard it before."

CHAPTER 53

LAYLA

That fall, when the leaves began to change and the air grew colder, Layla and Brian started playing together regularly. The bar they'd been playing at the night Josh came back had decided to go in a different direction, one that didn't include live music. But they'd lucked out, because Brian's friend had decided that having a free Saturday night a couple of times a month sounded pretty good, and they happily accepted the offer to stand in for him. Layla wouldn't have minded playing more than that, but it would do for now.

They were playing for a full house tonight. Tonya and Annie and their husbands were there. Josh's brothers and their wives were there, too. Layla's whole family had come, saying there was no way they'd miss it.

During the second break, Josh brought her a glass of water. "Next set?" he asked.

"Yep."

"Are you nervous?"

"Nope. I never get nervous. Not about music. Not even about this."

"Atta girl."

That made her smile.

"I love you," he said.

"I love you too."

He'd said it for the first time on the Fourth of July, right after they decided to go ahead and tell Sasha that her dad and Miss Layla were going to be spending some time together outside of school because they liked each other. Sasha had looked at them and said, "Okay. Can we go to the parade now?" So, they'd taken her to the parade and the carnival, and they watched fireworks and went back to Josh's.

"I guess that went okay," Josh said after he tucked Sasha into bed.

"I guess it did."

Later that night, when Josh said, "I love you," it felt right, and it felt good because she loved him, too, and she told him so.

Now, he gave her a little pat on the butt. "I think Brian's waiting for you."

Brian was already onstage, fiddling with his microphone. Searching the crowd for Layla. He caught her eye and smiled. "I think he is," she said, so she walked up onstage and joined him.

Right before they ended the set, Layla looked out into the crowd at the people she held most dear and said, "This is a song I wrote." She strummed the opening notes. "It's called 'Free.' I hope you like it."

It started so smoothly but ended so rough
Shined as bright as I could, but it wasn't
   enough
Gave you my youth, gave you my heart
But we were doomed from the start
Don't know why I cut you all that slack
'Cause those are the years I'm not ever
   getting back
Did I think I'd be a rock star
Well, I sure wanted to try
It wasn't meant to be
But back then I couldn't see
It was really about choice
And having a voice
I'm coming into my power
Gonna bloom like a flower
For a future that's brighter
You must be a fighter
Know exactly what you want
No room for nonchalance
You tried to break me, couldn't make me,
From the ashes, I will rise
Voiceless no longer

Because what doesn't kill you sure as hell
    makes you stronger
Now I'm free to lead
Free to choose
Free to dance
With the muse
Anytime
Anywhere
With all my heart
I'll be there

Layla could have made the song available to everyone. She could easily have parlayed the success she and Brian were having and gotten a lot more ears on it than she might have in the past. But this was her song, written about her, by her.

For her.

She had gone through every entry in her journal and she read the words she'd written in all their rawness and she listened to what she was trying to tell herself. And it turned out that she did have something to say after all.

When the song ended, Layla took a deep breath and then let it out, slowly. A long cleansing exhale was what she'd been working toward since the night she left Liam. Now she could see that life got bigger, not because of what you accomplished, but despite it. When she was twenty-three, the band had encapsulated what she wanted out of life, but it had also been her *whole* life. Back then she didn't know about the career she would grow to love, the people she would meet and surround herself with, and how they would expand her life in such a way that it was almost enough. And if she could sing, create, play the music that she loved, it would be more than enough.

Layla set down her guitar and looked for his face in the crowd.

He was there, of course.

And moments later, he pulled her into his arms.

The tears came then. Lots of them. Happy cathartic tears.

Layla Hilding didn't know everything. Life was unpredictable, and sometimes all you could do was hold on tight and go along for the ride. But what she did know was that life was a constant changing of the seasons and it turned out that she could handle them just fine.

ACKNOWLEDGMENTS

Heard It in a Love Song is my ninth book in approximately nine years. I am still in awe that I get to spend my days doing what I love and that there are people waiting to read my words. "Thank you" doesn't even begin to cover it. If you're reading this right now, please know that my life is infinitely better because of you.

I have been saying for years that I'd love to write a book that didn't require such a vast amount of research and I finally managed to make that happen. However, there were things I still needed to learn about and to that end I must give credit to Jackie Jones. Thank you for sharing the ins and outs of what it's like to supervise the morning drop-off line (bless you) and everything that's involved in teaching music at an elementary school. Thank you, also, for stressing how important and fulfilling performing is to someone with an educational and professional background like yours (and Layla's). Creative outlets really do feed the soul.

To my editor, Leslie Gelbman. You are a true partner and a kindred spirit. Despite the challenges presented to all of us in the year 2020, we persisted, and we prevailed, and I could not have written this book without you. You have my utmost respect and affection.

To everyone at St. Martin's Press. Words cannot express my appreciation for your continued support and enthusiasm. Special thanks to Sally Richardson, Jennifer Enderlin, Lisa Senz, Brant Janeway, Marissa Sangiacomo, Tiffany Shelton, and Katie Bassell. I'm so happy to be a part of your world.

Jane Dystel, Miriam Goderich, and Lauren Abramo of Dystel, Goderich & Bourret. You are truly the trifecta of literary-agent awesomeness. Thank you for all you do.

To Debby Garvis for cheering me on. It meant more than you know.

To my children, Matthew and Lauren. Thank you for never getting frustrated with my constant pleas for your patience and understanding as I worked through the many stages of writing a book. You are my two greatest gifts in life and watching you grow into young adults is the hardest job

I've ever loved.

To Christine Estevez for all your help with my newsletters, graphics, and anything else I didn't have time to take care of myself. You're amazing!

Honorable mention to the Marshall Tucker Band. This book may not be a literal interpretation of your song, but I will always listen to "Heard It in a Love Song" at an earsplitting decibel level that's well worth the risk to my hearing.

Thank you to anyone who has ever come to my book signings. Looking out into a sea of faces after worrying that there might be only one face — or worse yet, no faces — and seeing you there truly fills my heart with joy.

To the wonderful individuals who have written to me on social media or emailed to let me know how much one of my books has touched you — I am simply in awe that you took time out of your day to let me know.

To Ashley Spivey. Lady, you are one-of-a-kind. Your tireless endeavors and your amazing Spivey's Club group are so instrumental in spreading the word about authors and their books, and one of these days, I'll figure out how to thank you properly. In the meantime, please know that my appreciation is endless.

Special thanks to the book bloggers/bookstagrammers who have been so influential in my ability to reach readers. You work tirelessly every day to spread the word about books, and the writing community is a better place because of you. Jamie Rosenblit of *Beauty and the Book,* Kristi Barrett of *A Novel Bee,* Susan Peterson of *Sue's Reading Neighborhood,* Andrea Peskind Katz of *Great Thoughts' Great Readers,* Yvette from *Nose Stuck in a Book,* Jess from *Gone with the Words,* Hannah at *Bookworms Talk,* Sarah Symonds of *DragonflyReads,* Sarah Sabin of *Mama's Reading Corner,* Stephanie Gray of *The Book Lover Book Club,* and Elysse of *Compulsive Reader's Book Blog.* Your gorgeous pictures and posts are every bit as beautiful as your kind words and support. Thank you from the bottom of my heart.

To the members of my Facebook readers' group, On Tracey's Island. I love that you're still in my group despite my long periods of radio silence. I'll try to do better.

To those who discover and champion my foreign editions. It is thrilling to see your praise and to understand just how far around the globe my stories have traveled.

I want to express my sincere appreciation

to the book clubs who choose my titles, the booksellers who hand-sell my books, and the librarians who put them on their shelves.

My heartfelt gratitude goes out to all of you for helping to make *Heard It in a Love Song* the book I hoped it would be. Words cannot express how truly blessed I am to have such wonderful and enthusiastic people in my life.

And last, but certainly not least, my readers. Without you, none of this would be possible.

ABOUT THE AUTHOR

Tracey Garvis Graves is a *New York Times, Wall Street Journal,* and *USA Today* bestselling author. Her debut novel, *On the Island,* spent 9 weeks on the *New York Times* bestseller list, has been translated into twenty-nine languages, and is in development with MGM and Temple Hill Productions for a feature film. She is also the author of *Uncharted, Covet, Every Time I Think of You, Cherish, Heart-Shaped Hack, White-Hot Hack,* and *The Girl He Used to Know.* She is hard at work on her next book.

The employees of Thorndike Press hope you have enjoyed this Large Print book. All our Thorndike, Wheeler, and Kennebec Large Print titles are designed for easy reading, and all our books are made to last. Other Thorndike Press Large Print books are available at your library, through selected bookstores, or directly from us.

For information about titles, please call:
(800) 223-1244

or visit our website at:
gale.com/thorndike

To share your comments, please write:
Publisher
Thorndike Press
10 Water St., Suite 310
Waterville, ME 04901